Jenna Plural Wants You

David Parker-Ross

Tairis Anders Media LLC

David Parker-Ross

Jenna Plural Wants You by David Parker-Ross

Editors

Josette Quinlan Keelor, Madelyn Heatherington, Lisa Levy, Taylor Johnson

Art by Lara Wynter

Audiobook Read by Elliot Fitzpatrick

ISBN EBook 978-1-959138-24-2

ISBN Paperback 979-8-9859367-0-4

ISBN Hardback 979-8-9859367-4-2

ISBN Audio 979-8-8226199-5-1

Published by Tairis Anders Media, LLC

Dedication

For my daughter
Annette Jeannine Parker-Ross

Jenna Plural Wants You!

BY MICHAEL PHELKAR

A personal account of the rise of Jenna Plural

Dedication

This chronicle is dedicated to the two people who, without, I would not be here today, McKenna Anderson and Hannah Grant, who are genuine heroes of the Confederation.

From the Office of Michael Phelkar

Jenna Plural wants you!

Wherever you are in the solar system, there is no doubt you have heard of Jennacia Plularian, better known by her abbreviation of Jenna Plural. How you perceive her comes down to where you receive your information. Propaganda is a tool of politics and war and is a powerful one. With the enemy now in control of nearly all media, it is hard to separate facts from fiction. Jenna is portrayed as either an evil despot or an idiot fighting a lost cause.

My purpose behind this chronicle is to set the record straight. As a longtime companion and ally of Jenna Plural, I present you with this accurate and personalized account of who Jenna was and who she became. I hold nothing back. What motivates her, what drives her, and the reasons behind her beliefs so I can encourage you to play your part. She wants the best for you, and she wants to free you from the shackles of oppression.

As I write this, the war still rages across the solar system. Jenna Plural needs you! She is our future, a future you can be part of. You just need the courage to stand up for what is right.

Clear skies to you.

Michael Phelkar, OSC

First Minister of Civil Affairs

Chapter One

Welcome to America

T he European anti-aircraft guns could be heard through the toughened steel of the shuttle. I must admit, it unnerved me. I held on tightly to the straps that held me into my seat. My only assurance was the confident look on the pilot's face as he swerved and dipped and rose to avoid a direct impact from the antiquated shells and flak. "Sorry for the bumpy ride, Mr. Phelkar." The pilot said to me unnervingly, cheerfully with a huge grin.

"Bumpy?" I said as once more I flinched in my seat, watching various projectiles pass the windscreen in extremely near misses.

The pilot grinned again. "This is nothing. You should have taken a trip back when auto-targeted weapons still worked. This dumb fire is just a case of keeping us high enough so I can see what's coming at us." The Royal Air Force shuttle was equipped with the latest jamming and counter-jamming equipment.

It had been nearly a decade since the last auto-targeting weapon had been fired. Both sides had reached the peak of technology in blocking them. It required the blunt force of an unintelligent projectile fired from a cannon barely more sophisticated than one aboard an ancient pirate ship.

"How long before we reach American airspace?" I asked.

The shelling suddenly stopped, and he shrugged with a grin. "We just entered it, Mr. Phelkar. We are within shielded U.S. airspace." His amusement did not last long as a loud, ear-piercing alarm went off. He turned his attention back to the controls. "Bloody hell."

"What's happening?" I cried out as the shuttle began to shake violently.

"The flak must have caused more damage than I thought. We have lost the D.E. generator."

I was no engineer, but I knew that was probably the worst thing that could happen to us, short of blowing up instantaneously. The shuttle was a big block and not even remotely aerodynamically designed. As the gravity-repelling, artificially generated dark energy dissipated, the laws of gravity came back into play. We began to fall from the sky like a brick dropped from the Empire State Building. I gripped my straps so hard that my nails began to dig into the palms of my hands. I felt the g-forces upon us as we began to plummet. I said a silent prayer to whatever gods may be listening, believing that my diplomatic mission to the United States was going to come to an end before it even began. However, the pilot had other ideas.

There was a hiss, then an explosion above my head as the canopy flew off, and I saw the bright Virginia sky above me. Another sharp hiss of gas and my seat shot up into the air. I was out of the shuttle with the wind rushing past me. It was less than a couple of seconds, but the g-forces almost made me blackout. I struggled to keep myself calm as panic welled up within me. I was doing quite well until the straps, my emotional support, intentionally came unfastened, and the seat beneath me fell away. The back support remained in place while my ascension began to slow. I swallowed hard as I started my plunge toward the ground. Looking down, I saw lush green grass that the splatter of my blood would soon despoil. I screamed in sheer terror. Fortunately, thanks to the fast actions of that pilot, whose name I would never find out, I was not to die that day. Air rushed past me as I searched frantically for some sort of ripcord. There was nothing, but then I felt a sudden jerk at my shoulders, and I looked up as the parachute deployed automatically above me. A loud deafening crash made me look over my shoulder, where I could see the smoking ruins of the shuttle as it buried itself into the ground. I looked about to see if the pilot had ejected, but there was no sign of him.

I drifted down slowly, trying to remember the parachute drills I had been compelled to take almost twenty years earlier as a raw recruit in the Royal Air Force. "Bend your knees, Michael," I muttered to myself, looking at the ground and thanking God above that I was not coming down in a forest or, even worse, the Atlantic. The only break in the green of the fields was a long winding road. I looked eastward, and I could see the coastline in the distance. It enabled me to get my bearings. Fortunately, my training had stayed with me, and although I stumbled onto my knees, I did so without any injury. Automatically, the seatback fell away from me and immediately disappeared across the field as the wind picked up the chute and took it away. I sat down in the grass, breathing heavily, not so much from exertion but from the anxiety of the situation. I stared down at my knees for several minutes before pulling myself together.

I rose unsteadily to my feet and checked my surroundings. I looked over to where the smoke billowed out from the remains of the shuttle. I couldn't gauge how far away it was. I knew I could not walk away without at least checking if the pilot had made it. I had nothing with me; my trusty old traveling duffle bag went down with the shuttle. I had nothing but the clothes I stood up in.

The fifteen-minute walk seemed to take forever as I tried to calm myself from what I had just endured. There wasn't much left of the craft, but I was able to gain entry through a gaping hole in the side. The pilot was still at his post amidst broken steel and glass, and from the bizarre position in which he sat, it was clear his neck was broken. His seat was tipped at an awkward angle, and I saw that he had tried to eject, but one side had failed to release, securing his ultimate demise. I laid a hand on his shoulder and silently thanked him for his sacrifice.

I headed back outside and was surprised to see, amongst the debris, the large duffel bag that contained everything I had brought to the U.S. I picked it up carefully and dusted it down. Then I headed westward. Of course, in hindsight, I should have stayed with the shuttle, but I was somewhat dazed and confused and was fighting the onslaught of a massive headache, so forgive me for not thinking straight. The field continued up a slight gradient and disappeared. However, this was hardly the Sahara, and I was sure if I kept walking, I would find some form of civilization and be able to contact the authorities. Although the war had reached the mainland of the continental U.S., it was far in the South, and there were no enemy ground forces in Virginia as far as I was aware. The U.S. authorities would have been tracking us and known we crashed and would already be looking for us, but I did not know how long it would take.

Dusk began to descend, and I was surprised to find it was getting rather chilly, considering it was early summer. I had always imagined Virginia to be hot beyond what is comfortable for an Englishman. It was my first time in the United States, and I was already hoping it would be my last.

I decided to turn south and head towards the road which I had seen from the air. It was about thirty minutes before I reached it. The cold was starting to become unpleasant. The road was two simple lanes that had not seen any maintenance in some time. There were no sidewalks, as the Americans called them, and I continued along in a southwesterly direction. The bag was becoming heavy, and I regretted not bringing my backpack. After about another thirty minutes, I stopped and dropped the bag onto the ground and used it as a seat to take a rest. I sat there with only the sound of the cicadas to keep me company. It was almost dark when my solitude was suddenly broken by what was unmistakably some sort of small aircraft. I looked up to see it pass directly over my head. I recognized it at once. After all, my military career had been flying these devices. It was a drone, an American P57. It was about the size of an eagle. Although armed, it was primarily used for surveillance. Almost immediately after it passed, it slowed and turned around to face me, hovering several meters away. A bright light came on, shining directly into my face. I shielded my eyes as I stood up.

"Hands by your sides, mate. I gotta see your face." The woman's voice, emanating from the drone, was cheerful and had a strong Australian accent.

"Are you with the Americans?" I said, not immediately responding to her instruction.

"Ah, don't be a fucking moron, mate," she said with an impatient sigh. "Arms by your side. I won't repeat myself a third time. This thing may look like a toy, but it can make your day go real bad real fast."

I dropped my arm and squinted. "Actually, you only said it twice, so only repeated it once."

"Yeah, yeah, whatever," she replied disinterestedly as she piloted the unmanned vehicle back in my direction. It hovered in front of me, just out of my reach, and she said very cheerfully, "There you go, that's better. Well, how's it going? I'm Lieutenant Stacey Grant of the United States Navy. Would you care to identify yourself?"

"I'm Michael Phelkar of the British Ministry of Defense, liaison to the United States Marine Corps."

She shouted to someone I reasonably assumed was in her vicinity. "Boss, I found him. He's alive." Then Lieutenant Stacey Grant turned her attention back to me. "Okay, mate, we've got your location. You didn't make it easy for us. If you had stayed with your shuttle or your 'chute, we could have picked you up on the tracking system hours ago."

"Ah, sorry, I never thought of that," I replied sheepishly.

"You just stay right where you are. My boss is driving out to pick you up. Are you injured?"

"No, ma'am, I'm a bit shaken up, but that's about it."

"What about your pilot?"

"He didn't make it."

"Jeez, I'm sorry to hear that, mate." She sounded genuine. "We are dispatching a cleanup crew. We will make sure he gets back to Blighty. The boss is leaving now and should be there in about fifteen to twenty minutes. Look, I gotta get this baby back in the dock; she's running on fumes. Keep your chin up, and we'll have a nice cuppa and some tucker waiting for you when you get here."

"I'd appreciate that, Lieutenant," I said with a smile, only then realizing how hungry I was.

The drone turned, and I watched as it headed back the way it had come.

It was not unusual to find Australians serving in the United States military. Many who had escaped the annexation of that country had signed up with the allied military of the Pacific Alliance, primarily American and Japanese, and any of the other allied nations, including my own. However, very few held officer commissions unless they had a particular talent. I wondered what talent Lieutenant Grant had that made her invaluable.

I sat back down and watched the drone get smaller and smaller, then disappear over the horizon. It seemed to take forever before I saw the car coming. Its bright beams swept left and right with the curves of the road. I waited until it got much closer before I stood up. Pulling up next to me, a woman stepped out of the car.

This was the first time I laid eyes upon Jenna Plural.

As she stood in the glare of the headlights, I was immediately struck by how young she looked. Stacey had called her "boss," yet standing before me was a woman between her early to mid-twenties, probably barely out of some military college. I stepped toward her, offering her my hand. She stood at attention and delivered a sharp, crisp salute, and only then did she take it. I could not help but notice that her hand was soft, although her grip was firm. Rather unusual for an active servicewoman. However, what stood out the most was she was unbelievably beautiful. Her skin was fair, bordering on pale, and her hair hung over her shoulder in a light brown ponytail.

"Welcome to the United States, Mr. Phelkar." Her tone belied her appearance, for it was authoritative and confident and had a maturity that did not match her youthfulness. "I'm Lieutenant Jenna Plural."

"It is both an honor and a privilege to be here." I said with a warm smile, "And please, call me Michael. May I call you Jenna?"

Her eyes narrowed almost imperceptibly. "I honestly don't think that would be appropriate, Mr. Phelkar," her face maintained its passive severity. She stepped past me, and I could not help but turn to admire those long legs and trim yet athletic figure, for she wore a simple khaki tank with matching shorts and white sneakers. She seemed to tense momentarily, but I was sure I had imagined it. She picked up my bag and turned back. "My apologies, Mr. Phelkar. It wasn't the desire of the United States Marine Corps that you should be met on the side of the road near Virginia Beach."

"Think nothing of it," I said with a polite smile. "We are in the middle of a war, and sometimes events don't permit the normal social accouterments."

"Indeed. I must also apologize for being inappropriately dressed." If it weren't for the grimness of her expression, I would have considered this humorous banter. I was just in a god damned crash and did not exactly care that my ride was not in dress uniform. "I was off duty when we began the search for you." She opened the trunk of the car and dropped my bag into it.

Something about her simply did not add up, her age, her looks, her.... The penny finally dropped. Many women can be beautiful without having their DNA sliced and diced, but she simply appeared far too young to be in a position of authority. She was a GenMod, as they are colloquially referred to. She had been genetically designed in vitro with natural flaws programmed out. She appeared to be in her early twenties because that was when the typical human female reached her physical peak. Unlike the rest of us, her cells would not degenerate. Jenna Plural would never grow old, and, barring a violent act, she would never die. The Prague Convention outlawed human gene modification almost fifty years prior, so behind that stunning, youthful face was a woman of at least seventy years of age. I had never met a GenMod before, and I found myself staring at her as she opened the passenger door. After an uncomfortable pause, she said, "Are you coming, Mr. Phelkar? It's a long walk to Manassas."

Chapter Two

The U.S.S. Lewis Puller

A s I got into the car and she closed the door behind me, the seat molded around me to ensure the most comfortable ride. Yet I felt far from comfortable. GenMods were the stuff of legend, and in most cultures, they were the Bogeymen your mother would tell you would come and get you if you didn't eat all your veggies. It is hard to shake off the prejudice instilled in you as a child. As Jenna slipped into the operator seat next to me and told the car to take us to the military astrodome in Manassas, I could not help but wonder if she thought and felt like we did. The vehicle thanked us for putting on our seatbelts and silently turned around in the road, and headed back up the way my unusual companion had come from. Jenna looked at me with a frown. "Yes, Mr. Phelkar?" she asked, and I realized I had been staring.

I looked away and shook my head. "No, no, all is fine."

Jenna closed her eyes, laying her head back. I thought she was going to sleep, but she stated, "You should know, Mr. Phelkar, that I protested this oversight visit. Especially by a civilian and more so by a foreigner."

This wasn't an unexpected response to my assignment. "It's just politics, Lieutenant," I said with a shrug. "We are losing this war, and my government is rattling sabers before committing more troops to the cause. We don't want the public to see us as secondary allies in the conflict."

She opened her eyes, looked at me with disdain, and said, "You're judging the competence of an elite American unit and calling it 'just politics'?"

She was right, and I couldn't argue against her point. "To be frank, I'm not entirely sure what I'm assessing. I was diverted from another assignment in Reykjavík, and I didn't get a full briefing. All I know is I'm to meet with someone called James Royce and report back what a wonderful job you're all doing."

"That's the captain of my ship, the Lewis Puller," she said with an almost vicious growl, and although I found that odd, I let it slip by as something else had caught my interest.

"The Lewis Puller? That is a one-hundred-and-twenty-year-old cargo hauler." I said with surprise.

She raised a perfect genetically sculpted eyebrow and looked at me. "You know the Lewis Puller?"

"I worked in logistics and studied the specs of most U.S. ships we have records on. I only read the summary for the Puller. She did not seem worthy of further interest."

"Even so, recalling the Puller is rather odd." She looked disbelievingly at me. "The whole idea of it is that it goes unnoticed."

I tapped my forehead and smiled. "Eidetic memory chip. I have twenty yottabytes of memory storage."

Her frown deepened. "They are illegal, Mr. Phelkar."

"In the U.S.A., yes, they are, but not in the U.K. They are permitted in military use."

"But you're a civilian." She said the word as if it was some sort of derogatory term.

"I served in the Royal Air Force."

"But no longer?"

"No, I was invalided out nine years ago after an accident." I shrugged. "I transferred to the diplomatic department of the Ministry of Defense."

"So, you have total recall of everything you experience?" She sounded genuinely curious.

"Yes, just as if I'm there, but only when I choose to record them and if I choose to access them. It does not work like natural memory, which can come back when something reminds you. I have to access it with conscious thought, but the recall is in the finest detail when I do. Mostly I use it to access schematics, personnel files, languages, and the like."

She looked at me ponderously before saying, "Languages. So, you can speak French?"

"Oui, madam," I replied with a smile.

She grinned and waved a dismissive hand in the air. "Even I can understand that, idiot." It was a brief glimpse behind the veil of steel, and it was only fleeting.

I smiled back, but then an awkward silence fell between us until I asked, "You cannot have many in your unit if the Puller is your ship?"

"Forty." She replied curtly.

I frowned at this, it wasn't possible, and I thought she was being flippant. "The specs say the capacity is twenty-four."

"That's correct." She looked at me with those eyebrows raised again, waiting for me to work it out.

Then it dawned on me. "You have been kitted out with that new low berth transport technology?"

Jenna relaxed and lay her head back on the rest once more, "I prefer its official name of Matter to Energy Transit."

My eyes widened. The technology for M.E.T. had been around for several years; the Americans had it on most of their warships, but its use was still considered experimental in my country. It broke down the molecules of the human body into energy, making the storage of people and cargo virtually un-limited. Effectively they ceased to exist while traveling through space. To use the vernacular, the concept scared the shit out of me. Jenna, noticing my reaction, looked at me in surprise. "If that bothers you, what are you like on the battlefield?"

"I'm not relying on machinery to keep me alive. That's the difference," I responded defensively. "Have you seen the results of those things? At best, only ninety-five percent come out alive."

"We have improved on that; it is now ninety-nine percent," she said.

"The one percent of dead people will be pleased to hear that," I snipped.

"Compare that to the statistics of interplanetary travel before the M.E.T. You were more likely to die in an onboard ship accident," Jenna said with an edge of frustration in her voice. "And we are *always* relying on machinery to keep us alive. Advanced weaponry, scanners, medbots. All sorts of equipment help us achieve our objectives and reduce our chances of dying."

"The difference is we aren't off in some sort of limbo while using them." I refused to concede her point.

Jenna shrugged. "Would you like me to turn the car around? I'm more than happy to have you wrapped in cotton wool for your trip back to London."

I glanced at her. "A GenMod with a sense of humor, my oh my, wonders never cease," I said, unable to hide the sarcasm in my voice.

Jenna's eyes narrowed once more. Looking ahead, she gritted her perfect white teeth. "I don't appreciate that term, Mr. Phelkar."

"GenMod? Why not?" I was irritated now, my headache interfering with my need to be cordial.

"The term implies we aren't human." Her voice was now like ice. "It's offensive."

"It is not inaccurate. You were programmed and born in a tank." I shrugged, truly not understanding I was saying anything wrong.

"To parents who chose to ensure I did not have flaws or genetic mutation. Beyond that, Mr. Phelkar, I'm no different than you."

"Ah, Lieutenant Plural, our flaws make us human." It came out before I could stop myself.

Jenna turned toward me ever so slightly and rolled her eyes, which I now noticed sparkled bright blue just as her designer had intended. "Great, I'm working with another damn Anti-Gen."

"Not really." I frowned. "I just don't appreciate their superiority complex."

She looked almost amused by this and faced me full-on. "Really?" she smirked. "And just how many 'GenMods' have you met?"

I flushed slightly and said. "Well, actually, you are the first."

She nodded. "I see." Shaking her head slowly, she turned away. "I can assure you, Mr. Phelkar, I judge people by only two things. Their love of their country and their ability to kill Peons," she said, using a common derogatory word for Europeans. "The one thing I'm more than anything else is an American."

"That's nice," I said for want of anything else. Of course, I also was a patriot, but I did not wave the union flag the way Americans waved their fifty-two stars and thirteen stripes.

Jenna looked at me with a flash of anger. "Are you making fun of me, Mr. Phelkar?"

I sighed softly. "Not at all, my dear Lieutenant," I lied. "But what would you have me refer to you as?"

An intense look of irritation crossed her face. "I don't see why you need to label me at all. However, if you must, how about a loyal officer of the United States Marine Corps?"

I realized then that I was being a bit of an arse. I sighed and calmed myself before saying, "I'm sorry, Lieutenant."

"Forget it," she said aggressively, her eyes fixed ahead, looking out to the horizon.

"Seriously, I was out of line, and I'm sorry," I earnestly said.

She turned and fixed those sparkling eyes upon me. "Mr. Phelkar, I have to work with you, and you have to work with me. We aren't going to be friends... ever. We just need to tolerate each other. I cannot accept your apology because to do so will mean that I care, and trust me on this, Mr. Phelkar, I don't care. I don't care about you. I don't care about your assignment. I don't care about your paltry little country that we have propped up and defended for twenty years, only for you to dare come over here to see if we are good enough for you lazy, good-for-nothing British bastards. Am I clear?"

I sat there in stunned silence, just looking back at her. She turned away and looked ahead again. Eventually, I found my voice saying, quite meekly, "Yes, Lieutenant Plural, I understand you quite clearly." We rode the rest of the way in silence, and I couldn't help but think this would be a long assignment if she were going to be around.

The Manassas astrodome looked quite neglected. It showed signs of hasty repairs from frequent orbital bombardment. We may have had the power to jam technology, but nothing stopped the simple act of simply dropping a bomb from a low orbit. Fortunately, the Americans had improved their shielding of such bases in recent years. Nevertheless, it bothered me greatly that they, apparently, did not have the resources to restore the astrodome to its original condition. It was a sign that the U.S.'s fortunes were bleak. As astrodomes went, it wasn't one of their most significant. It bore two landing pads for interplanetary vessels, but only one of them was filled, and that was by some old derelict hulk, which I assumed was there for scrap. It was only as we drove right up to it that it dawned upon me that this was the U.S.S. Lewis Puller.

As I climbed out of the car, I stared at it in disbelief. A battle-scarred heap of junk covered in hasty repair patches. A large ugly black block of metal whose only color was the United States Navy emblems on various parts. This ship had certainly seen war in the twenty-year conflict with the Europeans. I found it hard to believe that it could leave the earth's atmosphere without breaking up.

Jenna fetched my bag from the car's boot as I stared up at the wreck. Ground crew buzzed around it, and I should have realized they were doing preflight checks.

My distaste must have shown, for someone to the side of me with a thick Australian accent said, "She ain't as bad as she looks." I turned to see a young officer. Stacey Grant wasn't how I had imagined her. She was noticeably short, and she wore her hair in an old goth style. The left side of her head was shaved, whilst the hair on her right side hung down over her right eye, covering half her face. Her hair was jet black and not what was likely her natural color. She wore many earrings of differing varieties, running up from the lobe to the top. Her most prominent feature was her mouth. She had an overbite of large, white, perfectly straight teeth that were almost always visible. Although fair-skinned, she had an ethnicity about her I could not quite place, and it was not until much later that I discovered she was of part aboriginal ancestry. Her neck bore the text of a tattoo that ran around from the front to the rear. I could not read it as her collar partly covered it, and I could only make out the letters "H.A."

She did not wear a uniform, and I still haven't seen her in one to this day. She has a fondness for skirts to trousers. She wears what I consider inappropriately short ones. On that day, she wore a short grey tunic over which she wore a long white trench coat that hung down to just below her knees. Finishing off her look was a pair of calf-high boots that ended at a point with thick one-inch heels that barely made a difference to her diminutive height.

"Lieutenant Grant, I presume?" I said, smiling at her.

"Got it in one, mate, but I'd prefer you to call me Stacey," she replied with a wide toothy grin and offered me her hand. Unlike Jenna, her skin was not soft and more in keeping with the military life.

Jenna handed my bag to a trooper who came up to assist. "Stow it aboard the ship," she ordered as another climbed into the car and drove it away. She turned back to us and gave us the formal introductions. "Mr. Phelkar of the British Ministry of Defense Liaison, please meet Second Lieutenant Stacefield Grant, our senior pilot." Stacey has a smile that lights up her face, enhances her looks, and makes you feel at ease. She also has what seems to be a perpetual grin that rarely disappears, as you will see.

"Is everything ready for launch?" Jenna asked her.

"As ready as she will ever be." Stacey shrugged in a not very confidence-inducing manner.

"Wait a minute," I said with concern as a light went off in my head, "when exactly are you shipping out?"

Jenna glanced at her watch. "In about two hours, Mr. Phelkar."

"Now, just a minute," I stated indignantly. "I'm here to do a review. How can I do that if you're off base."

With a slight, almost imperceptible smile of realization, she asked, "Were you not told we were shipping out today?"

I looked back at her incredulously. "I most certainly wasn't. I was told I was to come here, where I'd be further briefed. I have no intention of shipping out anywhere."

Her smile widened. "Why, Mr. Phelkar, how can you possibly assess us unless you go with us?"

I swallowed hard. "Where are you going?"

"To Mars, Mr. Phelkar. Our mission is to take out the European Union communications station on Phobos. It will open the way to taking out the Peons' Martian settlements. We are hoping to draw their attention away from their mainland incursion."

"I wasn't told of this," I said. I couldn't hide my discomfort at this news.

"We generally don't share mission details ahead of time."

"You're going into combat?"

Jenna raised her eyebrows with incredulity. "That, Mr. Phelkar, is what United States Marines do." She did not wait for a response; turning to Stacey, she said, "Show Mr. Phelkar around the ship. He should also check in with Doctor Archer for his preflight medical."

"You got it," Stacey replied, apparently amused by my reaction. Jenna stepped away before I could protest further and began giving other personnel instructions. "Come on, Phelks." Stacey headed up the boarding platform. I hesitated, then followed her.

The U.S.S. Lewis Puller had been an ore transport before being refitted for modern warfare. It was cramped with small corridors, some of which you had to turn slightly sideways to navigate. The low roofs frequently needed us to duck under beams. And it was black. Everything was black, from the metal floors to the walls and the ceiling, with low-level lighting. I couldn't help but wonder if the crew would need a therapist to overcome the grimness of this dilapidated vessel. Despite its small size, I felt lost as Stacey took me around the different corridors. As we went through the ship, I continued to protest fervently. "I really must insist I call back to London. There has been a grave misunderstanding."

"Chill out, Phelks," she said, laughing at me. "I'm not the one to ask about that. I just fly the Chesty. The captain or first officer are the only ones that can authorize calling off base."

"I assume that the Lieutenant is the first officer?"

"Then you assume wrong, mate. She is the second officer. It's kind of a weird setup. We're all part of Lieutenant Plural's covert ops team. However, because she's genetically modified, the law says she can't be put in charge of a ship. Something to do with some GenMod uprising in Russia a few decades ago."

"It was the Grozny uprising, and it was in Chechnya, not Russia," I responded informatively. "The Prague convention was held soon after. There was an international agreement that genetically modified people could no longer be created, and those already alive couldn't hold some positions in the military or corporate world."

"Yeah, well," Stacey continued, showing little interest in what I had just said. "It basically means that while Lieutenant Plural is in charge of ground operations, we need to have a different senior commander aboard the ship. We had a cool captain and first officer for the last four years. But the captain recently retired, and Addison, the first officer, moved on to bigger and better things. So, we just got our new first officer and captain, and this will be our first mission with them."

"So, how do you fit into this? A pilot is hardly part of a ground unit."

Stacey laughed. "Someone has to get them on the ground, ya moron. Jenna Plural recruited me after everything in Australia went tits up. Been with her on the Chesty ever since."

"Why do they call her the Chesty?" I asked.

"No idea." She shrugged. "Never given it any thought. They just do. I think it's something to do with the guy the ship's named after." We reached the Medical Center door, and she led me inside.

Chapter Three

The Dynamics of Command

The ship's medical officer, Dr. Carolyn Archer, was Navy, bearing the light blue uniform with a white medical coat over the top. She was possibly in her forties and had a permanently tired look. She was busy going through her preflight inventory as we entered, and she immediately stopped and came over to us. "Good evening. Who is this? A new crew member?"

"Nah! A pommy liaison from London who is shipping out with us," responded Stacey, grinning at me as I looked at her incredulously for the charming introduction.

I smiled politely at the doctor and offered her my hand. "Michael Phelkar, British Ministry of Defense liaison."

She took my hand and smiled politely. "Ah yes, I received your medical records this morning. I assume you're here for your preflight physical?"

"I'm not flying out with you," I said quite firmly.

Archer frowned. "That is not what I was told. Your Ministry of Defense has provided me with your medical history for active duty with us."

"Well, there is just a whole lot of misunderstanding then."

"For fuck's sake, Phelks, just go with it, will ya?" Stacey intoned. "We can sort all that out later."

"Please take a seat." Doctor Archer indicated the chair beside her. I looked at her, then at Stacey, but I gave up my protest. I expected Stacey to leave as I sat, but she leaned against the wall and folded her arms, observing me through her one visible eye. It was pretty odd, and I couldn't help but wonder what she was thinking.

"You appear to have had your medical nanobots replenished recently. Any negative reactions to them?"

She referred, of course, to the microscopic machines that were injected into the bloodstream and lay dormant ready to assist one's natural defenses or wounds or disease. They lasted about ten years and only needed to be replaced whenever they started to fail or an upgrade was required.

I simply shook my head in response.

"Your records state you had a spinal injury about nine years ago," the doctor said as she pulled out a small device and started to look in my ear.

"That is correct," I replied.

"Any problems with the organic disc replacements?"

"No, none. Though I'm not permitted to return to active service, I really shouldn't be shipping out." I lied. I was cleared for active service.

"Well, if you're looking for me to give you a pass, I'm sorry, Mr. Phelkar. You may not meet combat regulation fitness, but you meet flight requirements."

"I wasn't suggesting...," I started to say with indignation, but she interrupted me.

"Wow." She took a step back and looked at me quizzically. "You don't have an internal tracking transponder?"

"No, I haven't been in active service since before they were standard issue."

"Well, Mr. Phelkar, they are a legal requirement aboard a United States military ship. Any objections to me putting one in, or would you prefer to see one of your own doctors?"

Stacey did not give me the chance to say anything. "Sorry, Doc, he doesn't have the time. He has to ship out with us tonight."

"Yes, well, that hasn't been decided yet," I spluttered out. "I really should call my ministry."

Archer curled her brow in frustration. "All I know is that you will have to have a cranial transponder to launch with us, and you can't launch without it."

"Go ahead, Doctor," said Stacey, clearly amused by this. "We're not going to be able to leave without him, and we can't delay launching."

I relented, raising my hands in surrender. "Fine, go ahead."

It took a couple of minutes to prepare everything, during which time I sat silently. I felt uncomfortable under the constant gaze of Stacey Grant's grin, and I had to avert my eyes from her.

When she returned to us, Dr. Archer had a small gun-like object with a barrel as thin as a syringe. She placed what looked like a miniature shotgun cartridge in the back of it and then swabbed the side of my head with an alcohol wipe. "I can't promise you this isn't going to hurt. It's different with everybody," she told me, and I braced myself as she placed the barrel against the side of my head. There was a slight click, and it was like someone smashed the side of my skull with a small hammer, and I couldn't help but cry out, "Holy sweet mother fucker." I pulled my head away, but she was already laying the gun back down on the tray. "Excuse my language," I said, a tad embarrassed.

As the pain subsided, I scowled up at the doctor, and she gave me a slight smile, then tapped something into her tablet before turning to Stacey. "Can you test it out for me, please?"

Stacey nodded and looked down at her watch. "Tell me the location of Michael Phelkar?" she asked it.

A soft melodic male voice responded, "Mr. Phelkar is in the medical center." Stacey gave the doctor a thumbs up.

Archer stepped back and began to tap her notes into a tablet. "Well, Mr. Phelkar, I believe I can clear you for launch. If the two of you will excuse me, I have a lot to do here before we take off."

I thanked the doctor, more out of manners than appreciation, and shook her hand again before leaving with the young Australian.

Stacey led me past the crew cabins, of which there were only twelve.

"Where are the rest of the crew?" I asked.

"Most are already uploaded, ready for launch," Stacey told me. "The Chesty isn't capable of supporting more than about twenty people during the voyage. For now, we have a cleanup team out in the field to pick up your pilot. Other than that, only our senior officers, ship's engineer, and chief tech are still downloaded and will be the last to upload."

"No one stays awake through the journey?" I asked, hoping that I'd not have to be scrambled if I was indeed going.

"No, there is no need."

"Not even you, as our pilot?"

"Nah. Once the course is plotted and set, there is nothing needed from me until we reach our destination."

"What's it like?" I asked tenuously. "Being 'uploaded,' I mean."

Stacey shrugged. "It's like nothing. You cease to exist until you're reconstituted. To you, it's a flash of light, and it's suddenly six months later—or longer. You have no awareness time has passed."

"Sounds so dangerous if you ask me," I said, not at all happy.

Stacey grinned. "You remind me of a friend of mine. She was shit scared of the M.E.T. too. What about that British stiff upper lip?"

I sighed. "It's worried about whether it will come back attached to my face." I looked down at her highly amused smile.

"It's much safer than you would think. Should the ship get breached, the storage containers holding the energy matrix get ejected into space. Eventually, someone would pick us up."

"But what if the dematerialization system fails?"

Stacey chuckled. "Well, in that case, you won't even know it happened. Bloody hell, mate, there are multiple safety systems. You'll be as safe as you possibly can be."

"Mr. Phelkar." Jenna Plural came up the corridor. Her eyes narrowed quizzically at me. "I'm starting to get the feeling that you have never traveled into space." She now wore long khaki pants and a matching T-shirt, and her hair was now tied up in a bun on her head.

"I have, but only to the moon and back, and I was awake for the entire duration."

"But you said you're ex-Air Force?"

"I was. I sat in the comfort of an office in Colchester, controlling unmanned exploration vehicles. I never actually went to the front lines."

"In that case, Mr. Phelkar," Jenna said, looking horrified as if I had just announced I murdered babies, "I must protest most earnestly. You're a liability on this mission."

"Fine, let me call London, and I'll leave," I replied, looking deliberately over-enthusiastic.

She appeared to control her anger reluctantly and said, "Regrettably, Mr. Phelkar, that is not my call. We are on a communications blackout." She shook her head. "No personal calls until mission over. Security."

"I hardly would describe calling the Ministry of Defense in England a personal call."

"You should have said something earlier."

"I *did* say something earlier," I replied testily.

"Mr. Phelkar. Why are you choosing to be so difficult?" Her tone now became impatient. "Your government is aware of our situation and that you're going off-world. I assure you I would be more than happy to put you off the ship if I had a choice in the matter," she said with a dejected sigh. Then her shoulders slumped, and she looked away from me. "However, the captain wishes to meet with you, and then we'll need to prep you for launch. Like it or not, Mr. Phelkar, you're going to Mars."

James Royce was a man in his late fifties. He was portly to the degree that I couldn't help but wonder how he passed his annual physical. He sported a large black beard reminiscent of an ancient pirate. The cockpit of the U.S.S. Lewis Puller was small and cramped. The captain's chair was raised above the main controls, where two seats for the pilot and copilot were uncomfortably close together. The ship still had the old-style glass screen looking out the front of the vessel instead of the more modern monitors that access cameras from various parts of the ship's exterior. As I entered, with Jenna just behind me, he looked over his shoulder and jumped up from the command chair to face me. "Ah, Michael Phelkar, I presume." He shook my hand vigorously. "A pleasure to meet you, Sir," he said, strangely jovially for a military officer. "I hope Lieutenant Plural has made you feel welcome."

I glanced at the officious woman at my side, but I simply nodded to the captain and said, "Of course, she has been most delightful."

Royce laughed. "I guess there's a first time for everything then. Lieutenant Plural is not renowned for her civilities, but she is an adequate officer."

Adequate? Had the captain really just insulted his second officer in front of not only a stranger but a foreign diplomat? I glanced at Jenna, who was trying to hide her embarrassment behind an angry look.

"I'm sure that Lieutenant Plural is a great asset to your crew," I replied, trying not to show my disfavor at his lack of common courtesy. I may not have liked Jenna, but to humiliate her was uncalled for. She made no reaction to my comment, with her eyes still firmly locked on the captain, who had simply grunted noncommittally to my statement.

A tall, slender woman stood at his side with gaunt features yet warm, welcoming eyes. Although she looked older than Jenna, she was much younger. The sheer maths of the fact she wasn't a GenMod told me that. She bore the United States Marine uniform and a first lieutenant's chevrons. "Phelkar, meet Stephanie Morris, my first officer," Royce introduced her.

Unlike Jenna, Morris smiled warmly and offered me her hand. "Welcome aboard the Chesty, Sir. I hope you will find everything in order. She may be a small ship, but we're immensely proud of her. She's seen action many times over the last couple of decades."

"Yes, I could see that from the bodywork on the outside," I said coolly and felt Jenna stiffening in resentment at my side.

"I assure you, Mr. Phelkar, that this ship is as structurally sound as any in the United States fleet. Our workmanship is second to none," Jenna stated curtly.

"No offense intended, Lieutenant, merely observing the obvious damage the ship has taken over the years."

Royce chuckled. "You'll have to forgive my second officer, Phelkar. She is a rather zealous patriot."

"I can respect that. Isn't that something that has been sorely lacking in recent years?" I said, expressing an honest belief.

At my words, Jenna's head tilted slightly towards me with surprise, and there was a flash of a smile in her eyes. "Nice to see patriotism isn't dead, Mr. Phelkar. Maybe you're not completely objectionable, after all."

I smiled politely. "I will take that as a compliment, Lieutenant."

Royce slapped me on the back and said, "You should do that, Mr. Phelkar. It's the closest thing to one that you will possibly ever get from my second officer." Jenna's eyes turned passive once again as she looked back at her captain. Royce grew serious. "Well, Phelkar, I must say your arrival is unprecedented. Many of the crew won't welcome you warmly. Being assessed by a foreigner is not something we accept lightly."

"And I won't blame them for it, captain. I'm aware of the unusual nature of my assignment here, but I assure you it is purely a political one. The British are war-weary, and it's becoming a popular opinion that we are playing second fiddle to the Americans. So my attendance here, as with others doing the same as me, is simply to show that we are playing a significant role in our alliance. It is simply a morale booster. I'm not here to criticize or cause waves."

Royce nodded in acknowledgment, but his expression gave no opinion on my words. "My understanding is that I'm to assign you to one of my officers for you to tail as part of the assessment. So, I will assign you to my first officer here...." He stopped and glanced at his first officer and then at Jenna. He pondered a moment, and slowly, a smile crossed his face. "Actually, I think I will reconsider that." Jenna's eyes narrowed, realizing, as was I, what he was about to say. "I think it might be a good idea if you tail Lieutenant Plural."

Jenna stiffened, her eyes narrowed into an irritated frown. "Captain, may I remind you, I will be leading the ground assault on Phobos. If Mr. Phelkar is tailing me, he will have to drop into the combat zone."

Royce simply shrugged and chuckled. "He could hardly assess us sitting in the stateroom with the first officer going through crew rosters."

"No offense to Mr. Phelkar," Jenna continued to protest, "but we have planned this down to the last detail. We don't have the luxury to babysit anyone."

Rather than agree with her and potentially find a route out of this situation, I found my pride taking over my good sense. "Lieutenant, I can readily assure you I won't require babysitting."

As she looked back at me, it felt like she was trying to see the soul behind my eyes. I'm not sure, but I think I perceived the slightest smile, but she merely said, "We will see, Mr. Phelkar, we will see."

"Indeed, we will," said Royce, indicating how pleased he was with himself. "I will ensure that your M.E.T. bio download is linked to Lieutenant Plural. If she wakes up, you wake up."

I glanced at him and then looked back at the tall, severe, yet unquestionably beautiful young officer. "Looks like we will be getting to know each other quite well, Lieutenant," I said with a sigh, unaware of how valid my words would be.

She raised an eyebrow and replied, "I'm sure it will be most enlightening for you, Mr. Phelkar." I wasn't sure at the time if she meant that as a joke or not.

"You're dismissed, Lieutenant Plural." And with those words, Royce turned away. It was an obvious snub, and I saw her lips tighten. Her eyes narrowed ever so slightly in contempt at the back of her superior officer.

She turned about on her heel and, striding out, asked, "Have you eaten, Mr. Phelkar?"

"Don't go to any trouble on my account," I said, following on her heels.

"I'm not. I'm hungry and simply observing social niceties and inviting you to join me while I get something to eat."

Chapter Four

Up, Up, and Almost Away

"Does he always treat you like that?" I asked as I trotted to keep up with her swift strides.

"Like what?" she said, and her lips tightened.

"Like you're some kind of enlisted grunt."

She laughed at this, but it was dry and filled with irony. "I'm a GenMod, as you like to call me. What do you expect him to treat me like?"

"With the respect deserving of your rank, Lieutenant." I was starting to understand her extreme reaction to my inappropriate comments about her genetic modifications earlier.

"Don't be so naïve, Mr. Phelkar," she said, and with that, we turned into the mess hall.

The mess was basically a large, repurposed kitchen. As Jenna and I entered, two others were nursing hot drinks at a table.

Jenna introduced the older man. "Mr. Phelkar, please meet our engineer Rockford Harlow."

Harlow looked to be in his seventies and way past retirement age. He did not appear to be in the greatest of health. He had a slight rasp to his breathing and coughed frequently. Although he was polite, he had a grumpy demeanor about him. "Welcome aboard," he said, not bothering to stand or offer his hand. The aging engineer's uniform was stained with the chemicals required to operate the interplanetary engines.

He looked tired and weary. "Thank you," I said as I sat down at the table.

"The young lady is Gunnery Sergeant Helen Tracker, our chief tech," Jenna said as she stepped over to the counter. "Is this all we have?" She looked at a large plate of ham sandwiches. "We could at least have had one of Neuman's fry-ups before we uploaded him."

Tracker smiled at me. She had a pristine uniform covered by a clearly nonregulation pink hoodie. She had a skinny, anorexic look about her, appearing severely underweight. Her long, red hair hung down her neck but did not quite touch her shoulders. She had the matching pale skin and freckled nose that often came with her rare hair coloring.

"Nice to meet you, Mr. Phelkar," she said warmly, reaching over to shake my hand.

"Tracker is one of the best techs in the business. Possibly *the* best," Jenna advised me, and there was the sound of pride in her voice that I had not heard before.

"Really?" Without thinking how rude my following comment was, I said, "How come you're working here then?"

Jenna stared daggers at me, but Tracker just laughed. "It was my choice."

"Tracker is a graduate of M.I.T.," Jenna told me. "They wanted her to work in research, but she is a true Marine and wanted to be out here in the field."

"I believe it's the best use of my skills." Tracker shrugged.

"That's quite laudable," I said, genuinely impressed.

"Yes, well," said Harlow, grumbling. "Break time is over. We have to get back to it." He looked at Jenna. "Some of us have to work for a living." Jenna grinned at him, and he muttered something under his breath as he got up to leave.

"Very nice meeting you, Mr. Phelkar. I look forward to working with you," said Tracker as she followed her superior out of the mess hall.

Jenna passed me a plate of sandwiches and sat in the seat that Harlow had vacated just as Stacey entered. I tried to pull my chair closer to the table and noticed that it was bolted to the floor. There could be only one reason for this, and I looked up at Jenna. "You don't generate gravity on this ship?"

It was Stacey who replied. "We do, but it's nothing like you'd get on one of the more modern and bigger ships," she said. "We can only use it at certain times, so everything in the ship is bolted down." She poured herself a cup of coffee and offered one to Jenna, who nodded.

"My zero-g certification is long expired," I said, thinking this was my get-out opportunity. Stacey handed a cup to Jenna, then offered me one, which I accepted. Jenna smiled ruefully, rolling her eyes and shaking her head in disbelief before locking me in her gaze. "We also operate personal dark energy generators that will keep you on the ground when it can't be operated. I will show you before we lift off. I thought you had a photographic memory of the plans of this ship."

"I told you I only read the summary," I responded irritably. "I did not consider this ship to be of importance for further study."

Stacey moved to stand behind me and placed a hand upon my shoulder. "Don't pick on him." To my astonishment, she slowly began to massage my neck. "It's nice to have some eye candy on board."

Jenna snorted and looked away, taking a sip of her coffee.

"I would hardly call me that," I said, embarrassed.

Stacey leaned down until her cheek touched mine. "Take a look around, mate. Unfortunately, there are not exactly many men on this ship." It was only then I realized she wasn't flirting but was teasing.

"Very funny," I said, and I made to remove her hand. She simply laughed and, leaning in, gave me a swift kiss on my cheek before heading out of the mess hall with her beverage.

"You will get used to Stacey's...." Jenna paused, looking for the right word, "eccentricity. She is the best damn pilot around, which gets her a lot of slack."

"Nothing personal, Lieutenant, but your crew seem overqualified for an old vessel like this."

"She's an old harmless cargo hauler, and that is what we want the Peons to think. We are a special ops division. Our responsibility is to do the missions no one else wants to. Thus, we recruit the best from the Marines and other services. Our current mission to Phobos is to destroy the primary Peon communication center and find out what happened to an American agent who has been working for us for the past year. He went dark a few months back. In the fifteen years since the communication base was built, no one has come close to attacking the base despite many attempts. Tracker, however, believes she knows how to bring down the moon's defensive systems, so we have a green light to try. If we are successful, Mr. Phelkar, we will cripple the E.U.'s interplanetary communications and turn the tide of this war back in our favor. Now that, sir, will be a real morale boost."

She fixed those bright blue eyes upon me, and as I looked back into them, it made me ponder. Jenna Plural may have looked like a homecoming queen, but it is hard to explain; there were years of experience deep in those eyes. "If it is not rude of me to ask, how old are you?"

At first, Jenna looked surprised at what looked like the randomness of my question. She leaned her elbows on the table and rested her chin in her palm. She looked at me with a rueful smile. "Let's just say I was killing Peons while you were still wishing some cute high school cheerleader would notice you."

I couldn't resist my retort. "Oh, Lieutenant Plural didn't go for the pretty girls. They were always such bitches." Jenna got the intent of my comment, but she actually found it amusing and grinned back at me. I could have used this opportunity to ingratiate myself with her. Instead, I said, "So, you have never risen higher than your present rank because of the Prague Convention?"

Her eyes narrowed and then widened, and she laughed humorlessly as she sat back. "Not only do I not rise because of the Prague Convention, but I was also demoted because of it, my dear Mr. Phelkar. I was a general serving in the Pentagon when the Chechnian GenMod uprising happened. When the ban came, I returned to space." She shrugged. "And I'm happier for it."

So, she wasn't only alive at the time of the Grozny uprising but already a general. At the youngest, she couldn't have become a general until at least her thirties and even that was a stretch, but it now put this beautiful Marine in her eighties or nineties. "Yet, despite being screwed over by your country, you're still a patriot?"

Jenna shook her head. "My country never screwed me over, Mr. Phelkar. A-holes on Capitol Hill did that. Don't think government and nation aren't inseparable from one's love."

"I understand, but I would be bitter. How many decades have you put into the service?"

"Many, but I love my work," Jenna stated. There followed an awkward silence before she said, "I'm very concerned about your safety, Mr. Phelkar. This is probably one of our most dangerous missions. I pride myself on my record of bringing back most of my people. I believe that it will put them at risk if I have to concentrate my time looking out for you."

I looked at her, and I could see the frustration in her eyes. "I can assure you, Lieutenant, that I'm quite competent, but it is no more my wish to go into combat on Phobos than yours. However, if I must, I will do so with the utmost professionalism."

Her eyes fixed me with such an intrusive intensity that I wanted to look away, but I resisted. "Mr. Phelkar, I cannot guarantee your safety, and your death will be, at best, a diplomatic problem."

I sat back, smiled, and said simply, "Then I shall endeavor to do my best not to die and inconvenience you, Lieutenant."

She sighed softly and looked down at her coffee cup, saying quietly, "It is not a joking matter." There was another silence between us as she bit her lower lip and stared, deep in thought, at the swirls in her cup.

I was already coming to understand that there was more to this woman than the stern military officer I first encountered. "Look, Lieutenant, I don't know what will happen," I said, trying to sound reassuring. "However, I promise you this: If I do go down to Phobos, I will place myself under your command and obey your orders to the letter. And if that is to keep my head down and hide or run screaming at the enemy, I won't shirk, argue, or debate it."

She looked up, and her eyes narrowed as if she did not quite believe me. "You would take orders from an American?"

"I would take orders from the commander of the mission. It's in my interest and that of all our safety to do so." She still looked unsure. I raised my small finger and offered it to her. "Look, I'll even pinky swear if it helps."

She tried not to smile, but it came anyway. "Idiot," she muttered, then sighed and rose to her feet. "Come on, Mr. Phelkar, let's prepare for launch."

I had hoped to watch the launch from the cockpit, but it was too small, and there was no seating for me. Even Jenna had to take her place in a separate room. She led me into one of the crew cabins. It had four bunks with straps attached to hold the user in place. Jenna opened a cabinet at the back of the room and pulled a chunky-looking belt from a rack where several hung. "Ever used one of these, Mr. Phelkar?"

"What is it?" I asked as she held it up to me and pulled another one out for herself.

Jenna looked back at me, surprised I did not know what it was. "It's a dark energy belt. It pulls in or repels dark energy."

"Ah, an anti-gravity belt," I said knowingly.

She shook her head. "Not quite. It distorts millimeters of space all around your body. Pull dark energy towards you, and you repel gravity. Reverse that, and you get gravity where there is none. You fool the laws of physics."

I put it around my waist and struggled to fasten it, and before I knew it, she took it back from me. She dropped her own upon a bunk, stepped up close to me, and reached around to put mine on me. I looked down at her head which almost leaned against my chest. I could smell the apple blossom of the shampoo she had recently used. Her proximity had my hormones revved up like I was a high school freshman again. This piece of fine art from the hands of a team of master geneticists was so close, so alluring, even in her casual camo uniform. As she fastened the buckle, I hoped she did not notice my arousal. "Don't touch it until after we take off," she said casually.

My brain somersaulted, and I flushed. "Wait, erm, huh?"

"The belt, Mr. Phelkar." She looked up at me as she stood upright again. "Don't activate it until after we have launched."

"Oh, right. Yes, of course." I replied, relieved.

"Lie down on the couch, and I'll show you how to strap in." She casually indicated the top bunk, and she put on her own D.E. belt as I climbed up and lay down. She pulled the straps over me, tying me tightly down before climbing onto the bunk beneath me. "Try to keep your penis under control in the future, Mr. Phelkar. I prefer not to be the subject of your adolescent schoolboy fantasies." At that precise moment, Helen Tracker came in and stopped just inside the doorway, startled by Jenna's words. However, rather than get embarrassed by this, I got pretty annoyed. "Don't blame me for your parents making you sexually attractive, Lieutenant. I assure you any reaction by me is not by choice." I intended it as an insult, but to my surprise, she laughed. It was a soft, gentle laugh and the first thing she had done that was even remotely feminine.

"Touché, Mr. Phelkar, touché," she said, amused.

"Should I wait outside or something?" Tracker indicated the door.

"No, Gunnery Sergeant, you're good," Jenna responded. "Take your place." Tracker slipped onto a bunk beside me. "Did Harlow upload without complaint?" Jenna asked.

"Harlow does nothing without complaint," Tracker replied as she fastened herself down, and Jenna chuckled.

"G'day, Control," we heard Stacey say as she came over the ship-wide intercom. "This is Stacey Grant of the U.S.S. Lewis Puller to traffic control requesting departure clearance."

There was a brief pause, and then the voice of control came back. "Confirmed, Lewis Puller. Go for immediate lift-off. Clear skies to you, Stacey."

"That's a roger, Control. Keep a brew on 'til we get back. Igniting thrusters." I felt the boom of the engines igniting and felt that familiar vibration from the ship's hull. "External gravity compensators at twenty past ten percent." It was odd hearing Stacey sound so professional. There was that initial queasy feeling as the ship's dark energy drives came online. Then came that slight wobble as it repelled gravity. It felt like we were on the ocean. "Compensators at thirty percent and rising." The sea of dark energy beneath us wobbled us even more. "Seventy percent, now engaging thrust." The wobble was replaced by sudden upward momentum. I felt a moment of nausea as the g forces pressed down against my stomach. "D.E. compensators are at one hundred percent. We are in ascending freefall and increasing thrust." The Chesty shot up into the sky with a roar of the engines. It seemed to take an eternity, but I knew it was probably less than a minute until all went silent.

Stacey said, "We have left Earth's atmosphere and are floating free. Switching off external D.E. compensators."

I made a move to unbuckle myself, but Tracker stopped me. "Not yet, not until Stacey says it's okay. Safety protocols."

We waited a few more minutes until the young pilot's voice came over the speakers. "And the skies are clear, and the stars are shining brightly. At this time, you're free to unfasten your seatbelts and move about the cabin. Drinks will be served in the cocktail lounge in half an hour."

The three of us unfastened our buckles, and I sat up. Jenna sighed and shook her head with disbelief as I took off toward the ceiling. "Mr. Phelkar, you were told we don't generate gravity until out of Earth's system." I was embarrassed as I gently bounced off the ceiling and headed back down. I thrust my hand out to grab the wall but couldn't reach it. Jenna and Tracker reached up, grabbed me by the sleeves, and pulled me back down.

"Sorry about that," I muttered with humility.

"Idiot," Jenna said curtly, but Tracker laughed lightly. Still holding on to me, Jenna pulled me closer to her and adjusted the control on my belt with her other hand, then let go of me. Instantly I fell flat on the floor. As I raised my head, I found myself staring at her highly polished boots just in front of me. I made to get up, but she placed one of those boots firmly on my neck, pinning me down. "If this were a combat situation, you're now dead, Mr. Phelkar." Each time I made to get up, she simply pushed down harder. "Do you get my point?"

"Yes," I gasped. She stepped off and offered me a hand up, but I refused to take it.

I dusted myself down and glanced at Tracker, who looked embarrassed by what Jenna had done but struggled to hold back a grin. "Well, I best be getting back to the M.E.T.," she said and departed swiftly.

I rubbed the back of my neck and looked at Jenna. She had a smug look, and I wanted to punch her. "Come on, Mr. Phelkar, it's time to get you dematerialized before doing any damage to yourself." Before we could go anywhere, Stacey's urgent voice came over the intercom. "Tactical alert seven. Tactical alert seven."

"What's that?" I asked.

Jenna started out the door with me in tow. "That means the enemy is tagging us."

"Why would they tag us and not just follow us?" I asked.

"Near-Earth orbit, it's filled with space junk," Jenna said. "Almost impossible to get a lock on any ship leaving Earth. So, the Peons mine the area with probes that will lock onto anything not moving in an orbital direction. So, come on, let's get up to the cockpit and see what's happening."

Chapter Five

Interception

"Whoever has their D.E. belts active, turn the damn things off," Stacey shouted over the intercom. "You know they screw with the maneuvering thrusters."

"Damnit," Jenna muttered. It was her turn to look embarrassed as she reached out and deactivated mine, then her own, and we both floated again.

"Idiot!" I said in an awful imitation of her voice as I grabbed the wall.

I thought she was about to explode on me for a moment, but her anger immediately turned to a grin. "Dork," she muttered. "Do you want to wait here?" I shook my head. I was starting to feel queasy and desperately tried not to vomit, but I felt uneasy about being left alone.

As we made our way to the cockpit, pulling ourselves along the corridors, the ship lurched to the right and left. "That can't be an attack. It would draw the attention of our own fleets," I argued.

"It's probably not a ship, but Stacey is trying to maneuver away from something."

We reached the cockpit as the young pilot was making violent twists. The captain sat quietly, letting her do her thing. Jenna pulled herself up to his side. "What's happening?"

"Bloody Peon probe," Royce snorted. "One of the limpet kinds is trying to stick to us and burrow in. They will be tracking us to Mars if it attaches. Any element of surprise will be done."

"Hold on to your seats, boys and girls," Stacey interrupted, and I looked around for something to hold on to. Jenna, who gripped a handle on the wall fitted for such occasions, swiftly grabbed me and pulled me to her as she backed into the wall. Her arm wrapped around my waist, and she hugged me up against her. The ship spun and twisted in a one-eighty spin, lurched in many backward and forward movements, and then suddenly accelerated at full in-system speed. Jenna was pressed back into the wall, and I was pushed against her. Jenna's face was so close to mine, her blue eyes filling my vision, full of what can only be described as disdain. My heart pounded as that beautiful face studied mine. I could smell her minty breath and actually believed that was part of her genetic design and not her strict adherence to dental hygiene. Obviously, it was the latter.

"Why did you do that?" I asked uneasily.

"Because you were too slow, Mr. Phelkar," she said coldly, "Had I not, you would be splattered on the back of the wall. You said you would not be a liability in our assault. Yet here we are, not even out of Earth space. And seriously, Mr. Phelkar, more schoolboy fantasies when we are in a situation like this?"

"I'm sorry," I said sheepishly.

"Idiot." As the Chesty stopped accelerating, she pushed the tip of one finger into my stomach. Just enough to cause discomfort but not actual pain, and roughly shoved me away from her. I floated backward, stopping myself with the back of the captain's chair.

"Everyone can relax now." Stacey's cheerful voice announced. "I lost the bugger. Bloody hell, I'm good."

"Indeed, you are, Miss Grant," the captain said appreciatively. "Now, take us to Mars."

"Setting course. We will rendezvous with Phobos in seven weeks, three days, and thirteen hours."

"Close the shields," Royce ordered, and she hit a couple more buttons, and large exterior shielding came down over the glass screens. "Set ArtGrav to run for one hour."

"Bringing gravity online. Let's go get our molecules broken down." Stacey turned and grinned at me.

I was relieved to be standing on the deck again. I immediately excused myself and went out to find a bathroom. Locking myself in, I threw up violently. I then sank to the floor, trying to get my breath back. "Mr. Phelkar, have you quite finished?" Jenna's irritated voice came from outside.

"Just a minute." I washed my face with a damp cloth.

Jenna stood leaning against the bulkhead just outside the door. Her arms were crossed, and her head tilted to one side with a frustrated expression. "My understanding was that you were supposed to follow me. But, so far, all that is happening is I have to take care of you like some errant child."

"Sorry," was all I could think of to say.

"If it weren't for the captain, I would have you put in storage till we return to Earth." She shook her head slowly and most patronizingly at me. "Come on. The captain and Morris have already dematerialized." Then, without another word, she turned and headed briskly up the corridor.

The ship was designed in the days before dematerialization. The actual room proved little more than a repurposed storage area. Tracker stood at the console in the corner of the room, smiling at me as I stepped in with Jenna. I felt a tight knot in my stomach. Stacey followed us in and slapped me on the back, "Come on, you pommy bastard, it's not that bad."

"Ladies first," I said casually, but I felt far from relaxed.

Stacey grinned and started to pull up her shirt to remove it.

"What are you doing?" I asked, wide-eyed.

Helen Tracker replied. "You can't be dematerialized with nonorganic material unless you have special filters like your tracker and memory chip. If you mix synthetic with organic matter, it confuses the system."

"And you're happy just stripping off in front of anyone?" I said, startled.

"Mr. Phelkar," Jenna said impatiently. "You're the one with the problem. We are United States Marines and have been integrated for hundreds of years. If you have an outdated issue with seeing a woman naked or simply feel you cannot control yourself, I suggest you go outside."

I was about to respond when Stacey started to unfasten her bra. I hurried outside. Jenna called me back barely a minute later, and Stacey was nowhere to be seen. "Come on, Mr. Phelkar, we don't have all day. The gravity will go off soon." Jenna stated.

"I think you should go ahead."

Jenna rolled her eyes and shook her head slowly but in despair, not disagreement. "You're a most ineffectual man, Mr. Phelkar."

I shrugged. "Just think of it as my British eccentricity," I said sarcastically as I stepped outside again and waited until she disappeared too. As I stepped in again, something occurred to me. Was I expected to undress in front of this young tech? "I should probably wait until everyone else is gone. I'm an observer, after all," I said to her.

Tracker smiled at me. "You're the last one, Mr. Phelkar."

"Am I supposed to get undressed here?"

Tracker shrugged. "Get undressed wherever you like. Unfortunately, I still have to dematerialize you here. Don't worry. You don't have anything I haven't seen before."

"Yes, well, to use the old cliché, you haven't seen mine."

Tracker chuckled lightly. "Come on, Mr. Phelkar, let's get this over with. I have to recalibrate this to upload myself, which takes longer. If it makes you feel more comfortable, you're not my preferred gender."

Slowly and very uncomfortably, I started to remove my clothes. I kept glancing up at her to see if she was looking at me. Even though she paid no attention to me and continued to look at her computer screen, I still felt as if her eyes were upon me. Eventually, as naked as the day I was born with my clothes folded up in a pile, I stood waiting with my hands covering my embarrassment.

Tracker glanced up and nodded to my pile of clothes. "Put those in one of the lockers, if you please."

I turned to see about a dozen lockers fitted into the wall. "There aren't enough here for everyone." I noticed.

"Officers and warrant officers only. Everyone else undresses in the crew cabins," she said as I stuffed my clothes into one of the lockers.

Tracker indicated the circular disc on the floor and said. "Would you stand there, please?" I meekly complied, still holding my hands firmly in front of my humility. "You need to put your hands out at your sides and spread your legs so no part of you touches another part of you."

"You're not making this very easy, madam?"

"Are all English people this shy?" Tracker chuckled.

"Unfortunately, it's not my place to answer for the rest of my nationality, but..." Tracker rolled her eyes and hit a button. There was a blinding flash of light. It was so bright that it caused an intense glare on my retina, taking a few moments to clear. "Has something gone wrong?" I asked. I looked about the room as my eyes adjusted, but no one was there. Helen Tracker had vanished in the flash of light.

I waited indecisively for a good minute, looking around the room, expecting something to happen. Then I pulled my clothes out of the locker and put on my pants and shirt, and, sockless, I slipped on my shoes. As I stepped off the circle, there was immediately another blinding flash of light. I turned to see Jenna's naked form rematerialize. I instantly turned my back to her and blustered out in a long stream. "Somethings happened. Something went wrong. Tracker was trying to dematerialize me, and it must have hit her. She disappeared right in front of me."

There was a pause, and I heard Jenna sigh before she replied, "I'm starting to think you have some form of mental defection," she said casually. "I'm now clothed, Mr. Phelkar. You can turn around without your eyes burning out," she added, and as I turned back, she had moved to the M.E T. console. She was back in what she had worn before, but now her hair was long, loose, and hung around her shoulders, and without looking up, she stated, "We have been uploaded for three weeks. Tracker is not here because after she uploaded you, she uploaded herself and is still in there." Jenna indicated the M.E.T. equipment.

I admit this startled me as my whole experience was just that flash of light. However, something occurred to me. "We were supposed to be in there seven weeks. We are less than halfway to Mars."

"Give that man a coconut," she muttered sarcastically, not looking up from the console. "The system is programmed to rematerialize a senior officer should an urgent matter occur."

"So why would it wake me up?" Curious, I stepped up close behind her and looked over her shoulder, but she gently pushed me away with her elbow.

"As the captain said, you're observing me, and you cannot observe me whilst you are degraded into nothing. He had Tracker link us together."

"So, what is going on?"

She stepped away from the console and finally looked up at me with an air of mystery in her eyes, "That's the trillion-dollar question, Mr. Phelkar. Come on, let's go find out."

I followed her out into the corridor, and we made our way up to the cockpit. Jenna slipped into the pilot's chair and started to tap out on a screen in front of her. "It would appear that we are under attack."

The shields drew back from the windows, and I stepped up to stare out. "I don't see anything out there," I said.

"That is because the ship on an intercept course is still several hours away. The ship's computer calculates the distance, speed, and trajectory of other ships in our area." She pointed at a small screen on the console, which made little sense to me, and I could only assume that one of the little blips was us and the other little blip was the European ship. "In this instance, the ship has assessed that we can't evade the European cruiser that is now pursuing us. No matter what we do, they will intercept us."

"What *can* we do?" I said, trying to fight back the panic welling up within me. "We can't materialize the entire company."

"Correct, Mr. Phelkar, but we will materialize as many as possible to repel any boarders."

"What do you rate our chances?" I asked, not sure if I genuinely wanted to hear the answer.

Jenna shrugged and looked back down at the readout. "It's a modern European light cruiser. The crew will be little more than what we can carry dematerialized, but it is heavily armored."

"Is surrender an option? Should it look like a worst-case scenario?"

Jenna looked up at me with utter disgust upon her face at that idea. "I will pretend I didn't hear that, Mr. Phelkar. Even if it was an option, neither side can afford to take prisoners with ships designed with environmental systems to support only their crew."

I sighed softly. "So much for my little diplomatic mission for His Majesty's Government."

Jenna rose from the pilot's chair and turned around to face me full-on. "I'm going to need help in making the preparations, and I need to know that I can rely on you." She looked at me intently. "Be honest with me. I can always wake up someone else."

At first, I took this to be a condescending statement, but something in her eyes felt like she was giving me a chance to prove myself. She was right. I was probably a liability, for I had not faced actual combat. Call it pride or male ego, but something inside me wanted to prove I wasn't the ineffectual man she thought I was. I sighed softly. "I'll be honest with you. I'm afraid, but I will do whatever I can to protect the ship and her crew."

"I appreciate your candor, Mr. Phelkar," she said. Then heading out, she added, "Come on, let's do this."

Jenna led me down to a section of the ship I had not visited before. We entered an armory that was filled with lockers and sealed gun racks. She pulled her loose hair up into a pony and simply tied it in a knot. She turned back to me and looked me up and down. "What are your sizes?" she asked. I told her, and she opened one of the lockers. She pulled out a black flak jacket and a set of matching light armor combat knee and elbow pads. She tossed them over to me and instructed me to put them on. She did the same. She unlocked a gunrack, pulling out two snub nose, low-velocity Glock Pacifiers, pistols explicitly designed for shipboard combat and known euphemistically as "snap pistols" due to their noise when fired.

She handed one to me with a couple of clips and demonstrated how to load them. Then, with an almost pleasurable look, she said, "These babies are designed to be up close and personal. They have a low velocity to reduce the minuscule risk of hull penetration or hitting an oxygen tank and the like. But that pretty much makes them shit at long range." She handed me a holster for the snap gun. I looked at it, wondering how I could put it on with such a small strap until I saw Jenna wrap hers around her thigh.

I copied her and strapped my holster like hers. Then she reached into another locker, the contents of which I couldn't see until she withdrew two short blades in scabbards. They were too long to be knives and too short to be swords. "These darlings are made of murcuranium." She tossed me one, and as I fastened it about my waist, she explained, "Last-resort weapon, out of ammo, fighting up close." She drew hers from its sheath and twirled it in her hand to show me a plain cylindrical black fabric handle finished off with a silver disk top. "Slap the base, and you get a thirty-second electrical charge. It takes another thirty seconds to recharge before you can use it again."

I looked at the blade momentarily before finishing strapping it about my waist. I couldn't imagine the gruesome prospect of using it on another human being. Shooting someone from a distance was one thing, but sticking someone with this weapon was another. I put the thought from my mind and looked back up at her. "So, you don't think there's any way to stop them even trying to come aboard?" The jamming and counter-jamming had long ended ship-to-ship combat. Missiles could be deflected unless so close you could damage your own ship. Boarding was the only option left.

She shook her head. "None at all. If we plan well, we can stop them as they enter the ship. However, the only way we're getting out of this is if we counterattack and manage to board them somehow."

"Why don't we try that before they board us?" I asked.

"This ship simply isn't designed for assault." She turned her back to me. "Spot check, please." I stepped up and began fastening the buckles at the back of her armor as she continued. "We need to enter their ship via the method they use to board us. They will probably come through the hull with umbilical tubes, and we need to push them back and enter their ship via their connection."

"That's no small task," I said softly, and as I finished, I turned my back to her.

"No, it isn't, but we can do it," she said confidently as she tightened my buckles a little too tightly for comfort. "We have done it before." However, I wasn't sure if she was trying to convince herself or me, for it sounded more like a pep talk she would use to bolster the spirits of her troops.

As I turned back to face her, she placed a small pin under the collar of my shirt. "Don't let this get damaged, and don't lose it. We don't turn on the internal defenses unless we have no alternative, but if we do, this is the only thing that stops the mini-guns from targeting you as an enemy." She slapped me on the shoulder. "Come on, Mr. Phelkar, let's prep this baby."

Chapter Six

Repelling Boarders

We went around the ship going through the various defense systems and activating them in readiness for the assault. Compact mini-guns dropped out of the ceiling and hung there menacingly.

"Why can't we use these as our first resort?" I asked.

"Because the dunderheads at R&D installed them, forgetting our walls don't have a murcuranium lining in the hull. They would rip the ship to shreds, and there is a small possibility they will puncture the exterior."

We laid out uniforms, snap pistols, and swords in neat piles along the corridors leading away from the M.E.T. room. The Marines would be downloaded rapidly and vacate the M.E.T. as fast as possible. Realizing they would be coming out of that room as naked as the day they were born, I was starting to learn that life in the United States Marine Corps wasn't a dignified one.

We eventually returned to the cockpit, and I could now see the light cruiser closing in. It was sleek, white, and modern.

"I think it is time to download the captain," Jenna said unenthusiastically. She surprised me with some complimentary words as we headed back to the M.E.T. "Thank you for your assistance today, Mr. Phelkar. We worked well together."

"My pleasure, Lieutenant." I don't know why the words of this lieutenant, who so far I had found most objectionable, actually pleased me. But, alas, her following words completely undermined that.

"However, I have been thinking. Perhaps I should upload you until this is over, after all."

I will readily admit that I was afraid of the oncoming assault, but I was more fearful of dying in that scrambling device and never knowing it. "Lieutenant, I'm supposed to remain with you."

"No one considered we would be boarded, Mr. Phelkar." Jenna shook her head. "Things are different now."

I thought quickly. "I find your judgment of my ability quite offensive, Lieutenant Plural. If this ship is going down, I want to be part of its defense and not simply cease to exist inside some magic box which will turn me into protons." The latter part of this statement was probably closer to the truth.

Jenna studied me for a little longer. Her perfectly sculpted eyebrows knotted together before she relaxed and shrugged with a smile. "Just remember, don't leave my side, at any time, for any reason."

"What if you get killed?"

A wide grin crossed her face. Whilst a pleasant change, it made her look even younger and increased the challenge to take her seriously. "Then you cease to be my problem, and I cease to be yours, Mr. Phelkar."

"How reassuring," I muttered but returned the smile.

Jenna tapped in the codes, which resulted in a bright light again and the sudden appearance of the portly captain, a rather grotesque sight in his nakedness. Seeing Jenna and not Helen Tracker, who would typically be the first downloaded, he immediately knew something was wrong.

"Status report, Plural," he said, grabbing his clothes from a locker and hastily dressing.

"Peons are coming in, port side."

"Just what we need," he grumbled. "Okay, get Tracker out of there and have her send Grant and Morris to the bridge." He headed for the door, then added as an afterthought. "Oh, and join us yourself."

"Yes, Sir," Jenna responded coldly as he disappeared. She turned back to the computer console. There was another flash, and the young technician appeared. I immediately turned to face the other way, and Jenna briefed her on what was going on while she dressed. Tracker acknowledged her as Jenna gave her the captain's orders, and then we both left the room.

"Shouldn't Tracker be bringing out more than just the pilot?" I asked as we briskly headed down the corridor.

"She will. She's a professional, Mr. Phelkar. She knows we're in a combat situation and what is required of her."

We joined the captain in the cockpit, cursing under his breath as he watched the ship grow larger. "I don't need this. I'm too old for it," he said with irritation. As Stacey raced in, he stood aside, allowing her to jump into her seat in the pilot's chair. She started hitting a few controls before stating, "E.T.A. twenty-three minutes. I can probably gain you seven more minutes with some maneuvers."

The captain turned to look at Stephanie Morris, who was now standing in the doorway. She simply shrugged, unable to answer his unspoken question. Jenna stepped forward. "There's no point. It'll only delay the inevitable. We could be ready well before that."

"Morris, get your troops ready to repel boarders," the captain snapped.

Morris' eyes opened wide. "Sir, how do I do that?"

The startled look on the captain's face was picture-perfect. "You're my first officer and a United States Marine."

"Sir, before coming here, I was the second officer on board the John F. Kennedy. My duties consisted of supply lists and crew rosters."

"We are wasting time, Captain," Jenna snapped. "You know I'm the only person here who can deal with this. Get past your damned bigotry, and give me the go-ahead."

The captain's chubby face looked like it was about to explode with anger, but he just sighed. "Go for it, Plural."

Jenna spun on her heel and almost walked into Morris. She gave the first officer a contemptuous glare and waited impatiently for her to move. Morris hurriedly stepped out of her way, and I followed hot on her heels.

Men and women now filled the corridors, and I was surprised and relieved by how fast they had gotten into their uniforms. The buzz of conversation died as soon as the ones visible to us saw Jenna, and they jumped to attention. The second officer stood legs astride and hands behind her back. She waited in silence for a few moments, and the tension rose as all that was heard was the engine's hum. Suddenly, she swung out a fist, hit the intercom, and looked at her watch. Her voice boomed out all over the ship.

"Listen up, boys and girls. Seventeen minutes from now, Peons come a calling." She paused. "They want to take your ship." She paused again. "But just like the man who this ship is named after, we shall give them no quarter." Another pause. "We shall make them pay in Peon blood for every square foot of our ship." Her voice was rising in volume as she spoke. "They're coming from the port side, and we will expect full penetration." Someone giggled. "Stop sniggering, Paisley. We won't let these Peon bastards win the day." She then screamed out, "We are United States Marines. What are we?"

"United States Marines, Ma'am," they replied in unison, and it echoed around the ship.

"OORAH!" she screamed like a drill instructor.

"OORAH!" came the collective reply.

"Fall in on the port corridor and prepare for battle."

They ran in formation to where Jenna had commanded them. She came back to where I was standing like a fifth wheel. "Are you with me, Mr. Phelkar?" She gave me what I took to be an encouraging smile.

"Yes, Ma'am," I said, and I followed her. I was caught up in her confidence and positiveness and felt kind of proud that I was with this person who had such respect from her troops. The troops lined up facing the outer bulkhead holding their snub-nosed pistols at waist height pointed at the wall, for they couldn't extend their arms in the cramped corridor. Jenna led me around via the starboard side to join the rear of the line, as we couldn't fit past them.

Jenna raised her weapon, and I stood nervously at her side and raised my own. I hoped she didn't see my hand shaking. But, to my surprise, she smiled, and, glancing at me, she whispered softly. "Don't worry, Mr. Phelkar, we will prevail."

An eerie silence fell all around us, and only the slight hum of the engines and vibrations of the decks could be heard. We waited. I thought my heart would explode out of my chest, but I stood firm.

I did not realize the enemy hull hitting ours would be so loud. There was a boom, and it vibrated through the deck in an aftershock. Up in the cockpit, Stacey cut the Chesty's engines. The ship fell silent. The line of Marines tensed. "Easy boys and girls, just gonna be like squishing frog spawn," Jenna called down the line. "Ferris, stop scratching your ass, and Butterwick, hold up that ugly head of yours. You're killing Peons, not going down on your boyfriend." This brought a lot of snickering until the loud grinding and drilling began. The enemy was cutting their way into the bulkhead. "They won't drill all the way through," Jenna told me quietly. "That would make it too easy for us to get them. We could take them one by one. They can just do enough damage to weaken the hull and then blow it fast."

"Won't we get hit by debris?" I asked nervously.

She shrugged off that question. "Maybe some, but nothing significant. The explosive charge is a chemical that instantly destroys metal but not flesh. Otherwise, they'd kill their own troops waiting on the other side to come through. Even Peons aren't that dumb."

Further down the corridor, two Marines started to fire as a hole appeared in the wall, and I saw the first body fall through It and onto the deck. We had drawn first blood. Further gunfire was exchanged between our Marines and the Peons. The first casualty on our side was a young man who flew back against the wall and slumped to the ground. Butterwick, I think. Then there were more popping sounds along the corridor as holes opened along the bulkhead. It was almost deafening. I raised my gun towards the wall as it disappeared in front of me, and I fired into the darkness one, two, then three rounds.

Jenna opened fire too, and a shot came back, hitting the wall between us. I didn't even flinch, though I think it was more likely I was petrified by fear than Jenna, who showed stoic resolution as we continued to fire back. Suddenly, a small grenade was thrown into the corridor from the enemy ship. Jenna jumped at me, pushing me out of the way and onto the ground and covering me from the expected blast. Instead, a blinding flash of light came.

"Flashbang," Jenna said urgently, climbing to her feet. She reached a hand down to help me up, but I did not take it. Instead, I fired at the Peon, who, unbeknownst to her, was coming out of the opening. He staggered back, and Jenna spun around faster than I'd ever seen anyone move. Her leg raised to chest height, she kicked him up against the wall and shot him in the face. She turned back to me as his lifeless body slid to the ground. "Thanks," she muttered as she locked hands with me and pulled me up.

We moved away from the enemy entrances. I looked down the line to see that many of our troops had fallen. Then, Peons began pouring in, cutting us off from our own people as they retreated down the opposite end of the corridor. Jenna and I were now in a wider passage area, and we stood side by side, firing back down it. But as soon as any died, they were replaced by more pouring into the corridor like rats through a broken sewer pipe. "Damn it to hell," Jenna cursed. She hit the nearby intercom and shouted, "Tracker, start downloading more Marines and do it fast. Forget safety protocols."

"Aye, ma'am!" came the calm and professional reply of the ship's chief tech.

Jenna suddenly cried out and doubled over as blood spurted from her abdomen. Clutching at her gut, she went down with a cry. I stepped over my fallen companion, putting myself between her and our attackers. I fired at the bastards, killing as many as possible until I had no more bullets. As the empty gun clicked, I dropped it and stepped back over the lieutenant. I reached down and grabbed the collar of her shirt. She let out a scream of pain as I dragged her back out of the fight and around the bend of the corridor and immediate harm's way. I saw that no one was coming after us, unaware that that was unusual. I dropped to my knees and, pulling up her shirt, checked the wound as she muttered every expletive under the sun. The bullet had got her just below her vest. I admit I was in a panic. What was I to do if Jenna died? I certainly had no faith in the captain, and Stephanie Morris wasn't even backing us up.

"Med pack... on the wall..." Jenna pointed further up the corridor, and I raced along it until I saw it and pulled it off. I started to rip it open as I ran back to her. I did not see, against the black of the floor, that her blood had begun to pool. I slipped on it, falling feet first and kicking her hard in the hip with the flat of my shoes. She cried out in pain, clutching at her stomach with both arms. As I got up onto my knees, she laughed at me through the pain. "Idiot." She muttered.

I ignored the comment as I thrust some wadding from the pack into the wound.

"Got a stim pack in there?" she rasped.

I pulled one out and, biting off the cap, thrust its needle into her arm, allowing the auto-injector to do its work. Her face began to relax as the pain dissipated. I removed the wadding and mopped up as much blood as possible.

"Can you hold it together?" I asked, referring to the wound. Nodding and through clenched teeth, she held the puncture wound closed. I pulled out some sealant and sprayed the greasy mixture on it. In seconds, the combination bonded into an artificial skin layer. Her nanobots already had been starting to heal the wound, and although she would still have to see a doctor later to remove the bullet, it would do for now.

She pulled her shirt back down and glanced back up the corridor. "There should have been more coming," she said, her eyes narrowed with suspicion. "We have to get back there."

"You're not in any condition to fight," I implored, placing a hand on her shoulder as she tried to get up.

She looked up at me and gave a weak smile. "You forget, Mr. Phelkar, I'm not like you. I can keep going much longer than the average human." She looked back down the corridor with her eyes staring intently. "Why hasn't anyone come after us?" She almost said it to herself but turned back at me with a questioning look. "Can you hear that?" I listened but heard nothing, and I looked at her bewildered. She looked up at me with a very concerned expression. "Exactly. The fighting has stopped."

"Maybe it's just moved on."

She shook her head. "Oh, no, Mr. Phelkar. Not on a ship this small. We may not hear the snaps of the guns, but you would certainly hear the screams." She reached her hand out to me. "Help me up."

"I need to get you to Doctor Archer," I said firmly.

Jenna rolled her eyes at me, still holding out her hand. "My mother never mothered me, so I'm not about to start letting you, Mr. Phelkar. You can help me up, or I'll do it myself."

Reluctantly, I took her hand and pulled her to her feet. After retrieving my firearm and reloading it, we cautiously ventured back down the corridor. Bodies lined the floor, and when we could no longer walk two abreast, Jenna went ahead. Everywhere was so packed with corpses that we had no choice but to step on them to get over. She did pretty well but couldn't completely hide the pain, giving out stifled gasps now and then. To our surprise, the Peons had sealed the entry holes they had made. There was no sign of them, at least, not any living. Jenna stopped to examine the seals, reaching out to touch one of them as if she was making sure what she saw was real. "This isn't right. Something is so wrong here," she muttered.

I was startled when the ship-wide intercom came on with the gruff voice of Royce. "Lieutenant Plural, stand down. Purple sky, I repeat, purple sky. Stand down."

Jenna's already furrowed expression frowned deeper, and I asked, "What does he mean by 'purple sky'?"

"It's the passphrase to indicate that he is not under duress and that it is a genuine order," she said with bewilderment.

"So, what do you think is going on?"

She looked back at me. "To be honest, Mr. Phelkar, I have no idea."

"The Peons appear to have retreated?"

"Apparently!" said Jenna, as confused as I was, as we continued back toward the bridge, weapons still at the ready.

"Did we beat them back?" I asked hopefully.

She laughed and said, "No, we were dead the moment that ship started to follow us."

"But you said...."

She cut me off. "What did you expect me to say, Mr. Phelkar, 'Come on, boys and girls, let's go die today'?"

I was momentarily dumbstruck but eventually said, "You expected me to die today?"

She looked back at me with a grin and a shrug. "I offered to upload you, Mr. Phelkar."

Once more, the intercom crackled into life. "Lieutenant Plural, confirm that you have stood down. Report to the cockpit."

She stepped over to a wall intercom with an irritated grimace and thumped the switch. "Stand down confirmed," she snapped.

"What exactly is the issue between you and the captain?" I asked.

"He is a genophobe. Tried to get me replaced," she muttered.

"A genophobe?" I was shocked and tried to fathom how that would be relevant to officer interactions.

"Yeah," she said disinterestedly as we set off again.

After a minute, I asked, "Lieutenant, do you know what genophobe means?"

She looked back at me. "Hates GenMods. I thought you were an educated man, Mr. Phelkar." She turned away, and I just grinned to myself.

We made our way up to the cockpit, Jenna fending off questions from the surprised Marines that we encountered. "Get Tracker to download Doctor Archer to see to the wounded," she ordered a large thick-set man. Then she turned to another. "Start racking and stacking our dead in the cargo hold."

"What about the Peon dead and wounded?" the Marine asked.

"Stick them out the airlock," she barked, heading away from him.

"The wounded, Ma'am?"

"I don't like repeating myself, Sergeant Reeves," she said, not looking back. "They don't take prisoners in space, so neither do we."

Chapter Seven

Surrender

As we entered the cockpit, Royce was sunk back into his chair, looking melancholic. He did not speak. Morris was seated in the co-pilot seat. Seriously! She had not lifted a finger to help us out there, and I felt resentment. Stacey turned in her chair and looked up at us. Gone was the cheerful disposition that I had seen since meeting her.

"What the hell is going on?" Jenna demanded loud enough for Royce to raise his hand to his ear and lean away from her.

Stacey spoke quietly. "It just came over the interplanetary emergency broadcast. The United States has surrendered," her voice almost choked. "Britain, Canada, Japan, and all the allies are expected to follow."

I felt a knot in my stomach, and Jenna turned ashen white. "What the hell are you talking about?" she snapped.

"It's confirmed," the captain said. "It came over the interplanetary communications a few minutes ago. Those engaged in current hostilities are to stop and turn themselves over to European authority. The war is over."

Jenna grabbed my arm to steady herself, for she was shaking. "No, this can't be true. The president stated that we would never surrender as long as any American lived and breathed."

Royce sighed. "That's politics for you, Lieutenant, but she has surrendered, and Congress has endorsed her."

Spittle flew from Jenna's mouth as she screamed, "That's bullshit! Total and utter bullshit!" She then clutched at her wound and winced. Her other hand still gripped my arm. It was starting to hurt. I just stood there, unable to find the words that fit the situation. The inter-ship commlink started to blink, and Stacey turned back to her controls.

"There is an incoming call from the Peon ship, Captain," she said softly.

"Put it through, Miss Grant," Royce said dejectedly.

A thick French-accented voice came online. "This is Captain Matis of the Force d'Action Navale ship Jauréguiberry. I wish to discuss your surrender with your captain."

"Go ahead, Jangweberry, this is the captain of the U.S.S. Lewis Puller," the captain said with resignation.

"Bonjour mon Capitan. Can I assume that you've heard instructions about our hostilities ceasing?"

"You can. I'm willing to discuss terms of our surrender to your authority."

Jenna gripped my arm more tightly, her face a mix of anguish and anger.

The Peon captain chuckled. "Oh, mon Capitan, there are no terms. Your president has agreed to an unconditional surrender. You will disable all your weaponry. Disconnect your automated systems and prepare for my second officer to take command of your vessel. You will be towed to the nearest E.U. base and turned over for processing. Don't worry, mon Capitan. I'm sure you will soon be home watching baseball and eating hotdogs."

"Ow!" I could hold it no longer; Jenna's nails had broken into my skin. She looked at me sharply but then turned straight back to Royce. She let go and leaned her palms on the back of his chair as I rubbed my arm.

"I look forward to meeting you, mon Capitan," the Peon captain said quite jovially.

James Royce nodded to Stacey, who instantly cut the communication feed. "Peon bastard," the captain muttered.

Jenna stepped up beside him, her nostrils flaring and her face reddening with anger. "You're not going to turn us over to that Peon scum, are you?" she shouted angrily.

Royce spun his chair to face her so fast that she had to snap her hands back quickly. "Does it look like I have a choice, Lieutenant Plural? This is a direct order from your commander-in-chief."

Jenna threw her hands in the air. "She does not have the authority the capitulate to the enemy."

"Of course she does, you stupid girl," he sneered contemptuously.

Jenna pounded a fist down upon the top of his chair. "This is unacceptable."

"You're out of line, Lieutenant." He turned to Morris. "Shut down the automated defenses and inform the crew what is happening. Have the Marines return their weaponry to the armory and then go to the M.E.T. for immediate upload."

Then he looked back at Jenna Plural. "Prepare the main airlock to receive company."

"This is fucking bullshit!" Jenna said as she spun on her heel and strode out the door. I hesitated but sheepishly followed her out when all eyes turned to me.

Jenna walked briskly, and I had to trot again to catch up with her. "Reeves, leave the Peons. They can clear up their own damned dead," she barked before pushing past him and his team.

"You need to calm down," I said. "There is nothing you can do." I made the mistake of taking her by the arm.

She immediately snatched it roughly away and spun about to glare at me. "That is exactly why I cannot calm down, Mr. Phelkar," she shouted. She turned once more to stride swiftly away.

"You knew we were losing the war, and this was a possibility," I said, pursuing her as a couple of Marines watched us curiously.

She stopped and spun upon me once more. "You think so? Yes, I knew we were losing the war, but it was never to be lost as long as a free American lived and breathed and could hold a gun. We should have stood and fought to the last."

"That would cost us millions of lives," I said, trying to convince her.

"Better we all will die than live under a blue and yellow flag." Before I could respond to that, she turned away again and continued down the corridor.

"Where are you going?"

"To follow my fucking orders, Mr. Phelkar." She waved a dismissive hand at me without looking back.

We reached the airlock. She took deep breaths, pacing up and down in front of it with her hands on her hips. She eventually turned to the door and steeled herself before tapping in the unlock codes. Slowly the door slid open to reveal a tall, pleasant-looking man who smiled at her. He looked at the insignia on her shoulders. He nodded. "Bonjour, Lieutenant. The war is over, and we will all be going home. Today is a good day."

Jenna glared at him for a long while before speaking. "Surrender does not make us friends, Commander. Let's skip the pleasantries if you please."

Annoyingly, his smile widened. "As you wish, Mademoiselle. We shall do this officially. The captain of the Force d'Action Navale Navire Jauréguiberry lays legal claim to the U.S.S. Lewis Puller as a spoil of war. Your crew are now prisoners of the European Union and will be treated under the 24 Galle Convention." He entered the ship and stepped to one side to allow a line of his troopers to file in with efficient precision. One stood behind me and another behind Jenna. They each reached in from behind and removed our sidearms. The Jauréguiberry officer extended a palm down the corridor. "Lead the way, Lieutenant." I fell in step with Jenna as we headed back to the cockpit.

The Frenchman smiled again as the captain stood and saluted him. The fact he did not salute back spoke volumes about our situation. "Captain, you will power down all ship systems except life support and your matter converter. You will proceed to put all your crew into storage."

Royce nodded. "Already in process."

"Excellent." The commander positively beamed.

"I require medical attention before I can be uploaded," Jenna said determinedly, indicating her torn and bloodied shirt.

The Peon officer looked her up and down. "You look fine to me, Mademoiselle."

"Thanks to Mr. Phelkar's field dressing, it looks that way," she said with an innocent shrug. "However, there is still a bullet lodged in my abdomen. I can't go through the M.E.T. with a foreign object embedded within me."

The officer sighed. "Very well." He turned to one of the guards and spoke in French, of which, thanks to my memory chip, I had a fluent understanding. He told the man to escort Jenna to the medical center. The guard nodded, and, looking at her, he indicated to the door. As she turned and was about to leave, I noticed him look her up and down a little too appreciatively for my liking. It gave me an idea that I hoped would mean we were not separated. I stepped in front of the guard, who tensed defensively, and I spoke to the commander in his language.

"Is it protocol in the European Navy for a female prisoner to be escorted by a male one? Surely Monsieur, that is wholly inappropriate."

The officer was delighted that I spoke his language and responded in French. "Sir, you honor me." He stepped over to me and shook my hand with both of his. "But you don't sound like an American. What are you? English... Australian?" The others in the room, including Jenna, just stared blankly at us, not understanding what we were saying. However, Stacey perked up and looked at us curiously at the mention of "Australie."

"I'm with the British Ministry of Defense Liaison. I'm currently under the command of the United States Marine Corps."

"And your name?"

"Michael Phelkar."

"Well, Michael Phelkar, if you're so concerned about the wellbeing of the lieutenant, go with her."

I nodded and joined Jenna, but as we stepped out, followed by our escort, she glanced at me and whispered, "What was that all about?"

"I suggested that your virtue might be at risk if you went alone with the guard."

Jenna smiled for the first time since learning of the surrender. "Why I do declare, Mr. Phelkar. You be a mighty fine gentleman," she said in a mock southern states accent.

"I thought you said they would execute all of us, and yet they appear to be taking us prisoner," I said nervously.

"This is different. The U.S. has surrendered, and I'm guessing that has just saved our lives."

There was no longer any sign of our Marines as we made our way to the medical bay, just armed Peons staring at us as we passed. Most of the bodies were gone, but the occasional corpse was still lying, disrespectfully, where they had died. Two guards stood outside the medical bay, and our escort briefly spoke to them, explaining what we were doing. Inside, the ship's doctor was overwhelmed by the number of wounded and looked desperately at Jenna as we entered.

"I need more help. Tell these idiots that I need my team downloaded."

"They're not going to listen," Jenna said apologetically. "They will have you upload any wounded."

Doctor Archer looked horrified. "Half of these troopers have bullets in them. They can't be uploaded until I remove them."

"Do the best you can, doctor," Jenna replied. "But first, I need you to take a bullet out of my stomach." She lifted her shirt to show the doctor the rapidly patched wound.

"Sorry, Lieutenant, but you're still walking, and you have to wait your turn. I have other priorities of a more serious nature."

"I really must insist, Doctor." Jenna's tone indicated the seriousness of the matter at hand. "You need to remove a bullet, and you need to do it behind that curtain there." She indicated the privacy screen. The doctor was about to object, but Jenna placed a hand upon hers and shook her head. She briefly looked at me, and I nodded. She looked back to Jenna and sighed. "Come in then, Lieutenant. I don't know what shenanigans you're up to, but it better be good."

The doctor led Jenna behind a screen, and the guard made to follow, but I stood blocking his way, saying in French, "Sir, the lady will be in a state of undress. It is not appropriate for you to be watching. If you need a guard in there with her, I must insist it is a female one."

I was not sure it would work, but muttering under his breath, he headed towards the door to get one of his female colleagues.

I leaned back toward the curtain and said urgently, "I've insisted the guard find a female officer. You have until he returns."

"Quick thinking, Mr. Phelkar, thank you," Jenna replied.

"Stand still, Lieutenant," I heard Archer say irritably, "I will have that bullet out of there in a few seconds, but not if you keep moving." I heard some device, followed by a sudden gasp of pain from Jenna. "All gone," the doctor stated. "Sorry that hurt, but the wound had already started healing around it. Your nanobots are working at a pace that I have never seen before. Are you using some new experimental ones that I have not yet heard of?"

"It is not the nanobots," Jenna replied. "I have an accelerated genetic healing matrix."

The doctor sighed. "I cannot stop being amazed at the recuperation ability of the genetically modified. This will be healed in a few hours or a day at most. Though there will be a nasty scar."

"I don't scar, Doctor," Jenna said wearily.

"Lucky you," the doctor responded snarkily.

"Doctor, we don't have much time." The lieutenant spoke fast and urgently. "Can you get me some stim packs and deactivate the auto dosage so that we can pump it up to maximum?"

"But that will render someone unconscious or possibly kill them!" the doctor said.

"Well, duh," Jenna stated sarcastically. "That is my intent."

"I'm a noncombatant, Lieutenant," the doctor said curtly.

"That doesn't stop you from preparing equipment for me," Jenna said, struggling to maintain her patience.

The doctor looked quite put out as she stepped out from behind the curtain and headed to where she stored her meds.

"Are you still out there, Mr. Phelkar?" Jenna whispered.

"I don't have anywhere else interesting to be right now, Lieutenant," I replied.

"Give me a sitrep of the room. How many guards are there now?"

I looked around, trying to appear casual. "There is one by the door, and another just returned with a female. Judging from her epaulets, she is a junior officer. Hush, she's coming over."

"Are you the one that can speak French?" the officer said, walking up to me and speaking her language.

"Oui, Mademoiselle," I replied and gave a polite bow.

She looked around the room with a disdainful expression. "I'm making you responsible for the conduct of the people in here. You will convey my orders clearly and concisely. While my English is shaky, I know enough to know if you're not repeating my words correctly. Do you understand me?" She apparently wanted to say my rank, for she checked my shoulders, but then she frowned. "You have no rank, Monsieur. Why is this?"

"I'm a civilian, Mademoiselle, from the Ministry of Defense Liaison Office."

Her eyes narrowed, and she looked at me with contempt. "You're British?"

"Proudly so, Mademoiselle."

She cleared her throat and then spat straight in my face. I was startled and took a step back, wiping off the slime that ran down my cheek. "Nom de dieu de putain de bordel de merde de saloperie de connard d'enculer ta mère," she said to me, which was far too vulgar to translate here. It made Stacey look classy.

"Charmed, I'm sure," I responded.

"I hate the British!"

"I think I got the idea."

At that point, the doctor returned and went behind the curtain. The young woman pushed me aside and followed her in. Before any words were spoken, I heard the young Peon woman gasp, and seconds later, Jenna casually stepped out.

"What the hell are you doing?" I asked her in an urgent yet whispered voice.

"What I have to Mr. Phelkar. We are fighting back whether the captain wants us to or not. Are you with me, or are you with the captain?" I hesitated; my official duty was clear. Royce was in command of this ship, and she was disobeying his orders. However, I did not trust him. My next decision could mean facing a court-martial if there was still a military to speak of back in the U.K., but Jenna spoke again before I could reply. "I don't have time to wait for you to consider all the implications, Mr. Phelkar. Are you with me, or are you not?"

I sighed and made the decision that would irrevocably change my life. "I'm with you, Lieutenant Plural, to the bitter end. What do you want me to do?"

She grinned at my words. "Well, I will try to make sure the end is not too bitter, Mr. Phelkar." Her face then turned grim as she looked about. "There are two guards left in here and two outside the door. We need to incapacitate them and make our way to the M.E.T. room."

I nodded, but then I looked behind the curtain. "Is she dead?"

"No," said Doctor Archer, checking the pulse in her neck.

"Hey, you," Jenna called to one of the guards. "Something is wrong with one of your people here." She pointed into the curtain.

The guard came over and looked behind the curtain to see his officer on the floor. He hesitated long enough for Jenna to shove a stim in his neck. As she lowered him to the ground, she grabbed his pistol from its holster, then let him fall the rest of the way while spinning around to shoot a second guard. He fell back over a bunk where a recuperating Marine lay. Fortunately, the Marine wasn't so injured that he couldn't grab the man by the neck and twist it until it snapped. A cheer went up from the surviving troopers. If the gunshot hadn't attracted the guards, the Marines certainly did. The door opened, and another two guards came rushing in. The one in the lead instantaneously went down from another shot from Jenna. As the other went to return fire at her, my days playing rugby at school came into action as I went in for a diving tackle. As he went down, his gun turned to me, and he managed to get off a round, but, thanks be to God, he missed. He did not get a second chance, and the last thing he would ever see was Jenna Plural's boot coming down upon his face. With a sharp twist of her ankle, he was dead too.

"You're making a habit of saving my life Mr. Phelkar." Jenna smiled at me as she offered a hand up.

"It seems to be a mutual arrangement, Lieutenant Plural, but you're most welcome," I said as she helped me off the floor. I relieved the man of his firearm and slipped it into my holster.

Jenna turned to the Marine who had been of assistance. "Up for the fight, Private Mitchell?"

He looked delighted that she even knew his name but said, "Ma'am, I'd give anything to kill Peons right now, but...." He pulled back the sheet covering his legs and showed us the mangled mess of his knee.

"You always were a shirker, Mitchell." Jenna grinned and squeezed his shoulder reassuringly. "Listen to Doctor Archer, and don't grope the nurses."

He laughed. "I'll try not to, Lieutenant, especially as there aren't any."

Jenna noticed another young Marine who was wrapping a bandage around another's shoulder. She appeared unharmed. "What is your name, Private?" Jenna asked her.

"Dodgson, Ma'am," she responded, surprising me with a slight stammer. Jenna appeared unconcerned by it.

"You don't look injured."

"No, Ma'am, I'm not." The girl looked eager.

"You up for a scrap with the Peons?"

The girl stood up, letting go of her patient, who gave a little cry of pain. "Yes, Ma'am."

"Oh no, you don't," the doctor said to Jenna. "If you can't get me my nurses, you can at least leave Dodgson here to help me."

Jenna pondered this, and the girl looked quite despondent. Eventually, Jenna responded, "Carry on, Dodgson." Turning to the doctor, she said, "You have her for now."

"Give the Peon fuckers hell from us, Lieutenant," another Marine called over to her. She smiled at him and raised a defiant fist before stepping out the door with me once more in tow.

Chapter Eight

Mutiny

O nce back in the corridor, Jenna looked left and right as she slipped her firearm into the back of her pants and told me to do the same. "Softly, softly, Mr. Phelkar," she said quietly. "We will play along as if we are good little prisoners and hope they don't question why we don't have a guard."

"That's a huge risk," I said nervously.

"Trust me." We started to walk down the corridor casually. "Thirteen years in covert ops has taught me that you won't be treated as suspicious if you don't act suspiciously," she said before adding less confidently, "Well, most times. There was one occasion when Stacey and I...."

"Lieutenant, please don't tell me a story where your current tactic failed. I'm nervous enough as it is," I whispered. "What is it you plan to do?"

"If I'm to take this ship, I will need both Grant and Tracker."

"Why?"

"Tracker can shut down systems and start them up again from a computer terminal. She can fuck with the Peons big time. And Stacey, well, we can't fly the ship without a pilot."

"You only have one pilot?" I asked, surprised.

"No, there is also Neville Batty, but he's no Stacey Grant, and he is uploaded anyway. However, there is potentially one minor snafu with my plans." She held her thumb and forefinger slightly apart as she said it.

"What is that?" I asked uneasily.

"I have no idea whether Grant or Tracker will side with me. I have worked with Tracker for about six years now and four with Stacey. I trust them with my life. If you haven't already realized it, Mr. Phelkar, we are currently engaged in the act of mutiny, and that's a lot to ask of anyone."

I wasn't stupid. I had realized it, but I hadn't had time to think of its consequences. Thinking about the ramifications of our actions did nothing to calm my nerves. The only comfort I had was in the confidence of Jenna Plural, and it just damn well felt like the right thing to do.

There was a line of dejected-looking Marines lined up outside the M.E.T. room. A Peon guard looked at us suspiciously as we approached, but we simply joined the end of the queue and looked at each other, chatting casually. It seemed to put him at his ease. Many men and women near us turned and looked questioningly at Jenna.

"I'm not going to let you down," she said quietly, and it was all she said. I was amazed at the calm her words seemed to bring over them. These Marines trusted Jenna Plural entirely and utterly, and she had their respect and loyalty unquestioningly.

We saw Stacey near the front of the line, and her eyes met with Jenna's. Jenna nodded to her ever so slightly, and Stacey reciprocated and turned back to face the front. One by one, the Marines ventured in to be uploaded into the storage facility. Then it became our turn to go in.

A huge pile of clothes was stacked in a corner. Stephanie Morris was supervising. Stacey had somehow delayed being uploaded, and when it was just the four of us in the room. Jenna turned on the first officer.

"You're not going to accept this, are you, Morris?" she asked almost aggressively.

Morris looked vexed but would not meet the lieutenant's eyes. "Plural, this isn't time for your patriotic fervor. Get over it. We lost."

"You'll just give up like that?" The contempt on Jenna's face was extreme.

"It's not my call, and it's not yours," Morris snapped. Jenna fell silent as two guards came in to see what was causing the delay. Jenna stood there casually, her back to them as if she was waiting for something. As soon as they got close enough, she took a step back and thrust her elbow into the gut of the nearest one. As he doubled over, she pulled out her gun from her behind her and whipped him on the back of the neck, sending him to the ground. The other guard was already aiming for her head. Stacey swung out her arm, knocking his, and the shot went wide, narrowly missing Helen Tracker. Sparks flew up from her console. Jenna thrust her weapon into his stomach and fired. As he fell, she turned back to the man she had dropped to the floor. He was getting up, but Jenna pushed him back down with her boot and fired a single shot into the back of his head.

Morris cried out, "Jenna, stop this. You're going to get us all killed."

Jenna turned her weapon and pointed it at her forehead. "You're a damned traitor, Stephanie Morris."

Stacey grabbed up a gun from a dead Peon. There was a second of concern about what she would do, and I held my breath, only releasing it when I saw her point the gun at Stephanie. Stacefield Ellen Grant had chosen a side.

"I'm only obeying my orders, Plural." Stephanie looked terrified. "Just as you should be."

"Semper Fi." That was all Jenna said, and I tried to remember what that meant. It meant something to Morris, for she looked down at the ground. "Get undressed," Jenna ordered. All this time, Tracker had stood watching in bewilderment. "Get ready to upload her," Jenna ordered.

"Don't listen to her," Morris stated, and to my surprise, I saw tears in her eyes. "She is acting contrary to orders."

"Six years, Tracker. When have I given you a reason to doubt me?" Jenna said coolly.

Tracker hesitated momentarily, then with a nod to Jenna, she looked at Morris. "Sorry, Ma'am, but would you get undressed and step onto the circle, please?" Helen Amelia Tracker had also taken a side.

"I'll wait outside," I said, but Jenna gripped my arm.

"Stay where you are, Mr. Phelkar, and stop being such a goddamn idiot," Jenna snapped. "You're working with the United States Marines now." I followed her instructions, but I cast my eyes downwards.

Stephanie's wavery voice conveyed her tears as she undressed. "You will all be court-martialed for this."

Jenna laughed humorlessly. "By who? The Peons?"

Stephanie did not have an opportunity to reply. As she tossed aside her last sock, she disappeared into a flash of light, and the console sparked again.

Jenna turned and looked at Stacey, then Tracker. "Thank you, ladies. I'm glad I could rely on you."

Stacey Grant was clearly offended. "Bloody hell, mate. You had doubts about that?"

Jenna looked at her sheepishly and shrugged. "I don't know. Never asked you to commit mutiny before."

Stacey grinned at this, but Tracker did not look at all amused.

"Can we trust him?" Stacey asked with a single nod towards me.

Jenna glanced at me, then looked back at Stacey. "I think so. He has already proved himself several times today."

"I'm standing right here, you know," I said with indignation. "Whilst I cannot imagine the consequences of our actions, I have already committed acts of mutiny and treason. I'm a dead man for killing officers I had technically surrendered to. However, I think I have proved my loyalty and ability, so really—"

"Wow, you're such a long-winded pommy wanker," Stacey interrupted with a wide-eyed grin. "Maybe you should go talk the Peons to death. You're certainly killing me, mate."

Jenna turned to Tracker. "I need Harlow and Sakamoto downloaded now."

Tracker nodded. "I'll do my best, but there's a dirty great bullet hole in my console now. I almost lost Morris uploading her."

She tapped in the commands. I closed my eyes before the flash of light blinded me once again. When I opened them, the surprised, elderly chief engineer, as naked as the day he was born, was standing looking at the group of women surrounding him. "If you have woken me up for some weird sex party, I warn you, girlies, you may not be able to handle me," he said with a snort.

Jenna grinned. "I can't speak for the others, but I think you're a little past that, old man," she said, passing him a towel. "Get off the circle, and we'll explain what's going on in a minute."

He stepped off, and almost instantly, the short, wiry figure I would come to know as Sergeant Tomiko Sakamoto appeared. Stacey unwrapped another towel and passed it to her. I would later find out that Sakamoto was part of the Japanese Imperial Guard and posted here a couple of years before as part of a goodwill gesture between Japan and the United States, a bit like my situation. However, Sakamoto had chosen to remain part of Jenna's team when her time was up.

"What's going on, Lieutenant?" she asked grimly.

Jenna quickly explained the situation, and both looked shocked at the news of the surrender, but they had different reactions when they learned of Jenna's intentions.

Harlow leaned back against the wall folding his arms. "I have worked with you for thirty-plus years, Jenn." I was surprised to hear him talk so informally to her. "And still, you surprise me. You've always been straight with me, so I'll be straight with you. I'm not happy about this, not happy at all. But you know you're my gal, and I've got your back."

"That's appreciated, Rocky." Jenna smiled at the old man.

Sakamoto's reaction offered more outright support. "You know you can count on me, Lieutenant. Maybe now we can do things properly."

Jenna grinned. "The one thing I knew I could count on was your loyalty, Tomiko. Now there is much to do." She turned to Tracker. "Start bringing people we have worked with for some time—ones you think we can count on. We have a fight ahead."

Tracker looked down at the console and shook her head. "The M.E.T. has started fluctuating. I can no longer stabilize the patterns of anyone. We can't bring anyone else out without some workaround."

"Is everyone safe in there?" Stacey asked with concern.

"Yes, but I can't promise it will stay that way," the tech advised.

"Fuck!" Jenna snarled. "Okay, I guess it's up to us. Helen, is there any way you could block transmissions from the Puller to the Peon ship?"

"I can cause some temporary interference by networking into the primary computer," she said. "However, we can only make it permanent via the systems in Environment and Life. Security lockdown."

"Do it. We can't have the Jangle Berries captain informed of what's going on." As the tech started to work, Jenna turned back to the Japanese officer. "Get Harlow to engineering. Rocky, get ready to give Stacey all the power you can as soon as she needs it. The rest of you are with me. We will stop by the armory, then head for the Environment and Life room. I have an idea."

We were about to leave the M.E.T. room when the Peon soldier, bleeding out from his gut wound on the floor, groaned. Jenna went to withdraw her firearm again, but Stacey, who already had hers out, beat her to it with a single shot. Some viscera splattered onto my turn-ups, and I let out an involuntary gasp, stepping back against the wall. My sudden move startled Stacey. She looked up at me wide-eyed. "What's the matter, mate? You look like you're about to chunder."

"It's... It's nothing. You just startled me, that's all," I said, a little flustered. The reality was I found the casual cold-bloodedness of my companions somewhat unnerving. Stacey and Jenna had shot two injured men at point-blank range without any doubt or hesitation and were willing to move on as if nothing had occurred. It made me wonder what it took to become that unemotional and ruthless towards human life. I admit I was a little scared of them.

We knew that the Peons would secure the armory. As we approached via the adjacent corridor, Jenna pulled me forward. "You're with me, Mr. Phelkar. We will go ahead."

"Wow, you sure I'm the best choice?" I asked. I was quite proud that she chose me, but that didn't last long.

"You're the only choice, Mr. Phelkar," Jenna said casually as she chambered a round in her snap pistol. "We can't risk losing either Grant or Tracker."

"Well, thanks," I said dejectedly.

She looked at me and shrugged off my comment. "Well, you did ask, Mr. Phelkar."

And at those words, she pointed around the corner, and we stepped out and opened fire on two startled guards who were dead before they could get as much as a look at us. Just as we stepped into the armory, the ship-wide intercom came online with an irritated captain. "Lieutenant Plural, what the hell are you doing?"

Jenna couldn't resist, and she hit the intercom on the wall. "I'm doing my duty, Sir, as an American and a United States Marine."

The Peon commander's voice came on next. It was sickly sweet. "I understand your patriotism, Lieutenant, but this is a hopeless fight. Stand down now, and you will be treated fairly. If not, I have the authority to execute you and your entire crew."

"Listen to reason, girl," the captain added. "They know what you're doing. They found the bodies in the M.E.T. room. Why are you doing this?"

"Because I'm Semper Fidelis, *sir*." Her tone was now bitter. "Some of us haven't forgotten what that means, *sir*, but I'm about to educate you, *sir*. Plural out." She switched off the intercom. She turned to Tracker. "Anything you can do about our transponders? It is most likely the captain has given the Peon bastards our codes so they can find us quickly."

"I can hit them with a disabling pulse, but the nanobots in your system will immediately start repairing it. We will have an hour, two at the most."

"It will have to do," Jenna responded. "Go for it."

Tracker slipped a small device off her belt and held it up to each of our ears. There was a slight irritating buzzing but otherwise no apparent effect.

During this exchange, Stacey had unlocked the weapons and armor lockers. She and Tracker started putting on body armor like Jenna and myself. Jenna swapped the Peon guns for our own and gave us each four extra clips. Turning to the field ordinance, she grabbed up some limpet mines, which she handed me. I stuffed them into a backpack I had grabbed out of a locker.

"What do you plan to use these for?" I asked.

Jenna shrugged. "We will board the Peon's ship eventually and might want to blow stuff up."

"Second rule of a military life, mate," Stacey said with her typical huge grin, "always take what you don't need just in case you need It."

"What is the first rule?" I would immediately regret asking.

"Always make sure you know which of your teammates has the biggest dick." My biggest surprise was that Jenna had answered, and I looked at her wide-eyed. "Hey, it's Stacey's rule, not mine." She looked at me all innocently.

"You're learning well, my young apprentice." Stacey grinned at her, then, looking at me, said, "Spot check." She turned around, and I tightened the fasteners on the back of the breastplate. Jenna did the same for Tracker, who had remained quiet all this time. She did not have the others' ability to switch off their stress with a bit of mindless banter. To be honest, I was more like her than the other two veteran officers.

"Okay, listen up," Jenna said, all business again. "They know we're fighting back and will be looking for us. Any ideas on how we can get from here to Environment and Life without fighting our way there?"

"I can scan for nearby heat signatures so we can tell who's in the vicinity of wherever we go," Tracker suggested, pulling such a device from one of the shelves.

"That only gives us a heads up on who we are about to get into a fight with, but it's better than nothing. Anything else?" Jenna looked at me, and when I stared blankly at her, she just rolled her eyes and looked at Stacey.

"There is always the ventilation shaft. It will get us two rooms down from the Environment and Life room."

Jenna grinned at her. "Yes, you're the expert on ventilation shafts. You can lead the way." Stacey blushed slightly at her superior's comment, leaving me wondering what Jenna had meant.

The lieutenant then handed out a set of night vision goggles to everyone except Stacey. I looked at the young woman questioningly, and she just shrugged. "I eat a lot of carrots."

Stacey and Jenna moved some furniture so that we could climb it, and then Stacey pushed out the ceiling vent and nimbly disappeared into it. Jenna had Tracker go next and then me. Being a little bit older and out of shape, it was harder for me to pull myself inside, but with Jenna shouting at me, "Move it!" like a drill sergeant, I managed it. She came up behind me. We were cramped up together in a line. Jenna called ahead to Stacey, "What's the holdup?"

"There is one snag when you enter the vent via the armory. They seal off the bloody ends with more grates to stop people from getting in that way."

"Here, let me deal with this," said Tracker. It was too tight to swap places conventionally, and Stacey had to lie down while Tracker climbed over the top of her and lay upon her as she worked.

"Fucking hell, have you put on weight, mate?"

For the first time since this affair began, Tracker laughed. "Fuck you, Grant." She pulled out a tiny device that made a slight buzzing noise as it magnetically unfastened the screws. Then with a gentle push, she popped it out. She scrambled back off Stacey, who pulled herself up to her knees and continued on. The young Australian clearly knew where she was going as we turned a couple of times and, on one occasion, had to drop down to the second level of the ship. We had a couple of scary moments where we passed Peons talking near other vents.

After about fifteen minutes, Stacey stopped and pointed to the vent below her. She gave Jenna a thumbs up but then put a finger to her lips. The vent was larger here, and one could pass another, so Jenna scrambled up next to Stacey and looked down into the room below. Jenna stared for a long moment, then gave Stacey a most disgusted look. She then scrambled back and whispered something to Tracker that I couldn't hear. Tracker moved up next to Stacey. She, too, looked down, then rolled her eyes at Stacey as she pulled the little device out again. However, this time she left one final screw. Again, she scrambled back, and once more, Jenna went up and gave Stacey a final dirty look. The pilot just shrugged with an innocent stare. Then both turned around to place their feet over the vent. Jenna did a count-off with her fingers, and when she got to three, they both slammed their feet down hard.

The cover disappeared, and the two officers quickly followed as I tried to scramble up past Tracker. I was too late to see anything. Looking down into a toilet cubicle, I saw Jenna and Stacey standing over a dead Peon with his trousers around his ankles. Jenna looked up at me and waved for us to come down.

Then both left the cubicle to give us the room. I lowered myself gently, trying to avoid landing on the corpse or the toilet bowl. As I stepped out of the cubicle, Tracker dropped down behind me.

"You couldn't find somewhere better than a bathroom?" Jenna was saying.

Stacey shrugged. "I know it sounds weird, but it didn't occur to me that the Peons would need to use the loo."

Jenna just rolled her eyes, shook her head, and headed towards the bathroom door. She peered out at first, then stepped out, waving us along with her. Just two doors down, we were outside the Environment and Life room.

Chapter Nine

Taking Back the Chesty

Jenna tapped out the code, and the door slid back. The Environment and Life room was row upon row of computer banks filling every possible space in an area that wasn't designed for it. Tracker immediately stepped over to a screen and keyboard and logged herself in.

"Isn't that a little outdated?" I asked her.

"Huh?" Tracker grunted as a reply, not looking up at me as she worked.

"The keyboard. Why aren't you using voice activation? It's a lot faster."

"Voices can be recorded and imitated. The keyboard remains the best device for security."

Jenna hit the intercom once more, calling down to engineering. "Sakamoto, give me good news."

The lightly accented voice of the Japanese officer came back. "We had a minor encounter but made it safely." In the background, we could hear Harlow complaining about her getting blood all over his uniform.

"Good work Sakamoto. We are hopefully going to seal you in there so that you don't get any interruptions. Make sure Harlow is ready to fire up those engines if we need them. Plural out." She then turned back to Helen Tracker. "Cut the inter-ship communications so the French commander cannot contact his ship."

Helen's hand darted over the keyboard once more. "Done."

"Are you sure there are no crew members other than us, the captain, and in the med bay presently out of dematerialization?" Jenna stepped up beside her and moved me aside.

"Yes, Ma'am."

"Fine, start shutting down all the air systems everywhere except this room, the med bay, and engineering. Do it fast. They will know where we are even without our transponders once we start shutting things down." Helen Tracker's hands hesitated. She looked up at Jenna, her face filled with concern. "He has given us no choice, Sergeant. If you know of another way, any of you, tell me now."

I must admit that I had no idea how to resolve this abominable situation. When no one spoke, Jenna looked back at Helen Tracker, who still looked uneasy. Then, in a gentle voice that I had not heard before, Jenna said, "Stand aside, Sergeant. Tell me what to do."

Helen Tracker showed her, and then Jenna's fingers nimbly dashed over the controls. The intercom crackled into life with the captain's voice less than thirty seconds later. "What the hell are you doing, Plural? You stupid bitch."

She looked at me and nodded to the intercom as she worked. I turned it on. "You haven't given me much of an option, Captain." She said bitterly.

"What the hell do you expect to achieve, girl? Fight a war on your own?" He sounded almost hysterical now.

"I hope I won't be alone, Sir. I hope there are patriots like me who want to fight back."

"Mademoiselle," came the silky voice of the French commander, "you're achieving nothing here. I have sent my troops to your location right now. We will be out of here, and you will be dead in a matter of minutes. You will be remembered as an idiot if you're remembered at all."

"Hey, at least I'll be remembered as an *American* idiot.

"Zut! So be it." The intercom went ship-wide, and he ordered in French.

Jenna looked at me, and I quickly translated. "They are coming." She nodded in acknowledgment and said to the group, "This is it, boys and girls. It will take some time to open that door."

"They won't get a chance to," said Helen Tracker. "I have run a bypass through the defense systems using my back-door password. I can turn on the automated internal weapons right here, but there is a problem. It requires an officer of a command rank to authorize it."

"That is not a problem," I said, confused by what she said. "Lieutenant Plural is of command rank."

Helen Tracker flushed bright red, and Stacey looked the other way. There was a moment of silence before Jenna spoke in a cold, bitter tone.

"I'm a GenMod, Mr. Phelkar. I cannot be trusted with weaponry that could be turned on our own troops. Even as the second officer, the government won't allow me to do certain things."

I pondered this a moment, then looked back to Tracker. "But surely there must be emergencies where Lieutenant Plural can take command in the event of the death of Royce and Morris?"

"Yes, but neither of them is dead," she replied, confused.

"But does the computer know that?" I asked intently. "Can you update their records to say they are deceased?"

"I can, but Lieutenant Plural will still have restrictions based on her rank and genetic modifications."

"So, that's a start. Change the record to indicate that she's been promoted."

Helen Tracker looked uncertain but simply shrugged. "I can but try."

She tapped on the keyboard, and there was a long nervous pause before the ship's computer came online on the intercom.

"Attention all personnel," it stated in its melodic male voice, "with immediate effect, First Lieutenant Jennacia Louise Plularian has assumed command of the U.S.S. Lewis Puller with orders to immediately return to the nearest U.S. base."

"Bloody hell," laughed Stacey.

"Don't start celebrating yet," Tracker muttered as she continued to tap out on the keyboard. "If you went to the cockpit now, you would find that you could only set the ship to the coordinates of the nearest base. We probably have less control now than we had before."

There was a long silent pause, and then a grin crossed Helen Tracker's face, and she stepped back. The computer intoned once more, "Attention all personnel, with immediate effect Major Jennacia Louise Plularian has assumed command of the U.S.S. Lewis Puller."

"Well, that scared me for a moment there," Tracker said with relief. "It kept refusing to allow me to enter the rank of major. So, I told it there was an error in Lieutenant Plural's file and deleted the fact that she was genetically modified. Then, bingo, it let me update the rank as easy as that."

It was only then that I realized that Jenna had not spoken all this time. I turned to face her, and she was looking dumbstruck.

"Something wrong, Major?"

"Helen Tracker, I could kiss you," she said to the chief tech. I heard Helen mutter something about how she wouldn't complain about that.

Jenna pulled herself together and instructed Tracker to engage assault weapons at her leisure.

Tracker's fingers darted nimbly over the controls as she encoded the weapons system to target all life forms not currently wearing a Marine pin.

"I'm confused," I said quietly to Tracker as she started to tap once more into the keyboard. "You are unwilling to turn off the air, but you are okay activating the machine gun?"

She briefly glanced at me before returning her attention to the keyboard with a shrug. "I have no problem killing Peons. I do have a problem killing Americans."

We heard gunfire followed by the cries of dying troops. The sound was coming from all over the ship. Silence eventually fell once more, but still, we waited. It had been a Hail Mary decision. The risk to the integrity of the vessel, although small, was still a threat.

"Open up engineering and let Sakamoto and Harlow out and let's go," Jenna commanded.

As we headed back into the corridor, I was shocked to see how badly the walls, floor, and ceiling were shredded in gunfire. The ship looked like a giant cheese grater with gouges on all the walls. We encountered bodies of French troops whose remains were barely recognizable as human. We stopped at the mess hall, and Jenna led us in.

"So, how do we take the cockpit?" Stacey asked as she flopped into a seat.

"We don't," Jenna said firmly as she took a seat between her and Tracker. "If we take the Lewis Puller now, the captain of the Jangle Berry will become aware. To succeed, we must take the Jangle Berry."

I was making a pot of coffee at the counter as Jenna said this, but I turned to her with wide-eyed disbelief. "So, how exactly do you propose to take the Peon ship?" I asked as Sakamoto and Harlow came in. "These are insurmountable odds."

"Bloody hell, Phelkar, don't be such a gloomy guts," Stacey said, scowling at me.

Jenna looked at the young woman. "Stacey, you must have some ideas. Didn't you study Peon ship design as an air intelligence officer in the Australian Air Force?"

"Wow, that's bloody eons ago now. But yeah, now let me think about it. The Peon ship is a light cruiser of the Lafayette class. This means waking a crew that could be as many as forty-six, not counting troops that are probably in an M.E.T. However, it is most likely most were deployed in boarding the Chesty. She doesn't have internal defense systems solely relying on manpower to repel boarders."

I'd been passing around coffee whilst Stacey spoke, but as I sat down next to Jenna, I couldn't help interjecting my own thoughts.

"The six of us against forty-two? I don't like those odds."

"Oh, do shut up, Mr. Phelkar," Jenna ordered irritably. "Carry on, Stacey."

"The pom is right, Major. We don't have a chance in hell of assaulting that ship, not without downloading a lot more Marines."

Jenna looked to Tracker. "What're the chances of getting the M.E.T. back online?"

Tracker shrugged. "Honestly, I'm not even sure I can. I'm a programmer and an operator, not a repairman."

"You're a repairman now," Jenna advised. "But I'm sure Harlow can help you."

Harlow grunted but nodded.

"We're still talking several days." Tracker looked exasperated.

"That's your sole priority now, got it?" Jenna insisted.

Helen gave up the fight and, with a weary sigh, said, "Got it, Major."

"Oh, that's one less person," I said with a sigh.

"Mr. Phelkar," Jenna snapped, "you know I know how to break bones?"

"No, but it would be a reasonable assumption, given that you're a United States Marine," I replied.

"Well, if you don't knock off the negative crap, I'll start breaking yours. Do you understand me?"

"Yes, Ma'am," I said meekly.

She turned to the others. "There must be some way we can take that ship."

She looked at Stacey again. "Well, the ship does have one weakness that could compromise everyone inside. But, fuck, you're not gonna like it, Major."

Jenna's eyes narrowed. "Tell me."

"If we blow all six airlocks at the same time. The environmental defense systems cannot respond in time to sudden decompression. Unless someone is sealed somewhere, they're gonna be dead."

"So," Jenna said, looking confused. "Let's just do that."

Stacey hesitated a moment. "As soon as they secured the Chesty, they would have disconnected to take both ships wherever they wanted. There will be some distance between us and the Peon ship now."

Jenna went pale and leaned back wearily in her seat. "You're talking about a spacewalk."

Stacey glanced at Sakamoto, who immediately averted her eyes. Stacey looked back at Jenna. "Yes, boss."

"What's the problem with that," I asked, somewhat bemused.

Jenna sighed and colored a little. "There is only one thing that I hate, Mr. Phelkar, and that's leaving a ship in the middle of space."

I couldn't help but find the notion that Jenna suffered from astrophobia quite amusing. "You're a space Marine, and you're scared of space?" I chuckled until I suddenly saw stars of the metaphorical kind. It took me a moment to realize that Jenna had punched me in the side of the head. She was already talking with the others again by the time I recovered.

"That's our only option?" she asked Stacey dejectedly.

"No," Stacey said, shrugging, "but it's the only one I know of that leaves us with an intact ship to use afterward."

Sakamoto shook her head. "If we are aware of this, then the French are aware of this. It would be a standard tactic for taking out the ship."

"We have the elements of surprise," Stacey said. "They believe that we are currently under their control."

"They will know by now that communications between the two ships is down," Jenna replied.

"We can render the E.M.U. suits scanner invisible," Tracker said.

"The Peons cracked that technology more than ten years ago," Sakamoto said, frowning.

"Yes, but it still takes a couple of minutes for anyone to be detected, and that's after they start looking for them," Tracker said. "I would trust that the French will not be looking for us."

The following silence was intense as our leader stared off into space. No pun intended. Eventually, she sat up and brushed her hair from her face. "Very well, if that's what we have to do, let's do it."

"Don't get pissed at me, Jenna," Sakamoto said intently. "But are you sure you can do this? I have been out there with you before."

"I'll be fine." But the tremor in her voice did not instill confidence in the assembled group. "Sakamoto, I want you to take point on this one. We can't risk my issues getting in the way of the operation."

Tomiko Sakamoto nodded. "No worries, Major."

Jenna looked around the room. "We need six. That gives us a problem. I don't want to risk Tracker or Stacey, and Mr. Phelkar is bloody useless."

"Hey, that's not fair. I think I've played a good part so far," I protested.

Jenna ignored me and continued. "That means I have to take you, Mr. Harlow. It's a toss-up between you and Tracker, and I need her working on getting my Marines out of storage. Are you up to it?"

The old man grunted and shifted in his seat. "I was doing spacewalks before you girlies knew where to stuff a tampon. Of course, I'm up for it."

Jenna grinned. "I'm older than you, you grump."

Harlow snorted. "I was supposed to retire to a little farm in Kentucky after this mission, and now I've got a goddamn GenMod making me do a spacewalk."

I was startled at his aggressive attitude and calling her a Gen-Mod, but Jenna simply smiled at him. He seemed to be allowed to cross the line that the rest of us were not.

"That leaves just three more spaces." She leaned back and reached the intercom on the wall. "Doctor Archer, I need three Marines. What have you got for me?"

"I'm willing to release Kelsey Anthony, and you can now have Dodgson, but that's it," the doctor stated firmly.

"I need one more, doctor. If they can walk and hold a gun, patch them up and send them to me." Jenna ordered.

The doctor started to protest, but some man began talking to her in the background. We could not make out the words. The doctor returned to us with a sigh. "Sergeant Hardy will join you too. However, I will note that he has discharged himself against my advice."

"Noted, Doctor, thank you." Jenna turned off the intercom and turned back to us. "Okay, Marines, I want everyone ready in one hour. Stacey and Sakamoto stay with me to go over the ship plans. Tracker, keep working on the M.E.T."

"What do you want me to do?" I asked.

Jenna pondered that a moment, then raised her empty coffee cup and, with a smile, said, "Be a darling and refill this for me, would you, Mr. Phelkar?"

I sighed and took the cup.

An hour later, we were all standing in the cargo hold of the Chesty. Jenna, Sakamoto, Harlow, and the three troopers were kitted out in their environmental mobility suits. Basically, space suits, euphemistically known as Emus.

Jenna kept glancing at the large bay doors that would soon open to the vacuum of space.

I approached her cautiously. "Is there any way I can watch the progress of the mission?"

She seemed pretty distracted but replied. "Um, yeah. Get Tracker to hook you up in the V.R. training simulator. We use it for onboard exercises, but I'm sure she could patch you into my helmet cam."

I nodded and headed out of the bay. Stacey sealed the door behind me. "She's not as bad at this as everyone thinks, is she?" I asked her.

Stacey turned from the door and looked at me with wide eyes. "Oh, Phelks, that bitch is fucking bat shit crazy when it comes to spacewalks." Her words did not reassure me.

It turned out that the V.R. training simulator did more than just show you a visual from the camera.

"The whole idea is that you get a full experience," Tracker explained as she wired me up to various sensors. "I will hook you into the major's environmental recorders and even her health monitor. You will experience whatever she experiences."

"So, if she gets hurt, I get hurt?" I asked nervously.

Tracker laughed. "Well, it won't kill you, but the system will stimulate your pain receptors and other sensations. So, whatever she goes through, you will."

Before I could protest, she closed the V.R. visor over my eyes. I felt her touch my D.E. belt, and I floated up. I heard the door open and close and realized I was now alone. I found myself looking at the cargo bay doors, and I heard labored breathing. Then I heard Jenna lightly singing under her breath. "To Bombay, a traveling circus came. They brought an intelligent elephant, and Nellie was her name." She was unaware that I was now keyed into her comms. She stopped singing and muttered, "Keep it together, Plural, you're a goddamn genetically designed killing machine." She stamped her feet and pounded her chest.

"How are you doing, Major?" came Sakamoto's voice.

"As Stacey would say, 'fair dinkum, Ma'am. Let's kill some Peons.'" Jenna's voice sounded more competent than a few seconds before as she responded to the mission leader with an over-the-top bad Australian accent.

"Fuck!" Stacey came over the radio, "You have never heard me say that, mate!"

"Listen up, Marines," Sakamoto barked. "We are going to do this by the numbers. Give me a count off." The Marines counted themselves off, and Jenna was number three. "Okay, power up your packs."

I felt a slight vibration and heard the jets as Jenna switched on, for want of a better word, her jet pack. The cargo bay doors started to open, and Jenna took a step back. Her breathing became heavier in my ears, and she started singing again. "The head of the herd was calling far, far away. They met one night in the silver light on the road to Mandalay." The breathing became more desperate, and her heart pounded in her chest. She shook her head, taking another step back. "I can't do this!"

"Relax, Jenna," I found myself thinking aloud.

She stopped, her breath held, and there was a long pause before Jenna came back.

"Mr. Phelkar, you scared the shit out of me. I forgot you were going to be there. And since when do you get to call me Jenna?"

"Sorry, Major, I did not realize you could hear me. I will maintain radio silence," I said, embarrassed.

There was a long pause before she replied uneasily. "No, it's okay. You can distract me."

"What would you like me to do?" I said, eager to help.

"Just talk to me, Mr. Phelkar. Oh, and keep it a private line, okay?"

"Noted," I replied.

Sakamoto came online. "Move out, Marines," she barked.

Jenna looked down the line, and, in unison, they all moved out into the starry blackness of space.

Chapter Ten

Jauréguiberry

J enna started breathing heavily again. "So, how come you're afraid of space?" I asked

"Talk about anything but the current situation, Mr. Phelkar," she snapped irritably.

"Okay, okay, so... tell me, Major, is there anyone waiting for you back on Earth?" It was the first thing that came to mind.

"No, not really. My parents are obviously dead." She increased thrust to keep up with the others,

"I have a brother and sister back in Oklahoma, but we never talk."

"That's a shame. Are they older or younger?"

"Younger, but only by minutes. Mom wanted three kids all at once."

I saw the Peon ship coming ever closer. It was bizarre experiencing everything through the eyes of Jenna yet having no control over the situation. She made the occasional adjustments required to stay on course, and she had calmed considerably.

Sakamoto came online. "Time to break formation and head for the airlock you have been designated."

Two of the others came into my view as the group broke up, but I couldn't tell who they were.

Suddenly Jenna tried turning around inside her suit, her breathing labored. "Sweet Jesus, I can't do this."

"Yes, yes, you can, Major," I said firmly. "You have to keep going. Everything you believe in hinges on you doing this. Take a deep breath and close your eyes and count to ten."

Sakamoto's impatient voice burst online. "You're drifting off course, Major Plural. Do we have a problem?" She did not reply. I was only able to talk to Jenna in the V.R. gear, and her request I keep it a private line had been superfluous, but now I had to pull off the visor and hit my D.E. belt, landing with a jolt but still on my feet. I went straight to the comms panel.

"She's fine, Lieutenant Sakamoto. Just give me a minute."

"Kutabare! We don't have a fucking minute," Sakamoto screamed at me. "Everyone standby to abort."

"Belay that order," I shouted back.

"You're out of line, Phelkar!" Sakamoto said, spitting venom.

"I'm okay," Jenna suddenly came back.

"Major, you *will* keep it together," Sakamoto demanded.

"I got this," Jenna insisted. "Mr. Phelkar, you still out there?"

"Give me a sec." I turned from the comms and saw my visor floating near the ceiling. I turned off the D.E. belt and jumped, grabbing it before hitting the ceiling. I slipped the visor back on and once more entered our private channel.

"How are you doing?" I asked.

"Just keep talking. Get me through this," she said, a hint of nervousness in her voice.

"So, no husband, no boyfriend?" I asked.

Jenna gave a weak laugh. "Why? Are you interested in filling one of those roles, Mr. Phelkar?"

I chuckled. "I was just observing social niceties, Major Plural."

"That's what I said to you when we met. Sorry, Mr. Phelkar, but I was really pissed," she said, amused. "Not only did I have some upstart Brit coming to judge my Marines, but I was his damn chauffeur. I should have been more professional. But to answer your question. No, there is no one back home or anywhere else. I don't do relationships very well, Mr. Phelkar, and, to be honest, no one wants a serious relationship with the genetically modified person."

"Why not?" I asked with curiosity.

"We don't age. Do you want to grow old with a woman who has a twenty-five-year-old's face?"

"You're drifting slightly," I said, noticing the ship moving from out of view. Her breathing grew louder. "No, don't panic, just gently adjust," I said softly, and she followed my instruction. "There you go." And then I continued as if it had never happened. "I thought that was the fantasy?"

"Sure, if they're interested in just sex, but not to take to social functions or home to Mama," she said irritably. "At least not decent men. But what about you, Mr. Phelkar?"

"Well, you're technically my superior officer. Umm," I said awkwardly.

Jenna laughed. "Idiot. I meant, do you have someone back on Earth? Your 'little English rose' or whatever?"

Sad memories came back to me as I responded. "I was married once upon a time, but it didn't work out."

"I'm sorry to hear that," she said as she descended towards the ship.

"Oh, it is the old story." I sighed. "I got married too young and inexperienced."

"Do you have children, Mr. Phelkar?"

"I have a daughter, but she's all grown up now," I said dejectedly as images of my baby girl came into my mind.

"What's her name?"

"Kayleigh." I felt a slight jerk as I said it. Jenna had overcompensated on a turn and had brought it back too fast.

"Sorry about that." She took a deep breath. "Is she in the military?"

"Yes, she's doing her three-year national service, but she's not career."

"What branch?"

"Colonial Command. Last I heard, she was out on the moon Thalassa," I said, wondering what she was doing right now and how she was responding to the situation we now found ourselves in.

"You don't talk to her much?" Jenna sounded genuinely curious rather than just making small talk.

"It's a long story." I sighed.

"I understand. Where were you born?"

"A town called Hornchurch. You won't have heard of it. It's on the eastern border of London. Quite

a boring place, but I still call it home."

"East London? Shouldn't you be all, 'ello mate, 'ows you doin'?"

I winced at her appalling attempt at a cockney dialect, but I laughed, "A bit further east than that. Out in the suburbs. And, please, never do that again."

Jenna chuckled, "I promise you, Mr. Phelkar, I *will* get you home."

As the outer airlock door came up closer, she looked down, revealing the ring of limpet mines around her waist. "Be careful, Major. Apparently, it'll hurt me if you get blown up," I said teasingly.

"Tracker switched on the sensation monitors?" She chuckled. "That's too funny. I will try not to get my arm blown off or anything else, Mr. Phelkar. I wouldn't want to inconvenience you."

"Much appreciated." I chuckled. Jenna reversed her thrusters. She then cut them entirely and

allowed herself to drift until she hit the hull. She slapped a limpet mine on the door, keeping hold of it to stop herself from bouncing off and drifting backward.

Sakamoto came online. "Okay, Marines, they will have already detected us, but you have about three minutes before they will be ready to retaliate, so make it count." Jenna started planting the limpet mines along the seal of the airlock. "Give me a count-off when everything is in place." The Marines counted off after placing mines on each of the airlocks.

"Okay," Sakamoto said, "set the charge for one minute on my countdown. That's all the time we have, ladies and gentlemen. Three, two, one."

We could see troopers getting ready for our arrival through the airlock window. They were aware we were coming, but they thought we were trying to board conventionally. Jenna gave them a little wave and hit the reverse thrust on her suit. The sensation of accelerating backward at full speed was disturbing, and I closed my eyes. The minute seemed to last forever, and then a massive silent explosion took place, and seconds later, the shockwave hit Jenna hard, and the simulator slammed me into the wall. My visual flickered, and I lost communication with Jenna Plural.

I was in a panic as I pulled off the V.R. visor and adjusted my dark energy belt to sink to the ground slowly. I went back to the communications panel.

"What is going on out there?" I shouted.

"Phelkar, for the last time, will you stay off this line?" Sakamoto's voice was soft yet vicious with white-hot anger.

"We have lost the major. She's not responding," I shouted back.

"Shut up, Phelkar. Give me a count off, Marines." All but two replied to Sakamoto's order. "Plural and Anthony, give me your count off," Sakamoto said urgently.

My heart pounded up into my throat, and it seemed to take an eternity as Sakamoto repeated the command. Finally, a familiar voice came over the line. "Plural here. Well, that was unpleasant. I overcompensated on my reverse thrust and threw my systems out when the shockwave hit me. Damn, I have the worst headache."

Sakamoto simply acknowledged and then called out for Anthony once more, but no reply came.

I replaced the visor and once more entered the world of Jenna Plural.

"You still with me, Mr. Phelkar?" her voice came back, nervous and scared.

"I'm here, Major. With you all the way. I thought I'd lost you."

She relaxed a little at the sound of my voice as she turned around and headed back towards the Jauréguiberry. I noticed obstacles were coming toward her, and it took me a moment to realize what they were. She pushed the floating bodies and debris out of her way.

"See, it's like a walk in the park," I said.

"Remind me not to ask you to take me to see the parks in London if that's your thinking, Mr. Phelkar." Jenna chuckled.

"There are no parks in London. Hasn't been for over a hundred years."

"That's sad. I will have to take you to Oklahoma sometime," she said almost dreamily. "It's possibly the most beautiful place in the world, but of course, I'm biased." Her breathing seemed to relax as she got closer to the blown-in airlocks. Spherical silver repair drones with multiple arms and various tools were already out, rapidly trying to steal the entrance, but she could still get through the door. She reached down and slowly switched on her dark energy belt to one g and drifted to the ground.

"Well, that's a lot better," she said.

Unlike the Chesty, the Jauréguiberry was bright and well-lit. Jenna drew her snap gun and carefully walked into the main corridor. She suddenly fell to the ground with a thump, startling me. She reached down to switch off her belt.

"What happened?" I asked with concern.

"Stacey forgot to mention they have gravity generators on this ship," she responded with a hint of embarrassment. "With my D.E. belt on, I suddenly got hit by two g's when I entered the corridor."

"Idiot," I said, trying to sound like her.

Jenna laughed but muttered, "Fuck you, Mr. Phelkar."

"Okay, Marines," Sakamoto radioed in, "once more, by the numbers, confirm you're aboard." One by one, they sounded off again.

Suddenly there was a blast of sirens, and Jenna spun around, looking for danger. I felt nauseous by the rapid movement, but Sakamoto came back online. "That signals that the ship is sealed again. Head towards the bridge, but stay alert, and for God's sake, don't accidentally shoot each other."

Jenna moved cautiously forward, looking both ahead and behind as she started out. The going was slow, for there was no guarantee there weren't people that had been in closed-off rooms long enough to escape the sudden loss of air. Once again, she was unknowingly humming that funny song again.

"What is that song?"

She laughed, clearly embarrassed. "I didn't realize I was singing that aloud. It's a really old song for children, 'Nellie the Elephant.' My father used to sing it to me."

Before I could respond to that, a loud crash ahead made her stop and tense, weapon ready. Suddenly I felt a weird motion sickness as everything in my field of vision spun around. It took me a moment to realize that Jenna had jumped forward into a diving roll, and when she came up, she was firing behind her. I caught a glimpse of a Peon in a combat E.M.U. suit, ducking back behind the entrance to the corridor. Jenna looked about, but she had no cover in the large gleaming white hallway. The figure appeared again, and I made out from the shape that it was a woman. Jenna leaped to her feet and started running backward while continually firing to ensure her opponent stayed in cover until she could duck into a doorway. She gave herself a few seconds to catch her breath. But before she could return to the fight, we heard several more snapping sounds, and when she peered around the corner, Malcolm Hardy, the injured Marine from the med center, was stepping over the girl's body and coming toward Jenna. She stepped out.

"Much appreciated, Sergeant. I'm embarrassed to say I was caught by surprise."

"It can happen, Ma'am. Even to the best of us." He smiled at her with a twinkle in his eye. It was the first of many times I would want to punch him.

"I'm glad to have you at my back," Jenna said appreciatively. "Let's move out."

That was the first time I realized that I was developing feelings for the stalwart officer. A pang of jealousy that someone else had saved Jenna caused me to realize it. It was worsened by the fact that she now spoke to him and not me as the pair made their way through the maze of corridors. There was only one more excitement when Jenna shot a repair drone as it came around the corner, startling them.

"Okay, listen up," came Sakamoto's voice once more. "I'm at the bridge, and the door is sealed. I know you put me in charge, Major Plural, but I will defer this one to you. If we blow these doors, we risk damaging the control systems inside."

"Right. Well, we haven't come this far to risk losing the ship now," Jenna responded. "Mr. Phelkar, can you get Tracker on the line?" Less than three minutes later, Helen Tracker was patched into the call. "Okay, Tracker, here's the deal," Jenna began. "The cockpit doors are sealed, and we can't blow them open. Is there any way around this?"

"I could probably rig a bypass in the security system via the central computer room, but it would require me coming aboard."

"Get Stacey to set up a long-range umbilical tube. Now we are aboard, we can connect it this side. Get yourself into an E.M.U. suit and make your way over here. Mr. Phelkar, I know you're a noncombatant, but I'll feel better if Tracker has someone escorting her."

"On my way," I said and pulled off the visor. I met with Tracker, where we helped each other into our Extravehicular Mobility Units and checked each other's seals. Thirty minutes later, Stacey had us reconnected to the newly acquired ship.

Together we made our way through the airlock and entered the Jauréguiberry. We both withdrew our snap guns and made our way to the computer room, with Stacey, who had the deck plans back on the Puller, giving us directions over the radio. The ship was a rat's maze of corridors, and if we were ordered to get out of there fast, I had no idea of the way back. However, eventually, we found it. It took Tracker just a couple of minutes to open the sealed doors. As we got up to the bridge, Sakamoto urgently tried to call Anthony, but still, there was no response. Sakamoto looked at Jenna. "I will go see if I can find her." Jenna nodded, and Sakamoto headed off.

Tracker stepped up to the helm control, and Hardy dragged the dead pilot out of the seat and tossed the body aside so she could sit. As she did, she let out a long sigh. "The pilot was good.

He managed to lock out the controls during the decompression."

"Can you override it?" Jenna asked.

"If you give me a couple of years to learn technical French, sure."

Jenna looked at me. "Mr. Phelkar speaks frog, don't you?"

I stepped up next to her and translated the interface. "It's retinal scan protected," I said.

Tracker shook her head. "There is no way I can bypass this major. Not in time."

Jenna looked at her, and it was her turn to raise an eyebrow. "Don't give up that easily, Tracker," she said. "Would you give me a hand, Sergeant Hardy?"

They hauled up the pilot's body and held him over the retina scan. Dodgson came over and held open his eye. Everything started to come back online. As they let the body fall once more, I started translation for Tracker. Then Sakamoto called in. "Bad news, Major, Anthony somehow got entangled in cabling in her airlock and tore her air line. She didn't make it."

Jenna sighed. "Okay, Sakamoto, grab her tags and head back to the bridge." She then called our pilot on her earpiece. "Stacey, suit up and get that Aussie ass over here."

"Want me to go meet her?" I asked.

"No, Stacey can take care of herself."

"We have lost about ninety percent of total air supply," I said, translating the report.

Tracker said, "I'm venting all the remaining air into this room and the corridors leading to the airlock that Stacey has us connected to. We should be able to remove EMUs in about an hour." She then proceeded to tell me what needed to be done, and I translated it into French and typed it in. By the time we finished, our pilot had arrived at the bridge.

Jenna turned to see her enter. "Can you fly this thing?"

"I don't see why not," she said, slipping into the seat and running her hands over the controls. "Any way we can get these controls in English?"

"That's what I'm working on next," Tracker replied.

"I'm making you responsible for this ship, Stacey. I will leave Sakamoto with you. But the fewer people here, the longer the air supply will last until we can find a way to replenish the stores." She turned back to everyone else. "Ladies and gentlemen, I think we can consider this operation a success. We have ourselves a second ship."

It took about forty minutes for Stacey to dock the Peon ship with the Chesty once more, and as we set foot back on our ship, we helped each other off with our EMUs. Then Jenna hit the wall intercom. "Captain, we have secured the Jangle Berry. We ask that you now stand down and turn this ship over to my command."

Royce shouted back, "They'll hang you for this, bitch."

The Peon commander came on. "You have taken my ship? What about my crew?"

"Casualties of war, commander. If you don't want to be one yourself, turn over the bridge to us now."

"But...but how?" There was a tremor in his voice.

Royce shouted. "You have completely lost it, Plularian. You're insane, and those who follow you are idiots."

Jenna ignored the insult. "You have twenty minutes. After that, I will blow the doors off and take the risk of damage."

"How do I know you just won't execute me?" asked the commander.

"You don't. You must hope that I will show you mercy." She switched off the intercom.

Harlow headed back down to the engineering room. With Tracker working on the M.E.T., I was left alone with Jenna. "I think I could do with a coffee," I said. "Care for one, Major?"

"I think I can do with something a bit stronger than coffee at this moment, Mr. Phelkar," she responded. We headed to the mess hall, and Jenna unlocked a cabinet above the countertop, pulled out a bottle of whiskey, and poured out two glasses, handing one to me.

"So even if we have two ships, what exactly is it you plan to do next?" I asked as we took our seats.

"There are hundreds of ships and bases out there. I hope we can rally them and bring them back together into a new fleet and ultimately take the fight to Earth. If we can complete our mission to Phobos and destroy the major European communications network, the entire European Union will be in disarray. Their communications will take weeks, not minutes, to reach the outer planets, affecting their military strategy and commerce. Fleets won't be able to respond to emergencies. We will send out our own message to allied forces in a broadcast that will be picked up by every ship no matter how far away it is." She looked excited by the idea. Then as she realized something, her confidence fell. "Unfortunately, that is why Phobos is probably the most heavily defended place in the solar system. We are trusting the smarts of Helen Tracker to get us past the satellite defenses. If she's wrong, then we are going to die." She then downed her drink, reached the counter for the bottle, and refilled her glass. She nodded to me to finish mine, and I grinned at such an odd order. I downed the drink and let her refill it. "So, what do you think of my plan, Mr. Phelkar?"

"I will be honest with you, Major. I don't know if we have made the right decision today, but we have made the decision, and I will stand by it whatever may come."

"I appreciate that loyalty, but I appreciate your honesty more. It is easier to trust a person who doesn't sycophantically agree with you as some do." She smiled at me.

I smiled and raised my glass. "Here's to you, Major Plural."

She clinked her glass against mine. "Here's to the fightback, Mr. Phelkar."

Silence fell between us, and the lighthearted mood dissipated as we were lost in afterthoughts about the future. When the intercom buzzed, it startled us.

"Okay, Jenna, we will come out," Royce said.

Jenna grinned ruefully. "Did that shithead really just call me Jenna?" She downed the rest of her shot and jumped out of the seat, and I did the same. She hit the intercom. "Glad to see you come to your senses. Make sure your guards push their weapons out into the hallway as soon as we open the door." She released the button, looked back at me, and said, "Come on. Let's go deal with this."

Chapter Eleven

Breakfast with Jenna

"What are you going to do with them?" I asked as we headed to the cockpit.

"You understand we can't take prisoners," she said. "We don't have the resources for it." She was clearly trying to gauge my response to this.

"We can't store them in the M.E.T.?" I asked, uneasy about where this was going.

Jenna shook her head. "We no longer have the luxury of a home base, and the M.E.T. uses up a lot of power."

Jenna radioed Helen and ordered her to unseal the doors. Jenna had me stand on one side of the door as she stood on the other. She drew her snap gun, and I did the same. As they opened, several weapons were dropped into the hallway.

"Come out, one at a time," Jenna ordered. First, the two armed troopers came out with their hands raised. "Hands up.

Stand against the wall with your noses touching it." I translated the instruction, covering them with my firearm as they complied. Then the captain and the commander came out with hands raised, and the commander looked at Jenna.

"You will die for this, you stupid—" He never finished his words as Jenna raised her weapon and shot him directly in the face. Turning around swiftly, she shot both guards in the back of the head before they could react. I was startled by the suddenness of it all and the fact that Jenna did not even flinch as blood and brain matter splattered upon both of us.

Royce looked terrified and dived to the floor, covering his head. "You're completely fucking insane."

"Well, Captain. I'm just a dumb GenMod, aren't I?" Jenna stepped astride him. "Oh, and by the way, you don't have the privilege of calling me 'Jenna,'" she growled with such venom that she even scared me. Then she fired the killing shot into his forehead.

She stood staring down at his corpse until I spoke, "Are you okay, Ma'am?"

"I'm fine." She looked at me, frowned, then grinned. "I think you should say 'Major.' With that dumb accent of yours, you sound like you're calling me your 'mom.'" She bent down and dragged the body of the commandant away from the doorway, and we ventured into the cockpit.

Jenna slipped into Stacey's seat and called over to the Jauréguiberry. "Chesty to Jangle Berry, do you read me, Stacey?"

"That's an affirmative, boss," Stacey said.

"You will be pleased to know we now have control of the Chesty."

"And the captain?"

"No longer a concern. Come back over to the Chesty, please, and meet me in the captain's office for a briefing."

"Not a problem, boss." The line went dead, and Jenna sat back in her chair, deep in thought.

A short while later, Jenna entered the captain's office as if she had owned it for years. Like everything on board the Lewis Puller, it was small and cramped. Jenna sat down behind the desk. Stacey quickly pushed past me to grab the only other chair in the room using the long-obsolete term, "Ladies first."

Sakamoto, Tracker, and Harlow followed behind me. "Okay, so now we have control of both ships. What's the situation?" Jenna asked.

She looked at Harlow first, who grunted and said, "Engines running as normal on both ships. The only problem is I can't put a man in the engine room because there's no fucking air. You blew it all away just like you blow everything away, Jen."

Jenna smiled at him and shrugged. "It's what I do, Rocky." She looked to Tracker. "Anything we can do about the air situation?"

Tracker sighed and shook her head as she pondered the issue. "We can recycle it, but we can't create it. I can transfer the reserves from the Puller and section off engineering. That will least reduce what we need, but it's not a long-term solution."

"Do it. However, we need a plan to replace our supplies," Jenna said.

"There is a Peon resupply base orbiting Deimos," Sakamoto advised. "It is mostly automated and is most likely to have less than three or four crew."

"Surely it's not gonna be undefended," I commented.

"Mars can supply defenders long before anyone can get close enough," Sakamoto replied.

"Doesn't that make it rather pointless, seeing as we cannot defend against the Martian defenses at this moment in time?" I stated.

"Only if they see a Pacific Alliance ship, you moron." Stacey rolled her one visible eye at me. "The Jangle Berry is a Peon ship. A ship that the Peons think is still one of theirs."

Jenna smiled at Stacey, pondering a moment before replying. "Reckon you can take it with a few Marines, Stacey?"

Stacey shrugged. "Shouldn't be a problem. Fuck, give me a French speaker, and we may get them to refuel us without us even going on board."

Jenna nodded. "I will see what I can do. Do you think you can do it before the Chesty picks us up on Phobos? Once we blow that place, we need to get the hell out of Dodge."

"No promises, but I'll give it a damn good try." Stacey grinned.

Jenna turned to Tracker again. "How are things going with the M.E.T.?"

"It's not one hundred percent, but it's safe to download people. We just have to do it a lot slower than normal."

Jenna sat back. "I want to thank you all. What I asked you to do today was above and beyond the call of duty. Over the last four years, we have become a great team, and I value you and your loyalty to me." She then looked at me. "Even you, Mr. Phelkar, the one random element in this equation, are proving to be trustworthy and reliable, and I thank you for your support." She then addressed the group again. "I don't know what will befall us, but I know one thing: I don't plan on stopping until I'm either dead or we have victory." She stood up. "Let's get to work."

One piece of luck we had was a young enlisted man called Martin Neuman. His official job was as a field communications tech, working under Helen Tracker, but he was a superb fast-order cook. Awakening the next day to the smell of bacon and eggs looted from Jauréguiberry stores, wafting through the ventilation system, brightened my morning. I was looking forward to having breakfast with the troops. However, to my surprise, I was summoned to Jenna's cabin. When I knocked at the door, she shouted for me to come in, and as I did, I heard a shower running in another room.

"I won't be long. Help yourself to coffee and a bagel," she called out, sounding quite cheerful.

"I can come back later if you wish me to," I called back to her.

"If I wish that, Mr. Phelkar, I wouldn't have called you to come over now. I thought you might like to have breakfast with me."

An interesting idea, but I decided not to read too much into that. I always found it hard to relate to people I was physically attracted to. Especially when they were way out of my league, like Jenna Plural. It was so unlikely that I could ever enter into a relationship with someone like Jenna that it hadn't even crossed my mind, but that would change over the next hour.

Jenna was a true Marine regarding neatness. The room was spotless, everything neatly in its place. I looked down at the large desk where breakfast was neatly laid out: two cups and several bagels on a tray with a large pot of steaming coffee. I poured myself a cup, and I couldn't help but notice that it was the real stuff. The smell was distinct and not that synthetic crap we had been drinking of late. I took a moment to take in the aroma before taking a sip. This was the natural and expensive kind from South America, and I assumed it had been liberated from the Peons.

I heard the water go off a moment later. Jenna stepped out of the room dressed in nothing but a short pink towel as she used another to dry her hair. With her head tilted to one side, as she vigorously rubbed her hair, she smiled at the look on my face. I was in a state of shock and awe as I looked at her.

She misinterpreted my expression, saying, "That's good stuff, isn't it?"

"Huh?" I looked down at my cup. "Oh, the coffee, yes, it's excellent," I said, turning away slightly.

"Stacey had someone go through the Peon supplies. They lived like it was a luxury cruise liner. I need you to have everything distributed to the crew stores."

"I'm sure they will appreciate it," I said, trying to keep my eyes from looking back at those long, toned legs. She tossed the towel that she was using on her hair onto her bed.

"I hope you don't mind meeting with me here." She turned and retrieved a fresh uniform from a locker and laid it over the back of a chair.

"It is your prerogative to meet wherever you wish, Major," I said, chuckling.

She glanced at me with a faint smile as she stepped over and opened a drawer. "I wanted to thank you in private for what you did for me out there." She pulled out some undergarments, and before it clicked in my slow brain what was happening, she dropped the towel that she was wearing. I audibly gasped and turned away, but the image of that white-skinned, perfect body was burned into my brain. She spun around and asked urgently, "What's the matter?" But as I remained facing away, it dawned on her. "Oh, for fuck sake, Mr. Phelkar," she said, exasperated. "This is the United States Marine Corps. Men and women fighting side by side in the line of battle can't be worried about that sort of timidity."

"Yes, well, I'm not in the Marine Corps," I replied, somewhat flustered.

"No, but you're in active service with them." There was a pause where I said nothing, then she said with a resigned sigh, "You can turn around, Mr. Phelkar. I'm covered up."

I turned back to her to realize "covered up" meant she now had her underwear on. If I still looked uncomfortable, she did not notice it, for she appeared in no hurry as she continued dressing. Her long damp hair hung over her shoulders and stuck to her breast and flat stomach.

"As I was saying, I wanted to thank you for your assistance out there." She pulled on her trousers, and my comfort level started to rise.

"Not a problem." I smiled, dismissing the issue with a wave of my hand.

She frowned at this as she pulled a fresh khaki shirt over her head and tucked it in. "No, Mr. Phelkar, you not only saved my life but more importantly, you saved the mission." She took a seat at the desk where the breakfast was laid out and poured herself a coffee. "Come join me." I took the seat next to her but turned it to face her. She talked as she buttered a bagel. "Are you not eating, Mr. Phelkar?"

"I'm fine with the coffee, thanks."

"Your loss. These are fine bagels." She took a bite and sat back. Chewing softly, she studied me for a moment in quiet silence before speaking again. "I hope I can trust your discretion about how I reacted out there, Mr. Phelkar. I'm sure you can understand that it would severely undermine my authority should this incident become general knowledge."

"That goes without saying, Major. I can assure you no one will hear about the incident from me."

Jenna smiled, and her look of concern turned to one of assurance. "You should understand how much I appreciate that." And she briefly placed her hand upon mine, which was resting upon the desk. Sitting back, she tilted her head to one side as she looked at me. It was as if she was summing me up before she continued. "I would like you to work for me, Mr. Phelkar."

"I kind of already thought I was," I responded, unsure what she meant.

"I mean in an official capacity." She paused and shrugged. "Well, as official as possible in the new circumstances."

"Well, it's not like I can go home now." I grinned. "And to be honest, I would find it an honor to serve you."

Jenna smiled once again and seemed to relax considerably. "I want you to be my right hand. If I'm to achieve what I hope to, I'm entering an alien world. I'm a military person, Mr. Phelkar, yet I'm now stepping into a world of diplomacy and politics. I need you to be my guide and my conscience."

"You want me to be your Jiminy Cricket?" I chuckled lightly.

She understood the reference, for she grinned and said, "Will you be there for me when I give a little whistle?"

I felt a slight tingle of butterflies in my stomach as she said that, for the idea was quite alluring, although I was under no apprehension that she meant that in anything but a professional way.

"I can assure you, Major Plural, when you whistle, I will be there at your side doing whatever I can to assist you."

Her hand was on mine again, but this time it was for longer, and she said with her beaming smile, "I really do appreciate you, Mr. Phelkar. I just want you to know that."

I tried to suppress the pounding of my heart as she looked at me that way and touched my hand, and as she sat back again, I pushed from my mind the unprofessional feelings that were beginning to stir up within me.

"So, I'm not an idiot anymore?" I chuckled.

Laughing as she returned her attention to her bagel, she shrugged with a grin. "Oh, you're still an idiot, Mr. Phelkar, but you're now *my* idiot." She took another bite of a bagel, and with it still in her mouth, she looked up at me, saying, "Is that fair enough?"

Right then and there, I knew I would be her anything, but I more diplomatically replied, "It'll do for now, Major," I said, smiling back at her.

She lifted her hand and sat back. "I'm sorry for my attitude towards you when we first met," she said, now serious again. "It was unbecoming of me as a United States Marine and a decent human being. Which I assure you, Mr. Phelkar, I do endeavor to be."

"I accept your apology, and in return, I ask that you accept my apology or my comments referring to your genetic modifications."

She raised an eyebrow and smirked at me. "Only if you truly have lost your AntiGen bias."

"I must admit you have given me cause to re-evaluate my previously misconceived ideas. I do indeed now see you as a United States Marine and can look past your perfections."

Her smile faded, and whilst her attitude to me did not change, she looked somewhat disappointed. "One thing I can assure you of, Mr. Phelkar, is that I'm not perfect, and that is why I have asked you for your support."

I tried to lighten the mood. "Do I get some fancy title?"

The grin returned. "I don't know about fancy, but how does 'adjutant' sound to you?"

I wrinkled up my nose jokingly. "I was thinking of something more intimidating to people like The Hand of Jenna," I said ominously.

Jenna laughed, "Jenna is hardly an intimidating name, Mr. Phelkar, so I'm afraid adjutant will have to do. I will make the announcement this afternoon." She refilled both our coffees as she moved on to say, "We should discuss the situation regarding Stephanie Morris. I am inclined to leave her in the M.E.T., but Sakamoto thinks it would be too much for the crew to lose both the captain and the first officer." She put the pot back down and turned to me. "What do you think?"

"I think Sakamoto is correct. Not all the crew here have served with you long. I assume, whilst, in Manassas, you did a standard crew rotation?" Jenna simply nodded in response. "So, it is the case that at least a third of the crew may not have worked with you before and not have the same loyalty as the other crew members. It will be hard for them to adjust to the idea that not only have we surrendered, but we have also rebelled, so if you can get Morris on board with you, it would make the transition much easier." Jenna looked very concerned and sighed. "I thought you might say that, but I hoped you wouldn't. Personally, I'd like to put a bullet in her head."

I did not take her last comment as literal and merely an expression of frustration, but time would reveal that Jenna usually meant everything she said. "She may not even agree to support you," I responded. "But I think you should sound her out about it."

She sighed again and shook her head but said, "Very well, Mr. Phelkar, we will try it your way." She glanced over at the clock. "Is that the time? Shit. You'll have to excuse me, Mr. Phelkar, but I have a meeting with Stacey in about five minutes." She stood up and went back to the drawer where she had retrieved her undergarments. She picked up a locket from the dresser, clipped it behind her neck, and hid it under her shirt before pulling out a pair of socks from the drawer. "Meet at the M. E.T. this afternoon. I'd like you to be there when we download Morris."

"You need me there to stop you from hitting her?" I said, laughing.

She glanced up from pulling on a sock and grinned at me. "Ah, Mr. Phelkar, it's so sweet that you think you could stop me from doing that."

I rolled my eyes and stood up to leave. She pulled on her other sock and, with a final, very sweet smile, said, "Thank you, Mr. Phelkar."

With both ships now under our control, there was a lot of work to put them back in order. We had done considerable damage to the Chesty by turning on the automated defenses. As the ship's fifth wheel, I was now responsible for dealing with the dead. It was a grisly task. Jenna had separated the dead into two categories of Peon and American. She instructed me to dump the Peons out of the airlock. The Americans were to be stacked in the cargo bay and identified. Fortunately, I didn't have to do the physical work, just organized a couple of Marines who did the actual physical labor. I'm sad to say we lost twenty-three men and women in the battle for the Chesty. The Peons lost more, but I can't say how many since I never counted them.

I met Jenna and Tracker in the M.E.T. around 4 p.m., and we downloaded the former first officer. Of course, much to Jenna's chagrin, I faced away. As Stephanie Morris beamed back into existence, Jenna stood facing her. Tracker handed Morris a towel which she wrapped around herself. "How long was I gone?"

"Almost a day," replied Jenna, "but a lot has happened. I have taken control of both Chesty and the Peon ship. We aren't complying with the surrender order. I'm now in command of both ships." Stephanie frowned. "What about the captain?"

"He is dead."

Stephanie's eyes widened. "How?"

"He gave us no choice."

Stephanie grew nervous at this. "And is that to be my fate?"

Jenna shrugged. "There is a place for you on this ship if you accept my command."

The former first officer looked at me, then at Tracker, and then back to Jenna. "What is it you intend to do?"

Jenna stood erect and defiant. "Fight back whatever way we can."

"What will that achieve?" Stephanie looked confused.

"We must do something, Morris. We cannot let this be the end of centuries of our nation's history."

Stephanie pondered this a moment, then said carefully. "You know I outrank you."

"Not anymore." Jenna fixed her gaze with a 'dare you challenge that' expression.

A long silence hung between them before Stephanie nodded. "Very well. It is not my wish to lead such an endeavor, but I agree the situation is not one I'm willing to accept. I will join you, and I will recognize your authority in this matter."

Jenna simply nodded and folded her arms. "Your service is appreciated." She turned to Tracker. "We will start downloading the officers before we download the enlisted." She looked back to Stephanie. "I guess you can start by helping reorientate people."

That sounded simple, but in truth, it wasn't. Not everyone would agree to join Jenna, not because they weren't loyal to her but because they just wanted to go home. Some of the crew even got violent, and Jenna had to post Hardy and Dodgson in the room with Morris and Tracker as they conducted their interviews. I understood the ones who wanted to go home, but that was one place where Jenna had a blind spot. She just couldn't comprehend anyone being willing to accept a surrender.

To preserve the Chesty's resources, those who opposed Jenna's plans were re-uploaded, as were most of those on her side. However, we now had a crew that we could use, and for the first time, the U.S.S. Lewis Puller felt like a real ship with real people working on it.

That evening I was headed to Jenna's office, the one formerly belonging to Captain Royce, to give her the names of our dead as she had requested, but as I turned into the corridor, I heard her laughing lightly, and something made me step back. As I glanced around the corner, I saw her standing outside the office. She was leaning with her back against the wall, her arms folded. There was joy and happiness in her face and her eyes as she spoke. I felt my stomach turn over as, standing in front of her, inappropriately close in my opinion, was Malcolm Hardy, the barrel-chested Marine who was so full of himself. As they spoke about the Marines and past missions, I realized they had a bond I could never share with her. I felt sick as the new mood of envy overcame me. I moved back out of sight so they wouldn't notice me, and I lay my head back against the wall. I pondered continuing around that corner, interrupting them, but instead, I turned away and headed to the mess hall and into a situation that would eventually create more problems than I ever could have imagined.

Chapter Twelve

The Navy Way

I had hoped the mess was empty but was surprised to find Stacey sitting back with her white boots on the table, drinking some sort of whisky or brandy.

She looked up at me and grinned, raising her glass to me. "Well, hey, if it is not our resident pommy hunk." I harrumphed in response and threw myself into a chair. Stacey raised her eyebrows.

"What's got your undies all in a bundle?"

"I'm not in the mood for it, Stacey," I said sullenly.

"Wow, just messing with you, Phelks. Something's busting your balls. Come on, tell your Auntie Stacey all about it."

Stacey leaned down to pick up the bottle at her side. Her legs outstretched on the table and crossed at the ankles were quite exquisite. Unlike Jenna's, which were more muscular, they were soft and curved. Stacey's short white leather skirt inched dangerously close to revealing too much. I flushed and tried to avert my eyes. I looked at the bottle as she poured herself another and placed it on the table. "What's that?"

Stacey grinned again, "This, my good sir, is pure Australian ambrosia, the nectar of the Aussie gods." She turned the bottle to show me the label. "This is Portobello Brandy. One of the last bottles from Australia."

I raised an eyebrow. Everyone knew that Australians were renowned for making the finest brandy in the world for the last hundred or so years, and it had become extremely rare since the Peons had stopped all exports from the country.

I stared in amazement. "Wow, how much did that set you back? I heard they auction it nowadays!"

"Never cost me anything. Jenna got it for me."

My eyes widened. "Wow, that costs thousands, literally. Even before the annexation, it was beyond the average person's means."

"Oh, the American taxpayer picked up the bill on this." Her grin widened. "After the Battle of Cape York and the fall of Oz, the boss wanted to recruit me. I asked for this as part of my sign-on bonus."

"She must have really wanted you," I said, surprised.

"What can I say? I'm good at what I do, Phelks." She chuckled, and the one eye I could see amidst all that lacquered hair covering her face seemed to sparkle.

"You could've just asked for the money."

"What's the point in money if you can't go surfing on Bondi Beach?" She shrugged.

"Well, I haven't had the fortune of visiting Australia, and I'll certainly never got to surf."

"Well, I'll make you a promise. When we kick the Peons out of Oz, I'll take you surfing, but only if you wear a pair of budgie smugglers." Stacey winked as she poured me a drink.

I chuckled, and I'm sure I even blushed slightly. "Oh, my dear Stacey, I'm sure a delightful young man is waiting for you."

Stacey shrugged and gave me a sideways look as she handed me the glass. "Maybe, but he ain't here right now, and as I said, there's a big shortage of men on this ship." She yawned and stretched, her tight white shirt accentuated her curves, and I did not fail to notice.

"I thought you were on the Jauréguiberry," I said, swirling the liquor as I warmed it in my palm.

Stacey raised an eyebrow. "Yeah, I *really* don't like spending my off-duty hours amongst bloated corpses and eating in a mess hall with all the air sucked out. It's kinda bad for my health."

"I see your point," I chuckled. "I will send some Marines over there tomorrow to deal with the dead."

"Thanks." Then gave me a knowing look. "I plan on getting absolutely smashed tonight, so, hey, I might even end up fucking you." I brushed off that comment as her warped humor and downed my glass in one. Stacey's mood quickly changed, "Hey," she said irritably. "That's not some cheap Russian vodka."

"I'm sorry," I said, hiding that the brandy was now burning my throat. "I guess you should pour another and let me try again."

Stacey wasn't attractive in the traditional sense, but she was cute with an upturned nose that wrinkled when she laughed. However, there was something very sensual about her, and it is hard to describe. It was more her personality and that 'Don't give a shit attitude' that was somewhat alluring about her. Also, that accent was about the sexiest thing I've ever heard. She re-filled my glass, and to my astonishment, she let her legs slip off the table and onto my lap. I was unsure how to respond, so I picked up the glass, took a sip, and rested my other hand on her shin.

It was only then I noticed the grey, boring, functional bra hanging on the corner of her chair, and my eyes were instinc-tively drawn to her chest and the tight shirt that accentuated her otherwise modest breast. I only realized I was staring when Stacey said with a wide grin, "Enjoying the view, Phelks?"

"I have no idea what you mean." I lied, looking away, but parts of me were not hypocritical, and she was clearly aware of my arousal, which started to press against her calf.

"You're so full of shit, Phelks!" She chuckled and bit her lower lip provocatively, and rubbed her leg against the growing bulge in my trousers. I gasped ever so slightly, and before real-izing it, I found myself massaging her calf and filling with the strong desire to be with her. "Oh, that feels *so* good." She let her head fall back and held it in interlocked palms while I looked at her with less than pure thoughts in my mind. I slowly moved my hand up to Stacey's knee and looked to see if I got a positive or negative reaction.

I got no reaction and thought, *'What the hell? I'll take that as a positive sign.'* I gently ran my fingers up and down her thigh. She opened her eyes and looked at me with a lascivious grin.

Stacey put her glass down, slipped her legs off my lap, and stood up. Standing astride my knees, she sat down upon my lap, her wrists crossed behind my neck. She plucked the glass from my hand, lifted it to her lips, and drank the remains. My hands went to her hips without even thinking and grabbed her backside. I pulled her closer. She giggled and leaned down awkwardly. Her lips met mine, soft and gentle at first. But as we kissed, the intensity grew. She pulled back and whispered. "Get up, mister." She jumped up, pulling me to my feet. "Come on. I can think of one place where we can be alone that doesn't stink of greasy food and United States Marine sweat."

We ran down the cramped corridor towards her quarters. I was so sure we were louder than we meant to, but that didn't seem to bother us at the time. She clicked the door open and grabbed me by the shirt collar, pulling me through the door and into her quarters. Looking into my eyes, she said softly, "I want you, Phelks."

I smiled, looking down at her, and I reached up to push aside the black hair that covered her right eye. I suddenly tensed and let out a startled gasp. I saw a curved metal plate covering her hidden eye and a faintly glowing green light of a lens staring back at me. A thin pale scar ran down from brow to cheek. Her face, moments ago filled with joy, now looked upset at my reaction, and she tried to back away. I held onto her and pulled her back against me with a smile. She resisted slightly as I spoke, "Hey," I said gently. "it's okay. I was just startled. It doesn't bother me, honestly."

She hesitated momentarily, but then the smile slowly returned, and we kissed once more. Her soft young body pressed against mine, blowing off fireworks in my head and other parts of my anatomy. When our lips separated, she looked up at me with a wry grin. Her product-filled hair fell back into place, and she said casually, "You know, Phelks. I have never fucked an Englishman before."

I chuckled softly, "Well, there is a first time for everything, and hey if it helps, I have never slept with an Australian before."

"Then you have never lived, Phelks." She grinned. "It's a known fact you can't get better than an Aussie girl. Especially one from Wagga." I chuckled as she undid my belt, pulled it through the loops with a swift flick, and tossed it behind her. I squeezed my hands on her hips, letting out a low grunt. "Why, Phelks, I do believe you have gone right past boring and blushing and straight to bold." She whispered in my ear, her breath hot and still emanating the aroma of the expensive brandy. Her hands slid my shirt up over my head, and she took a step back. Almost admiringly, she said, "Wow. So that's what you were hiding under there. I'm impressed." She crossed her arms over herself and took hold of the bottom hem of her shirt, inching it higher before removing it completely and throwing it amongst the heaped clothes in the corner.

I closed the gap between us and undid the button and zipper on my pants as I did. I dropped them to the floor and stepped out of them as she slid out of her skirt, her regulation briefs tight against her skin.

My hand went to her breast, causing her to lean her head back, exposing her neck to finally reveal the tattoo with the name 'Harper' and a date four years previously. She suddenly lost her balance and, grabbing onto me, we tumbled down onto the bed, her on her back and me on top. It was the perfect accident. Without hesitation, she brought her hands up to either side of my face, and we started kissing again, lips and tongues going every which way with a fervent passion as my hands explored her body. She suddenly rolled me over and climbed on top, taking charge of the situation.

I'd been with women before—of course, I had—but none that could compare to Stacey. The way she felt when I was inside her and how she moved her hips. She nearly forced me to arrive too quickly, which would've been embarrassing. There's no way she was this good! Yet here we were. It seemed to last forever, and when we finally climaxed, it was like nothing I had ever experienced.

"I had fun tonight, Phelks," she panted as she flopped back on the bed beside me.

"You and me both," I replied, still unsure how normal old Stacey could've just rocked my world the way she did. It wasn't possible anyone could be that good in the bedroom, yet it had happened.

"I hope you don't think this means anything," she said, and I looked back at her questioningly. "You and me. This doesn't make you my boyfriend or anything." She bit her lower lip and waited uneasily for my response.

I wasn't sure how to respond at first. I wasn't expecting any sort of relationship with her. Hell, this was the furthest thing from my mind when I had entered the mess that evening. She was not remotely my type. I liked my girls with a tad more class who did not swear like a sailor. Someone a little classy, someone like ... well, like Jenna.

So, finding the correct response and considering her feelings, I replied, "If that's what you want." That way, I seemed to give her control even though I had no intention of getting involved as a potential long-term prospect. Not back then. I did not realize how much this little Australian firebrand would come to mean to me. At least ... not until she was no longer there.

"This was just a bit of fun. It's the Navy way," she said sheepishly. "If I led you on to believe it would be more than that, I'm sorry."

"It's fine." I smiled and stroked her cheek with the back of my hand. "I'm glad I shared this experience with you."

Stacey rolled her eye. "Oh shit, don't go mushy on me, Phelks. It was just a fuck."

I leaned in and kissed her, but it was a brief gentle one. "Don't worry. I know where we stand."

We fell asleep, and when I woke up, she had already left. As I dressed, I noticed a picture frame screwed to the top of the bedside cabinet. It contained a single picture of a young woman with long, light pink hair with her arm around Stacey. She was clearly someone special to the young pilot. It wasn't a professional picture, just one of those best-mate-type things. Stacey had a similar style of hair as she had now, but instead of being black, it was also pink, and I could see both her natural eyes. As I pulled on my clothes, I wondered who this young woman was and why she was so important to the young pilot. I then headed to my room to take a shower.

Chapter Thirteen

Assault on Phobos

It was another day before the various repair teams reported that everything was in order on the Chesty and our spoil of war. Jenna then prepared to transfer command to the new ship.

"The question is," Jenna said as we had our final meeting on the Lewis Puller, "who to leave in charge of the Chesty."

I pondered this for a moment. "Is there any other option than Stephanie Morris?"

Jenna's eyes narrowed. "Are you serious?"

"Indeed so. The crew will expect it, and it will raise concerns among them should they have even more changes."

She sighed and reluctantly nodded. "I don't trust her, but I will go with your judgment on this."

So, the command was transferred to Morris, and the young Neville Batty was made the senior pilot. This left Morris with a skeletal crew of the copilot and a couple of Marines. Her orders were simple. She was to wait for the report of a mission success on Phobos and bring the Chesty in to be ready to pick us up. Then Jenna, Tracker, Sakamoto, and I headed over to join Stacey on the Peon ship. Tracker opened the airlock on our side while Stacey opened it on the other. Jenna went through first, and I waited for the others to go through before I followed. Tracker came last, securing the Chesty's airlock once inside the umbilical. We had pumped the last of the Chesty's air reserves into the new ship to cater for the new personnel. It still left two-thirds of the vessel uninhabitable.

Stacey was there smiling at us as we reached her. "G'day Major, welcome aboard the Lady Liberty."

Jenna smiled back and nodded. "Lady Liberty? I like it. Let the record show I'm transferring authority to the Lady Liberty at this time."

On the bridge, Stacey slipped into her seat as Jenna took her place in the command chair, and although I couldn't pilot the ship, I slipped into the vacant copilot seat beside Stacey.

"Release umbilical," Jenna commanded.

Moments later, Stacey reported. "Umbilical released. We are floating free."

"How about those engines, Miss Grant?" Jenna asked. Stacey's hands darted off the controls, and the pleasing hum of the engines grew louder and louder.

"Engines online and purring like a kitten, Major."

Jenna grinned. "Well, Stacey, let's get this kitten to Phobos."

The following weeks would be laboriously dull for me. Jenna did mission prep with the Marines. Sakamoto worked with Tracker in practicing in a modern Peon E.M.U. suit she had found in storage.

Slowly but surely, we approached the minefield of satellites that protected Phobos. Stacey spent some time going through the modifications of the ship controls she'd made and had Tracker check everything.

"We're still sending out the ship's former name as its beacon," she told us at a morning briefing session. "The real issue is we don't know if the Peons have realized we have this ship. The sats will have been updated to attack us if they do."

"The moment we are compromised or mission complete, we need to broadcast as an American ship," Jenna instructed.

"I have hacked the transponder and set it ready to change once we formally identify ourselves after the assault," Tracker told her.

"The real problem will be getting us off of Phobos afterward. This ship isn't designed to land," Sakamoto interjected.

"That's fine," said Jenna. "By the time we are finished, the Chesty should be in orbit, and it can land for a pickup."

"It still won't be easy as it's an exceptionally low gravity moon, and it'll have to be a quick pick up," Stacey stated.

"You think Batty can handle it, or should I keep you back there?" Jenna replied with a frown.

"Nah, I don't think it'll be too much of a problem for him. He can handle it. Just warning you, it won't be a milk run."

"Understood." Jenna looked around at the assembled officers. "Is everyone ready for this?"

Everyone nodded, and Sakamoto said, "Just say the word, Major."

"Okay then." Jenna stood up. "Let's do this!" Everyone filed out and headed for their various duty posts.

There was a tense atmosphere on the bridge as we all took our places. Once again, I sat beside Stacey. Tracker stood just behind Jenna at the tactical console.

"Okay, Stacey." Jenna sounded almost ominous as she ordered, "Take us into the satellite system nice and easy, and try not to draw attention."

Slowly the ship moved forward, and I looked over at Stacey's screen displaying a readout of the dozens of satellites coming into range. Tracker spoke uneasily. "The first satellite is scanning us."

"Be ready to get us out of here, Stacey," Jenna said softly, as if the satellites could somehow overhear us.

"Aye, Major."

"Sending handshake signal now," Tracker advised. Then moments later, she added, "Handshake received. Waiting for response." She relaxed slightly when she next said, "Handshake acknowledged."

Sending the second handshake." There was a long pause before Tracker let out a sigh of relief. "Have received trusted transponder signal. We are accepted as a friendly ship and have been cleared to proceed."

However, tension still mounted as we moved in closer. A few minutes later, I slipped out of my seat and went down to join Sakamoto at the airlock. I helped her with the Peon E.M.U. suit, and we went through safety checks. I then called to let Jenna know she was ready. Sakamoto stepped into the airlock, and I sealed the door behind her. We waited patiently for instruction from the bridge, and when it came, my heart began to pound against my chest as Stacey spoke. "As close as I can get you, Tomi."

"You're all set, Sergeant," Jenna came back. "Clear skies to you, and don't take any unnecessary risks. Get in, get out."

Sakamoto acknowledged. "Understood. I'm opening the outer airlock now."

I saw the outer door open through the window, and Sakamoto stepped out into space. There was the flash of her propulsion boosters, and she moved from my sight. I ran back to the bridge, I had never moved so fast in my life, but even so, the young officer was already far away, heading towards the small satellite. Everyone held their collective breath as she reached it and held on to its side. Stacey switched on a forward camera and focused on her, and the image of her appeared on the window ahead of us.

Sakamoto was hanging on to a handle designed for such activity. "Easy does it now, Sakamoto," said Jenna. "We can't afford to screw this up."

"I've got the panel open," Sakamoto said.

We watched as she placed the device Tracker had made into the satellite system. The next few minutes went on like an eternity. Silence hung in the cockpit, and I felt a bead of sweat running down my forehead and wiped it upon my sleeve.

"Come on, come on," I muttered.

At last, she moved back and closed the panel. "Well, it's in. How effective it is, is up to you."

Jenna looked relieved and sat back. "Good job. Now get back to the ship."

"Um, Major!" Stacey looked up from the console. "We have a problem. The base on Phobos is calling."

"Do they know who we are?" Jenna looked concerned.

"No, they think we are still under the control of the Peons. They want to know why we are tampering with the satellite surveillance systems, as there is no scheduled work. If we don't respond, they will get suspicious and call backup."

Jenna turned to me, her eyes hopeful. "Mr. Phelkar, do you think you can bluff your way through this?"

I nodded and nervously stood over Stacey's shoulder. "Open a channel, please, Stacey." I then said in French, "Jauréguiberry to Phobos base, go ahead,"

An elderly-sounding man asked me why we had a technician out on the satellites.

"That's classified," I replied. "Who am I speaking to, and what is your security clearance?"

"I'm Doctor Valier, the chief custodian of this station. It is part of our responsibility to monitor the security systems around Phobos. Who am I speaking to? We were not informed of any servicing."

"Colonel Christian LeFevre of the First French Expeditionary Force, and I demand you keep this line clear for important transmissions. The president is about to make a serious announcement that must be heard throughout the colonies. We are extending the range of the transmitters. No further transmissions, please."

A pause seemed to take forever before he replied, "Understood, Colonel," and the line went dead.

I stood, staring in amazement. "What happened?" Jenna asked both eagerly and impatiently.

"It appears he fell for it. I ordered him to maintain radio silence for a presidential broadcast."

Jenna laughed. "That took some gall."

"Was that pun intended?" I asked, laughing.

"What pun?"

"Never mind."

Jenna spun to face Tracker. "Give me some good news, Miss Tracker."

Tracker did not respond at first as her hands darted over the controls. Her gaunt face almost contorted in concentration. Then she stepped back, and the expression became a smile.

"We have control of the satellite system. I have programmed it to only be friendly to the Chesty and us. Anything else will be subject to an attack."

Jenna smirked. "I could kiss you, Gunnery Sergeant."

Tracker grinned. "Hey, I'm not stopping you, Major."

Jenna had already turned back to Stacey. "Take us on to Phobos, Stacey."

"Plotted and set, boss," Stacey responded,

"I have programmed the satellites to block all the base's outgoing transmissions as soon as we move in for the drop," Tracker advised us.

Jenna nodded. "Stacey, ship-wide communications, please." Stacey nodded a confirmation, and Jenna barked her orders. "Okay, Marines, time to get ready to dropship. Gear up in primary cargo hold." She looked back at the pilot. "Stacey, you have command of the Lady Liberty. Once you drop us off, get out of range of any ground defense systems that may still be active. As soon as you have completed what you have to do at Deimos, head back to the Chesty and make sure Morris is ready to come in for pickup."

"Yes, boss."

Jenna slipped out of her chair, and Tracker and I followed her. I was nervous now. Jumping out of a moving starship onto a low-gravity moon wasn't exactly on my bucket list of must-do things. We joined the Marines in the empty cargo bay and pulled on our Environmental Mobility Unit suits before starting to run through safety checks. Jenna checked mine, and then I checked hers before she helped me switch out my D.E. belt for a more advanced combat one. My proximity to her was enough to feel her breath upon my face. I found myself staring into her eyes as she looked down at my belt. When her gaze came up and met mine, there was a questioning curiosity in them, and I realized I was staring. I flushed slightly, but to my surprise, she simply smiled at me.

"Everything is going to be fine, Mr. Phelkar," she said softly so that only I could hear. I returned the smile, and she turned away from me. "Remember, Phobos' gravity is not strong enough to hold you down. Your D.E. belt is all that stands between you and a thirty-minute trip into space and back."

We then turned our attention to our weaponry. Billings, the quartermaster, started handing out rifles. Jenna went through the weapon's multiple functions, and I have to admit most of it went over my head. However, I understood the basics. Point and fire.

"We will be using the new KK Ripper ammunition," Jenna told everyone. "They are designed to penetrate and shred environmental suits. They are only to be used where there is no atmosphere." It was a rather vicious technique. Its purpose was to cause a massive decompression in the environmental suit severe enough to be unable to be emergency patched, causing death from suffocation. "Once we're in the base, switch to regular ammunition." She paused and looked at the Marines, who stood ready. "Ladies and gentlemen, this will be the fight of your life. This mission's successful completion is the start of the rally against the imminent European occupation of our country. Success or failure today could mean all the difference to the future of our nation. It could even mean whether we even survive as a nation. This place is heavily armed, and they will give no quarter, and I expect you to give no quarter in return. We are at total war, ladies and gentlemen. We did not ask for it. We did not want it. But the damn Peons have forced our hand. You're the best-trained, toughest sons and daughters of a bitch in the solar system. I have faith in each of you to do your duty. Let's go to it."

As Stacey brought us down to the surface of Phobos, there was that weird lurching feeling as the dark energy compensators adjusted to the actual gravity of the moon. It was a sign that we were almost ready to jump. I cannot say enough about Stacey Grant's abilities as a pilot. As I have told you several times now, the Lady Liberty wasn't only not designed to land, but it was also not intended to go this close to a celestial object. However, Stacey smoothly brought us down to just thirty feet above the surface. We sealed our helmets, and the back wall of the cargo bay opened. First to leave was the compact all-terrain armored carrier, which held tech staff, including Tracker. It floated down with its D.E. field like a balloon, slowly losing its helium. Jenna stood in the entranceway, and with a wave of her hand, she counted them off as they went out through the exit, saying, "Go, go, go," until only the two of us were left.

"You got this, Mr. Phelkar." Jenna slapped me on the back, and when I hesitated at the edge, she gave me a gentle shove out of the ship.

It was a weird sensation. There was no need for parachutes or the D.E. belt. Phobos' low gravity meant I simply floated down until I finally touched the ground. Sort of. I immediately found myself sinking into the Phobian dust that covered the surface. I started to panic and reached down to my D.E. belt. Switching it to auto, I noticed my body vibrated slightly as it increased my apparent density to equate to one g or earth type. I thus found myself able to stand on the surface.

I looked around, and that feeling when you step onto an alien world came over me. It is something you can only experience and barely describe. Mars dominated the sky overhead with its brown rust appearance. I could see the lights of the cities spread across its surface. Hundreds of colonies by different nations had made Mars a second Earth. Rocky debris surrounded me, and it would be hard going. The lighting was dim, like a sunset in London, and I could not even make out the base we were heading for. Unbeknownst to me, it was actually over the horizon, with the moon being smaller than Rhode Island.

One by one, Marines checked in to confirm their safe landing. I saw Jenna land about a hundred yards for me, and I trotted up to her as she radioed. "One hundred percent safe landings. All troopers have confirmed. Let's tighten it up, boys and girls. On my mark, forward march." We started to head towards the base, with the troopers moving at an angle to bring themselves in closer with their commander. The silence was ominous, with the only sound being my nervous breathing within my helmet. I had to struggle to keep up with the more experienced officer. We made our way across the dust of the moon's surface until the base came into our sights along the horizon.

Tracker came online from the relative safety of the armored transport that followed us. "Okay, you have incoming bogeys. I'm detecting what looks like about two dozen Peons coming out of the base."

Jenna responded. "Affirmative. If our intel is correct, that would be their entire complement of troops. If we can take them down out here, our chances are severely improved. Safeties off, lock and load."

My mouth went dry, and my chest tightened as we continued onward. I eventually saw the light blue E.M.U. of a Peon trooper on the horizon against the starlit dusk. I was trying to make out the details when he suddenly fell. It took me a moment to realize he had been shot by one of our Marines.

What followed was a bizarre silent battle with no sound carried. It began in earnest as more of the enemy appeared and opened fire on us. I had very little peripheral vision inside that helmet, and I couldn't see our people fall, but I watched many Peons go flying back or up.

"Ready concussion grenades," commanded Jenna. I turned to look about and saw the whole front line of our Marines attaching the small explosive devices to the front of their firearms. "Fire!"

The line fired the grenades into the frontline of the Peon infantry, and they exploded without a flame or sound. Peons flew everywhere as if hit by an invisible force. Some were blown directly upwards and did not come back down, having been blown off the rock at escape velocity. Jenna waited for the dust to clear, and as I turned to look at her, I saw a Peon had flanked us and was aiming a weapon directly at Jenna. She had not seen him. Instinctively I grabbed her and put myself between her and the shooter, Jenna's back against my chest. She instinctively made to remove herself but stopped as I suddenly lurched forward against her. I felt a cold numbing pain in my left shoulder as the bullet hit me, and I instantly heard the inescapable sound of air rushing out of my suit.

Chapter Fourteen

The Call to Arms

I released Jenna, and she spun around, firing several rounds at the assailant until he fell. She grabbed my uninjured arm and pulled it downwards.

"Get down on the ground!" she barked at me, but I was panicking. She swiftly kicked my feet from under me and pushed me, face down, into the dust. I automatically tried to get up, but she planted her knee firmly in the center of my back, holding me in place with her whole body weight. I felt her jerk several times and realized it was the recoil of her weapon as she fired it. When it stopped, I felt the vibration of something on my shoulder, and the hissing stopped. Jenna had sealed my suit. Her knee left my back, and she knelt on one knee at my side. I raised my head and saw her take out several more Peon troopers. She pulled me up to my feet. "You wounded?" she asked. The bullet had pierced the E.M.U. but not the body armor beneath it. I shook my head. "Move out," she instructed, inclining her head toward our objective, and I fell in beside her again. I looked at my air gauge. I had lost about ten percent of my remaining air. It could have been a lot worse.

Onward we marched. Most of my shots missed their target at this distance, for I wasn't trained in this type of combat. The firefight grew more intense as the remnants of the two opposing parties closed in on each other. We lost two-thirds of the company that day, but the fighting ended as suddenly as it had started. A cheer came over the commlink, and others joined it. Looking around, I saw our Marines waving their weapons in the air. We appeared to have won the first offensive of this battle. "Don't assume anything, boys and girls," Jenna said, silencing them. "that was just a little too easy." As if in response to her words, far to our left, there was a massive silent explosion. Two Marines flew up into the air, one of whom never came down. "Freeze!" Jenna shouted. "Looks like intel dropped the ball, folks," she said with an irritated sigh. "They have a damn minefield. Tracker, on me."

"Affirmative, Major," Tracker replied as the armored vehicle trundled up. The hood of the terrain vehicle opened, and Tracker climbed out of the roof hatch. She leaned back in, and someone handed her a large device with both hands. She placed it on the roof before sitting cross-legged in front of it.

When Jenna and I approached the armored vehicle, Tracker hastily tapped into the device. "What's the holdup, Sergeant?" Jenna asked.

"High-grade jamming countermeasures, Ma'am. They are trying to block what I'm trying to do." She raised her head and scanned the roof of the dome. She pointed to a large dish almost hidden amongst other equipment on the roof. "Going to need you to take that out, Ma'am."

"Affirmative," Jenna said. She looked around and nodded to a trooper, Abigail Thompson, who I would later get to know quite well. She nodded back and slipped off a long sniper rifle from her shoulder. The trooper flipped open its stand and lay down on the ground before slipping a thin stiletto grenade into the barrel and activating the laser sight. She took careful aim, and moments later, what seemed like a puff of air came out of the muzzle. Almost instantly, a small dish erupted, and all attention turned back to Tracker, who again tapped out on the device she had and gave Jenna a thumbs up. "I'm in, but I cannot disable them," she told the major, "but I do have the option to detonate them."

"Heads up, boys and girls," Jenna barked. "Everybody, fall back." Everyone began to back away. Tracker's armored vehicle reversed with us until she banged on the roof, signaling for it to stop.

"Okay, ten seconds," Tracker instructed.

"Everybody down," Jenna said. Tracker rolled herself swiftly back inside the armored transport as we lay flat on the ground. Again, I heard nothing, but I certainly felt it. First, a large shockwave and then a rain of small rocks and pebbles falling slowly until everything subsided.

"Everyone check their neighbor for suit damage," Jenna commanded, and as I got up, she turned me around to check my back, and I did the same for her. She turned back to face the base. The ground was now pitted with small craters, and the dust in the low gravity seemed to hover and obscure our view. But Jenna simply shouted, "Onward."

As we cleared the dust, we could see the glass windows outside the base and started to make out moving figures of people watching our approach.

It wasn't like there was some grand entranceway to this base. The main entrance was on the other side of the donut shape of the base, where ships could descend within the base itself. The exit we headed for was used simply for an emergency. Jenna had Tracker patch her through on the communication lines of the base.

"This is Major Jenna Plural. We are coming in. We can do this the easy way, or we can do this the hard way. You can open the door for us, or we can simply blow it open. We prefer to minimize both damage and casualties. I give you one minute to respond."

Seconds later, the nervous voice came. "You may not have heard, but the war is over. I advise you to check with your own authorities to confirm this."

"Well, if that's the case," Jenna said, almost cheerfully, "there's no reason not to let us in, and we can all sit down and talk about it." No reply came. "Your minute is nearly up."

"I expect us to be treated following the Galle Convention."

"I promise you will be treated appropriately," Jenna replied.

After another pause, I found myself holding my breath with anticipation. The voice came back, discouraged. "Very well, the door is unsealed."

Jenna nodded at Neuman and then at the door. The Marine nodded in confirmation, then slowly headed up to the entrance. He carefully hit the panel on the door, and, accurate to the Peon commander's word, it slid open. Jenna then pointed to two more troopers and sent them into the base. Now was a moment of concern. The airlock could only fit two at a time. Of course, if the Peons tried anything while the troops were transitioning, Jenna could have blown both doors, and it would suck to be on the other side without an E.M.U. suit. She sent Hardy in next. "Once you have at least twelve on your side of the airlock," she said, "go take control of whatever operations room they have."

We went in last, about twenty minutes later. Jenna removed her helmet, and I did the same. Tracker then joined us, also removing her helmet. Two troopers went forward with their rifles raised, and we joined up with Hardy.

I will never forget the terrified faces of the prisoners as Jenna strode in and took in the scene.

We were in control of the Phobos base.

Tracker immediately sat down at a console and started to decode the communication system, and

I joined her in order to translate. Together, we managed to switch the system languages from French to English. As I left her to continue the deciphering, an elderly man stepped forward to Jenna. "I'm Dr. Vallier.

I'm in charge here." He stated in strongly accented English. "I assure you my people won't resist you, and I ask that you treat them with kindness. They are mostly civilians."

Jenna nodded to him. "Should any of my people encounter anyone carrying arms, we will assume you're resisting, and I won't be held accountable for anyone's safety." She then fixed her eyes upon him and asked more in a statement than a question, "Am I clear?"

"I assure you no one is going to resist."

Jenna turned back to her troops. "Okay, boys and girls, sweep the facility and round up any stragglers. Don't hesitate to use extreme prejudice if you face resistance. There aren't enough of us to take risks." She turned it back to the doctor. "You have a member of your personnel here called Toussaint. Where is he?"

At this, the doctor looked uneasy and said softly, "Your spy was caught about a month back. Unfortunately, he died under interrogation."

I was surprised that this did not appear to faze Jenna. I guessed that she must be used to this sort of thing. She appeared to be about to move on, but Tracker looked over at us. "What about her daughter?"

The doctor frowned. "What concern is that of yours? Bridgette is a European citizen even if her father is a traitor."

Jenna quickly stepped up to him, her face in his. "When one of my officers asks you a question, you will answer it with a Sir or Ma'am."

Looking nervous, the doctor stepped back, "Bridgette Toussaint is here on the base. She is being cared for by a very good European family....Madam."

Jenna looked at me. "Would you find her, please, Mr. Phelkar, and bring her to the Control Center?"

I nodded as the doctor spoke to Jenna. "Forgive my questioning, you, Mademoiselle, but the fate of this child is a personal concern to me, and I will question you taking her at the risk of my own life."

Jenna nodded. "Very admirable of you. As part of her father's agreement to help us, we promised the safe conduct of his daughter to allied space if anything happened to him. We are just following her dad's wishes."

"I see." The doctor sighed. "I hope you understand that I must protest. The rightful place of a French girl is among her people."

Jenna shrugged. "You can protest all you like." She nodded to me again to carry on.

"If you would please, Sir," I asked the doctor in French, "give me the location of this child?" He just stared at me blankly, then looked away. "Sir, you cannot doubt that we will find her in this base. You can either tell me where she is, or I will have the Marines search for her. I'm sure it will reduce her stress to meet with me than to be pulled out by United States Marines."

The doctor sighed and pondered this before replying. "She is in her quarters with orders not to open the door to anybody other than myself." He said in English.

"Then I suggest you give him the override codes for the room and the directions," Jenna said curtly. "I am running out of patience, Doctor Vallier." He glared at her but complied and gave me both the override codes and the directions to the room. I started to head towards the door when Jenna said, "Neuman, Thompson, please go with Mr. Phelkar and keep him safe." The two Marines nodded and complied, falling in with me as I headed out of the room.

I followed the directions until I came to the location stated by the doctor. I tapped in the override codes for the door, and it slid open. I am not sure what I was expecting, but it was certainly someone younger than the young woman who now stood before me looking terrified. Bridgette Toussaint looked fifteen years of age. Slightly taller than Stacey Grant, with platinum blonde hair, and was dressed in a plaid skirt with knee-length shorts and a white button-up blouse with a grey sleeveless cardigan over the top. She gripped her chair in her hands to defend herself but shook nervously. Immediately my companions raised their weapons, but I raised my hand for them to lower them. "It's all right. You're safe." She stared at me blankly, for without thinking, I had spoken in English, so I repeated the statement in French. The fluency of my use of the language seemed to make her relax a little. Yet she still gripped the chair. "You can put that down. No one is going to hurt you, I promise."

"You are American?" she asked uneasily, still holding onto the chair.

"No, I am British, but I'm here with the Americans."

Slowly she lowered the chair and placed it on the floor. Suddenly, she ran over to me and threw herself into my arms, much to my surprise. "Father said you would come for us, but that was so long ago I had given up hope."

I rubbed her back reassuringly, frowning at the smirks of my two companions. "It's okay. You're safe now. We're going to get you out of here."

I led her back out into the corridor, and she took my hand as we walked back to the Control Center. As we entered, Bridgette scanned the room as if looking for someone. "Charlotte Kensett is not here?" she asked.

Jenna recognized the name when I translated it for her. "Kensett is an intelligence agent. She used to work with me until about a year ago. I had no idea she was Toussaint's handler."

I explained to Bridgette that Kensett wasn't here but that Jenna was her friend. Bridgette nodded, but then her gaze fell upon Doctor Vallier. I have never seen such loathing and hatred in a child's face before. She let go of my hand, stepped up to him, and spat straight into his face. "You killed my father."

Vallier flinched and wiped his face with the back of his hand. "Your father was a traitor, child. A fine young French lady like yourself should understand that."

"I hope you die. My only regret will be not killing you myself," she screamed at him, and I grabbed her by the shoulder as she made to throw herself into an attack against him.

"Hey, hey, calm yourself, my dear." I quickly translated for Jenna, who looked half amused and half bewildered.

"Well, that's a first in twenty years," she grinned and, at my questioning look, added, "A Peon I actually like."

Bridgette did not take her glare away from the doctor until Jenna turned to Sergeant Hardy. "I understand there is a gymnasium here. Please escort our prisoners there." Hardy nodded, and he and his troops led them out.

Jenna came up to me. "This is it, Mr. Phelkar. This is make or break time. Either the remaining ships will rally to our cause, or it is game over."

Tracker confirmed she was ready to send the signal throughout the solar system. Even with the powerful Peon transmitter, it would take several hours for the message to reach everybody, with bases and ships being as far out as Pluto and even beyond.

Jenna took a deep breath, then spoke with an intense passion. "This is Major Jenna Plural of the U.S.S. Lewis Puller, calling out to all free allied forces throughout the solar system. We have chosen not to recognize the treasonous Pacific Alliance leaders who signed their surrender to the European Union and their functionaries. We call on our allies to rally to our cause and fight European imperialism's oppression. We will rendezvous at coordinates that will be encrypted and transmitted after this message. The time has come to decide: Live under European

Union oppression or be free once again. Please acknowledge this communication. Plural out."

Tracker switched off the communication, and Jenna stepped back and looked at me. "Well, at least this stage is a success."

I nodded hopefully. "It's just a case of wait and see what happens."

"Major," Tracker said, "we have a priority one message coming in from the U.S.S. Los Angeles. It's Captain Addison. She is asking to speak with you." She smiled at Jenna, and Jenna smiled back.

"You know this captain?" I asked.

"Indeed, I do. She was the first officer of the Lewis Puller before she was promoted just a few months back." She turned back to Tracker. "Put her through, Sergeant."

The voice of an older woman came over the speakers. "What the fuck are you playing at, Jenna?"

Jenna grinned widely at the informality of the question. "Good to hear your voice again, Claire," she replied rather jovially.

In response, the captain harrumphed. "Are we on a secure line?"

Tracker nodded to Jenna, who replied. "Secure line is confirmed. No one can hear us."

"Let's sort out one thing first," Addison said. "Since when did you become a major?"

"I assumed the rank to take command of the Lewis Puller upon the death and incapacity of the senior officers."

"So, it has not been officially assigned to you?" Addison said, sounding amused.

"In light of the fact there is no longer an effective United States government, nothing is really official anymore."

"Good point, especially as it is illegal for a GenMod to hold that rank." Addison laughed.

"You know well, Claire, that my rank was once much higher, and I'm more than qualified to hold command."

"Of that, I have no doubt. I have no hesitation in saying you're the finest officer I have served, both over and under. But let's get to the point. I understand your sentiment, but I do question your ability to achieve that goal."

Jenna tensed somewhat at these words. "I can assure you, as you should know, having served under me, that I'm more than capable of commanding a fleet."

"You misunderstand me, Jen. I'm not questioning your ability, merely the insurmountable odds we will face trying to achieve a victory. You know full well we were already losing the war. Now you're talking about uniting the remaining fleet without government support."

"I completely understand, but you have to look at it from the perspective of what the alternative is. If you don't want to retire to your home in New York and drink chardonnay under a blue and yellow flag instead of red, white, and blue, then join me and meet us at the rendezvous."

There was a long, tense pause. "I can see your point," Addison said, but before she continued, there was another long pause. "Very well, Major Plural. I'm aware that you're probably one of the few who could pull off such an audacious plan. I won't only meet you at that rendezvous, but I will recognize your authority in this matter."

Jenna smiled once more. "That is most appreciated, Claire. I promise you that whatever may come, those European bastards will have a fight on their hands. Have you received the coordinates?"

"Coordinates have been transmitted," Tracker advised.

"Coordinates received, Major Plural," Addison responded. "I look forward to seeing and serving with you again. Addison out."

"I have numerous other ships trying to contact you, Major," Tracker advised.

"There must be over a thousand ships out there. I can't respond to each and every one of them. Send out a standard message to anyone who tries to contact us telling them we cannot respond and to meet us at the coordinates you have transmitted."

"Aye, Ma'am"

"That was certainly most interesting," I said as Jenna stepped away from the console. "You have quite a history with this captain?"

"Addison served her first tour of duty with me in some of the bloodiest campaigns in this war's history." Jenna leaned back against a console and looked nostalgic and reflective. "We later reunited when she achieved the rank of commander and became the first officer on board the Chesty." She sighed, then looked up at me. "I think it's time we got off this rock, don't you, Mr. Phelkar?"

"Sounds like a plan to me, Major." I smiled.

She turned back to Tracker. "Put a call into Morris and tell her to come in for a pickup." "Aye, Major."

I returned my attention to Bridgette. She was standing to one side, looking around, confused. She had no comprehension of what was going on, and I explained to her briefly that we were working on getting us away from Phobos. We went into the base commander's office, and Jenna walked over to his drink dispenser.

"Coffee, hot, black." Nothing happened. Jenna glanced back at me.

I stepped up beside her. "Café, chaud, noir." A cup dropped down, and the drink poured out.

She took the cup, muttering, "Dirty, vulgar language," and sipped her drink as I repeated the order for myself. "Peterson, our demo guy, didn't make it inside. So, we need to get someone else to set up the explosives," she said as she slipped into a seat at the table.

"Wait, what?" I looked at her, confused, as I sat opposite her. "What about the prisoners?"

Jenna looked at me with wide eyes. "We are here to blow this base. That was the plan all along, and you knew that?"

"Whilst it makes sense now, I must be honest and say I did not think of it. I can't say I'm happy with it."

Jenna raised an eyebrow at me. "Then it is good that military strategy is not based on how happy you are with something." She looked over at Bridgette, who just stood there with her hands clasped together, looking at each of us in turn as we spoke. "How are your parenting skills, Mr. Phelkar?"

"You're going to make me responsible for the child?" I said with surprise.

Jenna looked at me with a smile and shrugged. "You are the only senior personnel who can speak French."

I sighed but remained smiling so as not to cause the young girl concern. Before I could respond, Tracker came on the line. "Major, I think we have a problem. You better come out here."

We hurried out into the Control Center. Tracker was looking towards us with her face ashen white. "Lieutenant Grant reports that the Chesty refuses to come to pick us up."

Chapter Fifteen

Stranded

J enna glared at me. Turning back to Tracker, she growled. "Get Morris on the line now."

"Already done."

"Lieutenant Morris, this is Major Plural. What is going on?" Jenna struggled to remain calm.

Morris' voice came online. It was cold and determined, yet nervous. "You're not a major, Lieutenant Plural. Whether you agree with it or not, the president gave a lawful command. I'm not going to be party to you bringing more suffering to the American people. We are setting a course for Earth where we will turn this ship over to the authorities and go home to our families."

"You said you would support me!"

Morris scoffed. "It was that or get a bullet in the head like the captain."

Jenna slammed a fist on the console. "You're just going to abandon us here?"

"The Europeans will be there eventually to take you into custody. You will be safe."

"Morris, you better start praying to whatever fucked-up god watches over you because when I get out of here, I will be coming for you, and I *promise* I will be the last thing you ever see!"

"Go to hell, Lieutenant Plural," Morris replied softly.

"She's cut the line, Ma'am," Tracker nervously advised the major.

Jenna threw her hands up in disbelief. "She has left us damn well stranded here."

"Is there no way that Stacey can land?" I asked.

"None at all. The ship's undercarriage is not designed for it," Jenna said, then turned to Tracker. "Is Stacey still online?" Tracker nodded. "Stacey, can you return to a Phobos orbit and still keep track of the Chesty?"

"That's an affirmative, boss," Stacey replied. "Mission accomplished on Deimos. Oxygen tanks full and plenty in reserve."

"Good work, Stacey. Let me know when you get here. We will try to work something out from down here. Plural out." She slammed her fist on the console once again and stepped back. "I knew we shouldn't have trusted that whore."

"It's my fault. I suggested she stay in command," I said weakly.

She spun upon me, glaring up into my face. "I know it's your fault, Mr. Phelkar, but it's not your place to judge yourself; it's mine. So, shut the fuck up until I ask your opinion."

I was pretty taken aback by the sudden rebuke. I almost thought Jenna was about to hit me, but instead, she turned away and called to one of the troopers.

"Go take an inventory of all the supplies they have here. Ensure we have enough food and water to last an extended stay."

"We probably only have a few hours until the Peons arrive," I said.

Tracker looked at me. "Did you forget I reprogrammed the satellite system? Their own defensive system will shoot them down."

It was as if my stupidity was the final straw, and before I could respond to Tracker, Jenna said, "I suggest you stay out of my way for now, Mr. Phelkar." She growled under her breath, not looking back at me.

Humiliated, I walked out of the Control Center, hearing her bark further preparation orders for our extended stay in the Peon base. I felt pretty annoyed at myself. I didn't know why her opinion of me bothered me so much. It wasn't that long ago that I hated being in the same room with her. However, we had been through much together in a very short time. I realized that my feelings were very one-sided. I walked around the base with my hands sunk deep into my pockets, cursing myself for suggesting Morris.

I went to a small cantina where I raided a bottle of whiskey from the Peon stores. I did not intend to get drunk. Just swig a few shots to take the edge off. As I turned back from the drinks cabinet, I saw Bridgette standing there. I had completely forgotten about her. "Hey, sweetie," I said to her in French. "Do you want something to drink?"

She stepped further into the room and came up to me. Looking at the bottle in my hand, she pointed to it. "Some of that would be good."

I grinned at her. "Yeah, that's not going to happen." And for the first time, I saw her smile.

She sat down at the table with me as she shrugged. "Meh, it was worth a try. I don't want anything but thank you."

I opened the bottle and poured myself a glass. "So, how did you end up on Phobos?"

"My mother was Chloe Toussaint. Have you heard of her?" I shook my head. "Well, she was a rising politician in the National Assembly. However, she started a movement dedicated to bringing an armistice between the European Union and the Pacific Alliance. When it started growing in popularity, she was arrested for treason." Bridgette stopped talking for a moment, swallowing hard as she tried to hold back her emotions. "She never came home. It changed my father and me." She looked up at me, "My country betrayed my family. My father started working for the Americans against the government. I don't know if it was just revenge or if he had meaning to it. However, my country killed my father, and my country killed my mother. I hate them."

"I understand," I said reassuringly. "We will take care of you now and do what we can to honor the sacrifice of your parents."

She stared at me for a long moment before speaking. "Will I be able to kill Peons?"

The question took me by surprise. "I'm sure you'll be able to join the military when you are old enough."

She snorted divisively. "I am not sure if I can wait that long." But before I could respond, she added, "I'm tired. Do you mind if I return to my room and get some sleep?"

"Of course." I made to get up, but she raised her hand to me.

"I know the way." She stood up and headed for the door, and I was about to let her go alone, but I put in a call to Abigail Thompson to check that she made it safely there and establish a presence outside her door. I was concerned for her safety, but something in the back of my mind made me worry she might get up to something in retaliation to those she saw as her captors.

I sat alone in that large room where the base personnel would have sat and had their meals, talking about their homes and families only days before. Maybe even celebrated birthday parties. I took a couple more shots, and my head began to buzz. I concluded that sitting here only increased my negativity, so I headed back to the Control Center.

I was surprised to see most of the Marines were no longer there. Jenna had sent most of them to find quarters for the night. Jenna, Tracker, and Malcolm-bloody-Hardy, that testosterone-filled grunt were the only people there were.

"I can't believe they don't have any form of escape from this moon," Jenna was saying.

"It is less than a two-hour trip down to Mars and back," Tracker replied. "There wasn't any necessity since the base could be easily evacuated."

"Ma'am, if I may be so bold?" came Hardy's deep, nasally voice.

"Speak freely, Sergeant." Jenna nodded to him.

"I don't know Lieutenant Grant well, but I know her reputation. Is there surely no way she could find a way to land?"

I snorted derisively. "Stacey could be the greatest pilot in the galaxy, but you can't change that the Lady Liberty has no landable undercarriage, D.E. launch compensators, or launch thrusters," I said it so sarcastically that even Jenna raised an eyebrow at me.

Hardy was unfazed. He looked down at me both literally and metaphorically. "Well, let's hear your plan then, *Mister* Phelkar." He emphasized the word 'mister' as if it were a derogatory title. I hoped that Jenna would have stepped in, but everyone just stood there staring at me.

"I don't have one, Sergeant Hardy," I said quite aggressively.

"Hardy does have a point," Jenna said and smiled at him. My stomach tightened in a knot. "The solution does have to be around the Lady Liberty."

"I don't see how." The aggression was still in my voice, but while it was aimed at Hardy, it came across as if I was dressing down Jenna. "Whether a mile away or a thousand light-years away, there is nothing that ship can do for us."

Jenna scowled at me. "Watch your tone Mr. Phelkar. I don't appreciate it."

I felt flustered and unsure of how to respond. "I'm sorry," I said simply.

"I'm sure that, as a civilian, Mr. Phelkar is simply unable to handle the stress of the situation." Malcolm Hardy said as if in my defense, but he was clearly patronizing me.

Jenna looked at me, sizing me up under the weight of his words. I so want to slap Hardy. "Are you intoxicated, Mr. Phelkar?"

"I had a drink or two, but I'd hardly call myself intoxicated," I replied defensively.

"Your words are slightly slurred, and you're swaying some-what. You should go and lie down," she
   said coldly.

"I'm perfectly fine, Major," I replied a little too defensively.

"It wasn't a suggestion, Mr. Phelkar. Go find a cabin and sleep it off or find an Alcorin pill." She said, referring to the drug that negated the intoxicating effects of alcohol.

I went to protest, but instead, I gave up. "As you wish, Major," I said, now defeated.

"And, Mr. Phelkar, refrain from imbibing for as long as we are on this base."

"Yes, Major."

I turned to go, and as I reached the door, I heard Hardy say, "I don't know what they were thinking, forcing you to bring a civilian on this mission. He is a liability."

If that wasn't bad enough, she replied in a most disappointed voice. "Yes, I realize that now." Then, as if I had never existed, she asked Tracker to give her a situation report.

I headed down the corridor but suddenly found myself flying across the hallway with the sound of an explosion. I landed in a heap of rubble with twisted metal, glass, and other debris falling all around me. But darkness enveloped me as I slipped from consciousness.

The first thing I became aware of was the racking pain throughout my body. I gasped and tried to get up, but a pair of hands on my chest gently restrained me. "Stay still, you idiot." It was her voice, but it was soft and gentle rather than scolding like before. I looked up at Jenna standing beside the bed, looking down at me. On the other side was a Marine paramedic.

"What happened to me?" was what I intended to say, but instead, all I could get out of my mouth was, "What? What?"

"It appears we didn't get everyone. Someone was still in the base. You happen to walk by the life support just when he took out the oxygen recyclers. He either got caught in his own blast, or it was a suicide plan. Either way, he is dead."

"You're lucky to be alive," the paramedic said. "Piece of shrapnel just missed your heart, but don't worry. I've removed it and patched you up. I have shot you up with rejuv. You should be good to go in an hour or two but get a checkup with Doctor Archer when we get back to the Chesty."

"The bad news is no more recycled air," Jenna informed me as I realized she was holding my hand. "Tracker is working out how long it will be before the lack of air affects us."

"There's no chance of repairing it?" I asked.

Jenna shook her head. "None at all. Tracker said it is a total write-off."

"But why would they do it? They are killing their own people."

"We have shut down their entire communication system throughout the solar system. Ships are out there running blind. They have lost contact with their supply runs and their forces. I assume whoever did this saw this as a greater priority."

"Killing off forty or so civilians to save a communication station is a bit harsh to me."

Jenna shrugged. "Get some rest. Meet me in my office when the medic lets you out of here."

I got about two hours of sleep while Jenna continued to try to resolve our predicament. My body felt like I'd had a marathon. Still, it was amazing, considering I had been in an explosion. Even in the last fifty years, the advances in medical technology have been phenomenal. It is impressive what advances humankind can achieve when trying to annihilate each other.

Hardy turned out to be my next visitor. "Move out to the Control Center, Phelkar," he ordered.

"Why? What is going on?"

"Gunnery Sergeant Tracker is sealing off these rooms. Everyone has to be in the Control Center now."

"So, this is it. We've come to an end?"

Hardy snorted. "Are you going to cry, Phelkar?"

"Fuck you, Hardy."

Hardy grinned, but it was almost a sneer. "So the little Englishman has some balls. We have about six hours of air left. Tracker reckons if we seal ourselves in the Control Center, she could extend it to twelve."

"Not much point is there, Sergeant?"

"Well, I did suggest that we could extend it even further by eliminating nonessential personnel."

He was obviously referring to me. Most childishly, I replied, "That will be quite a noble sacrifice on your part."

"Just get moving, Phelkar. I've wasted enough of my time on you already."

When I returned to the Control Center, Jenna and Sakamoto were standing just behind Tracker and looking over her shoulder.

"We are royally screwed," Sakamoto was saying. "Whoever did this knew exactly where to plant that bomb in life support."

"Is there nothing you can do to repair it?" Jenna asked.

"There is nothing to repair. The room is nothing more than scrap metal now."

The major sighed, and she stepped back; her shoulders slumped, and it was Sakamoto who voiced what we were all thinking. "How long do we have?"

"Well, with the twenty-three of us and forty or so prisoners." Tracker did some swift mental arithmetic. "We have about two days until the air runs out. However, with the nitrogen buildup, we will be incapacitated long before that."

The major gave a stern look toward Sakamoto, then back at Tracker. "What if there were only the twenty-three of us?"

Tracker looked puzzled by the question, but she immediately responded. "Five or six days." Sakamoto and Jenna exchanged glances, and Tracker's eyes widened in realization. "You can't possibly be thinking..."

"Not if you find me an alternative, Sergeant," Jenna said coldly. She turned away and headed towards the office door. "Sakamoto, Mr. Phelkar, with me."

We followed her into the office, and Jenna closed the door behind us. As Sakamoto and I just stood there, she sank back into the chair behind the desk. A silence hung in the air for what seemed like an eternity. My mind was racing with the implications of that last question they had asked Tracker.

"Suggestions?" Jenna asked curtly.

"We bring down the Liberty," I said sharply. Even though I knew that was impossible, I did not want to countenance the idea that was on all our minds.

"No point. It cannot land," Sakamoto said.

"But the Chesty can. Any chance they can take it back in time?" I knew I was grasping at straws.

"Stacey is the best damn pilot I have ever known, but she is no Marine," said Jenna. "Anyway, she has a skeleton crew, and

Morris has access to all the troops in the M.E.T. who chose not to side with us."

"I see no other options," I said, hearing the shaking in my voice.

"You know that is untrue, Mr. Phelkar," said Jenna grimly. "As loathsome as the idea is, it needs to be discussed."

"Such an act would be a war crime," I said, my voice barely audible.

Jenna sat back and stared at me for a moment and then studied Sakamoto, whose face remained impassive. Looking back at me, she said, "These people were dead whatever happens, Mr. Phelkar. We cannot take them with us as prisoners, and we cannot leave this base intact so they could repair their communication systems."

"You accepted their surrender, Major," I said. "The rules of the Galle Convention do still apply."

Jenna looked at me exasperated and threw her hands in the air. "We are now a resistance force and standard rules no longer apply."

"They have brought this on themselves," Sakamoto said curtly. "They blew up their life support,
indicating a willingness to sacrifice their own lives to stop us having control of this base."

"We don't know who did it. Many of them could well be innocent bystanders, considered to be collateral damage by their government."

"I agree, Mr. Phelkar," said Jenna, "but we aren't responsible for European collateral damage brought on by themselves. The Peons have already killed themselves. I'm just saving the Americans."

"They will all be dead soon anyway," Sakamoto advised.

"That is not the same as executing them," I said with a raised voice.

"It is exactly the same," Jenna insisted. "Dead is dead. However, we have the chance to save the lives of our people. It is not a pleasant task, and if I had any alternative, I would take it."

"But..."

Jenna did not let me continue. "I have stopped giving a little whistle, Mr. Phelkar. I have heard your counsel." I did not know how to respond. I just stared, dumbstruck at the idea. Jenna fixed her gaze upon me. "I understand how you feel. But I need to know that you have my back. I cannot have anyone on my side who is not hundred percent with me."

I let out a long sigh, then steeled myself. "Major, as your adjutant, I believe it's beholden to me to disagree with you when necessary, and I only hope one day you will stop asking me about where my loyalty lies."

Jenna looked at me long and hard, and I had no idea what she was thinking. Eventually, she looked at Sakamoto. "Come on, let's go do this."

Chapter Sixteen

The Stacey Grant Solution

My decision to be present was, in some twisted way, the right thing to do. I had been part of the decision-making process, and even though I had disagreed with the decision, I was still responsible for it. We approached the gymnasium door. Jenna entered first, followed by Sakamoto and Hardy, then me, with the six firing squad members bringing up the rear. The people, speaking in French, fell silent as all eyes turned to us. I tried desperately not to make eye contact with anybody so as not to make this harder on myself, but I failed. My eyes matched with a scared-looking tech. She could have been no more than twenty years of age and reminded me of my daughter. Her eyes were filled with fear as they met mine, and I looked away as nausea began to well up within my stomach. Sakamoto ordered those seated upon the floor to get up, and they complied.

As the single line of Marines marched in, lining up in front of them, murmurings began again. I looked at Jenna and could read nothing in her stoic face as she stood legs astride with her hands behind her back, surveying the room. People began to back away as they realized what was happening. The murmurings turned to gasps, and I heard some people cry out in French along the lines of, "No, don't do this. Please, we beg you. "

"Squad ready," Sakamoto ordered, and in unison, the Marines brought up their rifles. People started to panic and ran to the other side of the room. She sped up her commands, "Take aim." People were crying now; some were falling to their knees. I fought back the desire to vomit. I wanted to walk out of there. I wanted to run away and pretend this wasn't happening. But in some crazy, fucked up way, I thought I was doing the honorable thing by staying.

Just as Sakamoto was about to give the final command, the room's intercom burst into life. Tracker shouted urgently, "Major! Grant thinks she has a solution."

Jenna raised a hand to stop Sakamoto. "Speak fast, Helen." When Tracker didn't respond right away, Jenna added, "If you have an idea, now is the time to tell me."

"Look, it would probably be easier if I put Grant on," Tracker replied.

A stricken silence now filled the room as dozens of fearful eyes stared back at Jenna and her soldiers. After the desperate cries from a few moments earlier, it was an eerie change and made the seconds of waiting all the more torturous.

Finally, the young Australian came online. "You ain't gonna like it."

"Spit it out, Stacey," Jenna snapped.

"I do a flyby. I come in on a low-level skim. You turn off your D.E. belts and jump into the ship."

"But that is insane," I said in disbelief.

"Shut up, Phelkar," snapped Hardy.

"But..."

"You heard the man, Mr. Phelkar. Shut up," Jenna said without even looking at me. "Stacey, you cannot possibly come in slow enough and low enough for us to jump."

"Last night, I was working out some calculations with the tech Helen gave me. Although she agrees with you, I think I can trim off enough speed to achieve this. There is hardly any gravity on that moon. If you jump, you're gonna go up and up. If we time it perfectly, I can pretty much scoop you up in the docking hold."

"Tracker," Jenna called, "is anything she is saying in any way feasible."

"While it is not impossible, it is highly improbable that she would catch even one person," Tracker replied.

"With all due respect, Sergeant," Stacey said curtly. "I'm the best fucking pilot in the solar system, or at least that is what everyone tells me. You know how I have pulled your fat out of the fire many times. I know I can do it, mate."

"It would be insane to try," I said, bewildered by this suggestion. "We would be splattered into the ship or lost in space. It's too risky."

Hardy sneered at me. "I understand your fear, but none of us can wetnurse you. If you don't think you can do it, I suggest you stay here for pickup by the Peons." To make that patronizing comment a million times worse, Jenna chuckled, and the Marine grinned at her.

"I said it was risky, not that I wouldn't do it," I replied, but my confidence wasn't as big as my words.

"It is risky," Jenna said. "But it may be necessary."

"For fuck's sake, boss," argued Stacey. "How often have you seen me do what everyone calls impossible with a spaceship? Think of it this way; what's the alternative?"

Jenna managed to smile. "You make a good point. If you pull this off, I'll up your coffee ration."

Stacey laughed. "I will hold you to that, boss."

Jenna looked at Sakamoto and nodded towards the door. Sakamoto ordered the men to leave the room and followed them out, leaving just Jenna, Hardy, and myself standing there with the group of prisoners. They looked decidedly relieved, even as some still shed tears and others tried to calm their colleagues.

Their leader came up to us. "What is going on, Mademoiselle? Is this some sort of game?"

"You know we have to blow this base, don't you?" she said, not answering him.

"My people have been celebrating the end of the war and that they had survived it, and now we have encountered you," he said softly, though his voice wavered. "Is there no way around this?"

"I don't think so. The destruction of this base will put the E.U. into chaos, giving us a fighting chance. The freedom of my people is my only concern."

"Have you no soul?"

Jenna stared at him for a long moment. It was an unfortunate choice of words. Many people in religious communities often debated if GenMods had souls. "I'm afraid I've had to put my soul on hold ever since I heard the words 'we surrender' from our president."

She turned and headed towards the door, and I followed close behind her, but as she reached it, she turned back and looked at Doctor Vallier. "Are there any other children on this base?" When Vallier shook his head, she gave him a single nod and stepped out of the room.

Returning to the Control Center, she summoned everyone together. There was now hope in their eyes.

"Okay, boys and girls. Stacey has a plan. Those who have been with me a while know that that bitch has wings. She has pulled our butts off the hot plate more times than I can count. She is the best, and I trust her with my life and yours. Yes, it's a long shot, but if we stay here, we're dead anyway. And damn it to hell, we are not going to die while our country needs us. Get your extravehicular mobility suits on double time. Prepare to move out." She turned to Malcolm Hardy. "Are all the explosives in place?"

"As per your order, Major."

"Good work. Set them to detonate in one hour."

"Yes, Ma'am"

She then turned and looked around the room and saw Abigail Thompson. "How do you feel about taking a passenger with you?" At first, I thought she was talking about me. "I don't think our young Bridgette is going to manage this on her own. You are one of the highest-rated with an E.M.U. suit, and I would like you to take her with you."

Thompson nodded. "Yes, Ma'am."

Then Jenna looked at me. "What are you standing there for, Mr. Phelkar? Want me to dress you? Suit up."

A chuckle went up around the room from all except Hardy, who shook his head at me in patronizing disgust. I said nothing and complied with the order, picking up my mobility suit, which I now saw had been stacked with the others in the corner of the room. I quickly changed.

"Okay, boys and girls, this will be a tricky evacuation. Timing is everything; we're going to do it by the numbers. Give me a count."

Each Marine counted off. "When you hear your number, you're to deactivate your D.E. belt and take the jump of your life into the Lady Liberty's cargo bay. It will be about twenty to thirty feet above you. Timing is everything, as the Lady Liberty cannot hover. Stacey will have to fly by repeatedly. Miss your cue, and there will be nothing we can do about it. We can't wait for you to come back down. Does everyone understand me?"

The Marines all banged the butts of their rifles on the ground. I headed down to Bridgette's room with Thompson and explained what would happen. To my surprise, she did not look too concerned as we took her back to the Control Center, and Thompson sorted her out with one of the Peon E.M.U. suits they had in storage. Together we helped her put it on and checked its safety features.

"Okay, everyone," Jenna commanded. "Let's do this. Let's get out of here."

Back out on Phobos's surface, my heart began to pound. I did not have the Marines' training, and I was terrified that I would miss my cue. It was eerie to watch the Lady Liberty silently come down towards us. "Okay, I'm coming in for the first run." Stacey swept towards us faster than I ever imagined.

Jenna slapped two Marines on the back. Looking up, she waited before shouting, "One, two, G.O.!" The first two Marines shot off into the air, and I breathed a sigh of relief as I saw them disappear into the open cargo hold. It was going well until we were down to about ten people. Jenna had started to look hopeful and had clearly not expected the rate of success we were having. Then all our hearts fell as one of the Marines momentarily hesitated. He smashed into the ship's undercarriage as he went up, and bits of him floated down in separate parts. There was a moment of silence as we all stared, stunned. Not for the first time, I wanted to throw up, and fear was pounding in my chest as my mouth dried, and an intense desire to pee overcame me. Eventually, it was just Hardy and Thompson with Bridgette, Jenna, and me left.

Hardy looked at Jenna. "Do you need any assistance, Major?"

Her response made me smile widely. "What? Do you think I'm some rookie?"

He hesitatingly apologized, and as Stacey came around again, he disappeared into the sky and into the docking bay, much to my disappointment.

I nervously looked at Thompson, but she looked quite confident behind her visor as she strapped Bridgette to her suit. As Stacey came in for another run, the two flew into the air, and I watched for an eternity until I saw them safely enter the cargo hold. Now there was just Jenna, and myself left.

We waited for Stacey to come around again. I jumped on Jenna's order but had hesitated for just a second. Jenna grabbed me from behind, and I hung there like a toy balloon in the air as the Lady Liberty overshot us.

"Idiot. You would have missed," she snapped, and once more, I found myself apologizing, embarrassed by my mistake. She pulled me back down, and I went to switch the gravity belt back on, but she told me, "No." She placed an arm around my waist, pulled me against her hip, and told me to stay still. She looked up at the ship again as Stacey brought it in for a final run, and then Jenna jumped, taking me up with her.

The added mass made it tricky, and we did not land straight into the cargo bay. We almost missed, but she managed to grab hold of the strut that held the bay door. We were hanging from it like a flag flapping in the wind as Stacey started to pull up.

"Hold on to me, Mr. Phelkar!" Jenna cried in pain as the muscles in her arm strained. I wrapped my arms about her and clung on for dear life as she let go of me and tried to grab the strut with her other hand. She screamed out in frustration as the ship slipped out of Phobos' orbit. With a greatly strained effort, she finally grabbed hold. She swung us into the cargo hold. She hit her D.E. belt, bringing us down on the deck. I landed sprawled on the deck of the cargo bay while Jenna descended neatly upon her feet. As I got up, Jenna sighed, looking at me and shaking her head, clearly embarrassed by my lack of competence. Then she turned to her troops. "Okay, boys and girls, well done. Go get yourself a last meal before you get ready for upload." They filed out as Jenna turned to me. "That was abysmal form down there."

"I'm sorry," I replied a little sheepishly.

"I cannot be continually looking over my shoulder and checking on you. You need to get it together."

"I will endeavor to do better, Ma'am."

"See that you do, Mr. Phelkar, see that you do, and stop calling me Mom." With that, she strode out, leaving me to my thoughts.

My priority was to settle Bridgette. Having moved my quarters to the first officer's room next to Jenna's so that I could be on call at a moment's notice, I gave her the room next to mine, which was another executive suite. She looked surprised to get such exclusive accommodation, but I was not about to move her anywhere that was far from me.

"I did not pack anything or bring anything with me," she said, facing me. "The only clothes I have are what I am wearing."

It was more of a question than a statement, and I did not have a straightforward answer." I will see if there is any way I can find you some clothing, but we will have to make do."

She did not look particularly happy with this answer, and I assessed that she was used to getting what she wanted. However, she moved on. "Where am I to go? What is to happen to me?"

Good questions, neither of which I had answers to. "For now, you will stay with us, and after we make our rendezvous with the fleet, we'll have to reassess the situation."

"Maybe it would have been better if you had just left me on that base to blow up with everyone else," she said with a little aggression in her voice.

"Bridgette, I don't know what will happen, but I promise you this. I will make sure everything is all right for you." I did not allow her to respond, moving on quickly. "I will leave you to settle yourself, and we'll check back on you later." She did not respond but simply shrugged at me as I turned and left.

I showered and headed up to the cockpit where Stacey had already laid in a course after the U.S.S. Chesty and Stephanie Morris. "Do we have time for this?" I asked Jenna, who sat quietly in the captain's chair.

"We will make time for this, Mr. Phelkar," Jenna stated firmly. "That's my ship that she's taken." "Our E.T.A. with the

Chesty is twenty-two hours and twelve minutes," Stacey informed us.

"That's enough time for you to be practicing proper use of a D.E. belt down in the hold, Mr. Phelkar," Jenna said, her voice as cold as on the day we met. Not once did she look up to meet my eyes.

It was a dismissal, and I simply said, "Yes, Major," and stepped out of the corridor. I couldn't help but wonder how long she would hold on to my failure. I prayed that I had not lost her faith in me. I did not, however, go to the damn hold and practice with a damn D.E. belt. Instead, I went to the mess and found the liquor cabinet unlocked. I took a half-full bottle of whisky back to my room. I spent the night drunk and the next day in bed. I woke in the late evening, having slept it off.

As I headed back towards the cockpit, I happened to run into Abigail Thompson. "I hope you don't mind, Sir, but I took it upon myself to arrange meals for Bridgette. I have managed to find a couple of our personnel with similar sizes to the young lady. Once we're back on the Chesty, they can provide some options for her." Although the young sniper maintained both a polite tone and manner, I could see the judgmental look in her eyes.

"Thank you, Corporal," I said, embarrassed that I had not seen to these matters and instead had chosen to wallow in some self-pity.

"My pleasure." She nodded and continued heading down the corridor in the opposite direction to me.

"Thompson," I called after her, and she stopped and half-turned back to me. "I really do appreciate it. I am sure my own daughter can attest that I do not make a very good father." Thompson nodded and smiled ruefully and then continued to head away from me.

I once more joined Jenna in the cockpit. "How goes it?" I asked, standing at her side.

She kept her gaze fixed ahead. "Just over an hour to go." She sounded tired as if she had been sitting there for the whole twenty hours since I last saw her.

"Major," Stacey said intensely. "The Chesty has just begun transmitting a distress call. She's reporting us as an enemy combatant attacking her vessel."

"I won't shoot that little whore; I will hang her slowly," Jenna said venomously in barely a whisper.

Chapter
Seventeen

Jenna's
Justice

The Lady Liberty slipped into the side of the U.S.S . Chesty. Jenna left her seat to go down and join the Marines for the assault, but I stepped in front of her before she could leave. I was nervous about standing up to her, but I had nothing to lose in our current situation. "This isn't your job anymore," I said. "What do you mean?" She did not wait for an answer and made to push past me, but I stood firm. I heard Stacey gasp as she saw me grab Jenna by the upper arms. "You're in command now, maybe not of just a ship, but of the entire resistance to the European occupation. We can't risk losing you. Who will lead these people if some stray bullet takes you out?"

Jenna looked like she was about to deck me, but I did not back down. Her expression then faltered, and she looked down and sighed. "I guess you have a point. Fine, I'll stay here."

I let go of her, and she turned back to Stacey, who was bringing us closer to the Lewis Puller. "Here we go," Stacey called out as she overtook the ship and then swung us into its side. The ship juddered, and there was a grinding of metal which didn't stop until Stacey managed to match the same speed as the Chesty. There was a tense moment as the Chesty tried evasive maneuvers, which Stacey had to match to keep the two ships together. Her former copilot was no match for her, and there was another sound of grinding metal before Stacey fired the grapples into the Chesty.

"The Lady Liberty and the Chesty are attached," she cried out. She cut the engines, and the larger mass of the Lady Liberty began to slow the Chesty. "Come on, Batty," Stacey said to herself, "you know you have to cut your engines, or you'll burn them out."

He did not do it, though, and there was a tense moment until Stacey hit the commlink and called over to the pilot of the Chesty.

"Cut your engines, mate. Are you some sort of rookie? You're going to burn up. Now don't be stupid."

Surprisingly, a cheerful voice responded. "Good to hear your voice again, Stacey. Morris just left the bridge and can't hear me. Tell me now if there is anything I can do to assist you."

Jenna looked at me, her eyes wide with surprise, and then she grinned and turned back to the commlink. "You're the voice of an angel, Batty. Can you shut yourself off in the cockpit?"

"Aye, Major." There was a pause before he responded. "I'm sealed in the cockpit. Morris is going to be so pissed."

Jenna chuckled at the copilot. "I just bet she is. Don't worry, Batty, you're not going to have to put up with her for much longer. Can you tell me how many of the resident crew remain loyal?"

"Most of them. Hell, it's not exactly inspiring to be given the orders that we ought to go back to Earth and surrender to the Peons."

Jenna laughed but then became serious. "So, what resistance should we expect?"

"Well, everyone will obey their orders whether they like them or not. There is no one to rescind them."

I stepped up. "Can you patch us through the ship-wide comms?"

"Sure can," Batty responded.

Jenna looked up at me. "What are you thinking?"

I smiled and shrugged. "Try ordering the crew to stand down. It can't hurt the situation."

Jenna nodded. "This is Major Jenna Plural of the Lady Liberty and your commanding officer. We already have control of the Chesty, and I'm ordering you to stand down. This is your chance to be patriots, ladies and gentlemen. Stand down and place Stephanie Morris under arrest."

We seemed to wait an eternity before a young stammering voice finally came on. "This is Private Emma Dodgson. I have Commander Morris in custody."

We couldn't help laughing and sharing a round of high-fives. We had taken back the Chesty without a shot fired. "I think I love you, Private Dodgson," Jenna said unprofessionally, giving Stacey and me a good chuckle.

"Um, I guess that's appreciated, Ma'am," Dodgson replied with a nervous laugh.

"Clear the portside. We are coming aboard."

"Aye, Ma'am."

We could have detached and created a formula umbilical, but a sense of self-preservation made us wary of a potential trap. We had a couple of Marines burn their way through the bulkhead. There was no trap, and the Chesty's crew cheered us as we boarded. We immediately made our way up to the cockpit, and Batty let us in. He smiled at us and stood at attention, giving Major Plural his best salute.

Jenna slapped him on the back. "At ease Batty. You're a goddamn hero today." He beamed widely at this praise and returned to his seat as Jenna took her place in the captain's chair.

"So, what do you think, Mr. Phelkar? The Lady Liberty is the superior ship, but it's still a Peon ship. Should I assume command from here, or should I assume the command from there?"

I leaned over Batty and hit the intercom switch. "Stacey, can you switch on the Lady Liberty's transponder to signal we are an American ship?"

"Sure thing, Phelks." And after a short pause, she replied, "We are now beaming to the solar system that we are an American ship."

I looked at Jenna and smiled. "She's not a Peon ship now."

Jenna grinned back at me. "You're a complete dork, Mr. Phelkar," she said, chuckling. Then her face grew grim. "We have to deal with Stephanie Morris."

"Do you wish me to arrange a special court-martial?" I hoped she wouldn't stick to her words and that they were said in anger.

"You heard me on the ship, Mr. Phelkar. We need to make an example of what happens to traitors."

I sighed softly. "As you wish, Ma'am." I tapped the intercom. "Hardy, have Morris moved to the cargo hold."

His voice abruptly returned. "Is that the major's orders?"

"It is."

"I would rather hear it from the major."

Jenna sighed and snapped irritably. "Yes, Hardy, it's my order. Mr. Phelkar is my adjutant. His word is my word. Now stop wasting my time." I could have skipped and whistled my way to the cargo hold.

Hardy was already in there with the Marine we had spoken to over the comms. Emma Dodgson was just nineteen. Your typical American kid born and raised in Phoenix, Arizona, who joined the Marines to avoid conscription into the regular infantry. It turned out that this was her first tour of duty. She was a tall thin girl with dark rust-colored hair that hung down in a plait to her lower back. She had a wide-eyed deer in headlights look about her, and when she spoke, she had that slight stammer. This belied the true confidence of the young Marine. She gave Jenna a smart salute as we entered, which the major returned.

Stephanie Morris stood in the center of the room, her hands bound behind her back. She struggled to maintain her composure, but the terror in her eyes was unmistakable. Jenna walked straight up to her and slapped her hard around the face. "You disgust me."

At my side, Dodgson stifled a gasp. I turned to her and whispered, "Do you want to wait outside?" She steeled herself in the at-ease position and shook her head.

"Look, Jenna," Morris said between anguished sobs, having quickly abandoned all composure, "you don't need to do this. Let's just talk about it. Let me out of here, and I will follow you anywhere you want to go. I will accept your authority. I'm begging you, please don't kill me."

Jenna folded her arms and paced up and down in front of her. "You're a complete coward, aren't you?" she said with bile in her tone. "You think I will just sit back and forget what you did to me?"

Stephanie visibly shook, and Jenna suddenly stepped back in horror as a wet patch appeared at the former first officer's crotch. I started to feel a little sorry for her as Jenna turned her head towards Hardy.

"String her up," she muttered.

Hardy nodded, and I noticed that he already had a cable waiting for her. He threw it over a beam in front of her, and I saw it had been formed into a slipknot.

"Let's leave him to it," I said for Dodgson's sake, but Jenna thought I was talking to her.

She shook her head. "You can leave if you want, but I promised Morris I would be the last thing she sees, and I won't be faithless."

"As you wish, Major," I replied, but I remained at her side. As did Dodgson. Apparently, neither of us wanted to be seen as faithless to our commander.

Tears streamed down Stephanie Morris's face, and Dodgson moved in to help her to remain standing as Malcolm put the noose around her neck.

"Raise her slowly," Jenna commanded and moved to stand directly in front of her with her hands behind her back and legs astride. Malcolm nodded and pulled her up about half a foot from the ground. As the tips of her toes left the ground, Stephanie Morris struggled with her legs, unable to do anything with her bound hands. Her face quickly turned red as the air supply was cut off. I wanted to turn away but was afraid of what Jenna would think of me. She watched with intense contempt and loathing. Dodgson watched with fascination, and Hardy looked like it was just another day in the Marine Corps.

We remained there in silence for several minutes as Stephanie continued to struggle. Eventually, Jenna sighed, pulled out her sidearm, and shot her squarely in the chest. Stephanie momentarily stiffened and then fell limp as the front of her shirt turned red. Jenna remained, staring at her for a full minute. Then, turning away, she strode to the door without looking back, muttering the order, "Throw her out of an airlock."

"That was unexpected," I said, stepping up to her side and leaving with her.

"Guess I'm going soft in my old age," she growled contemptuously.

When we returned to the Lady Liberty, we headed up to the cockpit. Our pilot disconnected us from the Lewis Puller and set a course for the rendezvous. Tracker was sitting next to Stacey, monitoring communications. "Ma'am, I'm pleased to report that we now have a hundred and forty-two confirmed ships heading towards the rendezvous point. However, Admiral Baines of the U.S.S. Constitution has claimed that he is going to assume command upon arrival."

"He did, did he?" Jenna almost growled.

"Yes, he is constantly demanding to speak to you, Ma'am," Tracker said.

"Yes, well, inform him I'm busy. I'm not going to be overheard in some power game until I'm good and ready."

Jenna sat back and crossed her legs. She sighed wearily and closed her eyes. I said nothing and stood beside her, trying to look like I was supposed to be doing just that. "I think we can call that a successful mission," she said without opening her eyes. "Don't you, Mr. Phelkar?"

"Quite," I replied.

"I think we should take some time out for a little R&R," she said. "It's been stressful, and we should celebrate our victories so far. I assume the Peons left us some liquor?"

"Yes, we have a fair stock," I said uncomfortably. Planning a party less than an hour after cold-bloodedly executing a former colleague seemed rather distasteful.

"Inform the crew that a little libation will occur in the officers' mess. Open to all ranks, casual dress." She paused and looked up at me with a grin. "Then have someone find out where the officers' mess is on this ship and get us ready for a party."

"About time!" said Stacey enthusiastically.

"As you wish, Major." I grinned at the pilot and left to make the arrangements.

For her part in capturing Stephanie Morris, Jenna promoted Dodgson to corporal. She was then assigned to work as an aide to me in carrying out my duties which had become primarily logistical. She was more of an adviser since I did not know the workings of the USMC, and it became her job to turn my plans into a reality. I asked her what was involved in throwing a United States Marines party. Her eyes lit up with a huge grin, and she said what would become my favorite words. "You can leave everything to me, Sir." And I did.

Everything appeared to be going well. Most of the crew seemed to be in good spirits, knowing a good time was to be had. However, as I was headed to the mess for some lunch, the ship's klaxons suddenly blared out, and the ship's computer intoned in its soporific male voice, "Escape capsule number seven has been launched. Repeat escape capsule number seven has been launched."

Jenna's voice immediately came online. "Security to Evacuation Preparation Center on the double."

A few minutes later, an uneasy voice came back. "Um, Major, we have a situation down here. We strongly recommend that you come down and deal with it."

"On my way," Jenna responded.

I headed down there myself, curious as to what was going on. The evacuation area was not very

big and bore only ten life pods. Well, nine now. In the center of the room, Stacey Grant stood there looking sheepishly as I entered. Standing around were three Marines.

"What's going on?" I asked, looking at Stacey just as Jenna entered behind me.

Stacey shrugged and looked just like a little girl caught with a hand in the cookie jar. "I was just making sure they had a good time. "I didn't know the alarms were gonna go off. We've never used the life pods before."

Jenna's eyes narrowed, and she looked furious. "What did you do this time, Stacey?"

Stacey looked down at her feet when she twisted her heel back and forth. "You see, we were gonna have this party, right? You also told the Chesty to do the same, but Batty told me they have no liquor on board." Her voice trailed off.

"Stacey?" Jenna intoned in a deep growl.

"I stocked up a life pod with some of our liquor and jettisoned it while Batty put the scoops on and pulled it into the Chesty." She shrugged. "They should have a good time too."

There was a long moment of silence, and it looked like Jenna was about to explode. "Give me the room, please, gentlemen," Jenna said coldly, and we all filed out, but once the three Marines had left the area, I stepped back and listened to the door. To my surprise, I heard the pair of them laughing but could not make out what was being said. Jenna had surprised me in many ways lately.

To be honest, I was not familiar with the appropriate dress code for a rank-and-file party for

American troops. It was not as if I had a lot of options. The trustee duffel bag I brought over from the Chesty did contain formal clothes, but there were more suitable ones for formal functions. I decided to go with a simple pair of dress trousers and a white button-up shirt without a tie. Fortunately, Dodgson arranged for these to be laundered and pressed for me in time for the party.

Chapter Eighteen
The Major Event

I t kicked off at eight the following day. The Liberty's officers' mess pounded to the music of the latest hits from the U.S. A. Not quite my taste, but the atmosphere was electric. I arrived fifteen minutes late, and almost the entire crew, excluding those on the Chesty, were present. Jenna had yet to arrive, and two duty personnel, one of whom patrolled the corridors and the other who remained on the bridge. I had arranged for them to be rotated out every two hours so all could attend. Civvies were the order of the day, and I noticed Tracker, conservatively dressed in bell-bottom grey slacks and a matching button-up vest, dancing with a young man I did not know, and from the looks of it, he was way more into her than she was into him. All around were the elite of the USMC in the best party gear they could keep in their footlocker. Dancing, drinking, and acting like war was a word they had never heard of.

Stacey had taken over serving at the bar, and I was startled to see her in a sleeveless white blouse with a ludicrously short, pleated tartan skirt. Standing at the table opposite her was Bridgette. She was dressed in a basic U.S. Marine uniform with the insignia removed. However, I immediately noticed Stacey pouring her an inappropriate drink. I stepped over to them and, reaching around Bridgette from behind, took the glass from her hand whilst glaring at Stacey. Bridgette glared at me.

"You are no fun, Mr. Phelkar," she said in French.

"That's life, I'm afraid, Miss Toussaint."

Stacey said nothing and moved on to serve someone else with a huge grin. Bridgette glared at me once more, then flounced out of the hall, head held high with indignation.

Suddenly the music stopped, and all looked around, wondering why. A large beer keg rolled into the room, followed by another. A cheer went up, but I was just plain confused. Dodgson noticed me and came over. "It's a Marine tradition ever since the first Marines were sent into space. Just watch." And as if on cue, Jenna Plural stepped into the room, and my brain about exploded. It was the first time I had seen her out of uniform since we met that day on the road. She wore a tight black skirt above the knee with a matching, almost translucent sheer collared shirt. Her hair was tied back in a ponytail with a white scrunchie and a gold chain with a locket that hung down over her breast. She sported a pair of three-inch pumps with black stockings and a gold anklet on one ankle. She looked as far from being a Marine as one could. Everyone except me stood at sharp attention and saluted.

Jenna stopped at attention at the entrance and returned the salute. Then the familiar tune of the Marine Hymn began to play, and all but myself and the few Navy personnel began to sing, "From the Halls of Montezuma." "The Star-Spangled Banner" immediately followed this. All the while, no one moved from their rigid spot at full attention. Then silence fell, and I watched Jenna waiting for something to happen. She then lowered her head, and everyone followed suit, and the voice of what I can only describe as an angel began to sing 'I Still Call Australia Home' acappella. I stared in disbelief at Stacefield E. Grant as she concluded her anthem. I turned back to Jenna and was surprised to see that she was looking at me questioningly. I shook my head vigorously. There was no way I would torture everyone with my tone-deaf rendition of "God Save the King" or "Jerusalem." A grin twisted at the corner of her mouth, and she moved into the at-ease position. Everyone immediately copied her.

"Boys and girls of the United States Marine Corps. As your commander, I ask nothing less than your best. On Phobos, you gave me nothing less than your best. So, the beer is on me." It was only then I saw she carried a snap gun, and raising it, she fired once into each keg, and a cheer went up, and Marines grabbed up their mugs to get what was called The Commander's Fill as it gushed out over the floor.

Dodgson looked up at me, and I nodded to her. "You are off duty, Corporal. Go enjoy yourself." She grinned and dived into the melee around the beer.

As I turned back to Jenna, I saw her hand her gun over to a steward, and she approached me with a smile. She was a stunning vision of perfection, and my heart began to pound as she stopped in front of me. "Good evening, Mr. Phelkar," she said with a broad smile.

I raised an eyebrow. "So, am I back in your good graces, Major Plural?"

She laughed. "Oh, you never really left them. You can be a most infuriating man, and I often forget you are not one of my Marines." Then a coquettish expression crossed her face. It was bizarre and different from anything I had ever seen from her. She gently placed a hand on my arm. "How can I stay mad at my favorite Englishman?"

My mind was doing cartwheels. Was Jenna Plural flirting with me, or was my ardor deceiving my senses?

I chuckled. "How many Englishmen do you know, Major?"

She tilted her head knowingly. "Oh, I have known quite a few in my time Mr. Phelkar," she said, making me wonder, once again, about her age.

"Really?" I replied. "I can't believe they were all negative experiences."

Jenna frowned. "I don't believe I said they were."

"I got the impression that your opinion of the British was rather negative. After all, it is a 'paltry little country of lazy bastards.'" I smiled.

Jenna flushed slightly. "Oh, dear. I did say that to you when we first met, didn't I?" I nodded in response, my grin widening. "I was angry, Mr. Phelkar," she said, almost brushing it off. "You can have my full and unreserved apology." At that moment, the tempo of the music changed to a slow number. The drunken revelry took a sidestep for a smooch with the partner of choice, or whatever person didn't have a partner. "Mr. Phelkar, it appears we are the only ones not dancing," she said softly, looking up into my eyes.

I was about to comment that although the vast majority were indeed dancing, many weren't. Stacey, for one, still stood behind the bar, and various others stood around the room, but as I looked back at her, she bit her lower lip and tilted her head to one side, looking up at me with a wry smile. I returned the smile. "Would you care to dance, Major?"

Jenna feigned surprise at the question. "Why, thank you, Mr. Phelkar. I would be delighted." She took my arm, and we stepped out onto the dance floor. As we turned to face each other, she placed her arms over my shoulders, crossing her wrists behind my neck, and I slipped my hands down to her waist. I had no idea what she was thinking, but it was a most intimate moment for me as my hands rested upon her hips. We drew the attention of those around us as we moved in time to the music. I'm not much of a dancer, but this was hardly difficult. All I had to do was ensure I did not step on her toes, and I'm pleased to say that I achieved that. She looked up into my eyes, and I looked down into hers, and I was lost. For me, the room became empty, and it was just us for that moment. I felt that tingling in my stomach, standing so close to the woman I adored. I wanted it to last forever. Judging from her expression, she appeared to have enjoyed it, but as the tempo increased, we took our leave of the dance floor. "May I get you a drink, Major?"

"Sure, why not."

I turned away and headed over to the bar. Stacey was finishing serving Neuman but grinning inanely at me. "Hey, Phelks, you trying your luck with a good major there?" she said.

I blushed and gave a cold stare to the trooper until he stopped grinning at her words and hurried away with his drink. "Don't be silly," I told her.

"Ah, come on, Phelks, you have to admit she has great legs. Even I get tingly looking at them, and I'm as straight as straight can be." She sighed. "Can't you just imagine them wrapped around your back?" Then, widening her eyes, she said with the broadest grin. "Or better still, your neck?"

I narrowed my eyes in disgust. "You can be pretty crude, you know? Give me a couple of brandies, if you please."

"Just telling it like it is, mate." She chuckled at my expense as she poured out two large glasses. "Anyway, looks like you've lost your chance," she said, handing them to me, and I turned around to see that barrel-chested fucker Malcolm Hardy walking up to Jenna. That cold feeling of a sudden shock flowed down me as I took one step back towards them, then hesitated.

"Good to see you again, Major," Hardy said, grinning like some rabid hyena. Yes, I know I'm biased, but you know what it's like when you see some guy hitting on the girl or guy you like. Anyway, he was killed not long after this, so maybe I should cut him some slack. Actually, no, damn that fucker.

Jenna looked up at him. Yeah, even in those heels, the bastard towered over her. "Hey, Sergeant," she said, smiling warmly, too fucking warmly for my liking. "Sorry, I never got the chance to thank you for your help when we took this ship."

"Oh, I was only doing my duty." He stepped closer to her, looking into her eyes, and she reciprocated with a slight smile. "And it's an honor to serve you and your cause."

I thought I noticed Jenna glance over at me but decided I had imagined it. She looked up at him again and said girlishly, "Well, there's nothing better than a man who knows his duty."

He stepped in closer to her, and I felt my stomach tighten. I wanted to punch him out then and there. Fight for her in a testosterone-filled haze. The reality was that he could probably pulverize me in a single punch. What gutted me the most was that she did not step back or act in any way, to indicate that this was inappropriate. "Maybe we can get together sometime and discuss strategy?" Let's be honest, he wasn't talking about strategy, and it was such a lame line there was no way she was going to fall for it. She was way too bright and—

"Maybe you should come over to my quarters sometime to talk about it?" She smiled at him in a way that I could only describe as seductively, and when she spoke, her voice was like silk, soft and inviting.

He stepped even closer, and she gave a very uncharacteristic giggle.

OH MY GOD! NO, NO, NO...

I turned away, standing like a pillock with the two drinks held so limply in my hands I almost spilled them. My humiliation entirely amused Stacey. "Oh, never mind, Phelks. Hey, there is always Dodgson. She's been checking you out since you got here." I turned to see young Dodgson. She was dancing with some guy, but she looked over at me. As our eyes met, she flushed and looked away.

I looked back to Stacey, downed one of the brandies, then placed both glasses upon the bar. "I don't think that will be very appropriate to fraternize with the enlisted, do you?"

Stacey shrugged. "You're not military, mate. You can fuck whoever you like."

I shook my head in disbelief and, with a final glance at Hardy and Jenna, who looked as though they were about to kiss, I strode from the room.

Returning to my quarters, I paced up and down for a good hour, trying to relieve my anger and frustration and push Jenna from my mind. You know that was hopeless if you have ever been infatuated with someone. Eventually, I decided the only course of action was to go to bed and sulk like some lovelorn teenager.

As I started to unbutton my shirt, a knock at the door came. I hastily fastened it up again and headed to open it, annoyed someone was choosing to visit me in my current state of mind. As it slid open, I was dumbstruck to see Jenna standing there in her stockinged feet with her heels dangling from her pinky finger by the straps. She looked at me through what seemed like sulky pursed lips. There was a moment of silence before she spoke. "Where is my drink, Mr. Phelkar?"

I struggled to find a reply to this, and she appeared to find that amusing, for a slight smile crossed her face as I um'd and ah'd.

"I don't exactly consider myself an expert on English culture, but I believe it is as offensive in your country as it is in mine to ditch a lady you were dancing with." Despite the words, she spoke in a tone of amusement.

"You seemed to be preoccupied," I said uneasily.

Jenna raised a perfect eyebrow and gave me a perfect smile. "Really? And what makes you think that?" I was squirming uncomfortably inside as I could not refer to her encounter with Hardy. "All I know is that you just walked out on me," she continued.

"Well, I um," I said dumbly, unsure where this was going as my thoughts were doing somersaults in a now fogged-up brain.

An almost mischievous smile crossed her face. "Do you often stand women up like that?"

"To be honest, I don't often have the opportunity." She looked at me, into my room, then back at me. "Oh right," I said and hastily stepped aside to let her in.

As the door slid shut behind her, she tossed the shoes onto my desk chair. "They should use those things to torture people in interrogations," she muttered. She then spun back to me. I was just standing there mutely confused by this visit. She gave me a dry smile and said, "Are you intimidated by Sergeant Hardy?"

"No, of course not," I blustered out indignantly.

Jenna chuckled. "You liar!" I felt my face grow hot as she flopped back down in my armchair, crossed her exquisite legs, and studied me. "I must confess that I enjoyed teasing you, but I never expected you to give up so easily."

"So..." I started uneasily.

As my voice trailed off, she grinned and chuckled again. "Go on, Mr. Phelkar."

"That... you and Hardy... that was all an act?"

"I was playing with you." She shrugged. "I was being a tease."

"And Hardy was in on it?"

She frowned, looking quite confused. "No, he was hitting on me. Why would he be in on it?"

"Never mind," I said, realizing she had no idea that she had been teasing Hardy too. "So, you and Hardy are not...?" my voice trailed off again.

She scrunched up her nose. "Eww, no. All brawn and no brain is hardly a turn-on, Mr. Phelkar." She stood up again, and there was a slight sway to her hips as she stepped back toward me. "I prefer men with a little more ... up here." She ran her middle finger up through the side of my hair. "Though you really should work out more."

"I get my ten thousand steps in every day."

She chuckled. "Well, doesn't that just get a girl tingling?" She stood just inches from me, looking up into my eyes. She may have been sarcastic, but she certainly had *me* tingling. "So we just going to stand here, Mr. Phelkar?"

"I'm not sure what you're talking about," I lied.

"Really?" Her face was so close I could see the blue speckles in her eyes. "So, you're not attracted to me?" She feigned a disappointed look as she bit her lower lip seductively. "Well, that certainly would be a first for me."

"What do you mean?"

She shrugged. "I haven't met a man who was not attracted to me." She saw my incredulous look and smiled, "Just a statement of fact, Mr. Phelkar, not arrogance."

"That being said—"

"Come on, Mr. Phelkar, deny it right to my face," she interrupted, grinning and stepping even closer, her body almost pushing me back against the wall. As she looked into my eyes, my heart pounded, and my manhood stirred. Her lips were millimeters from mine. A silence hung between us, and each hot breath, smelling of a mixture of alcohol and her peppermint mouthwash, only aroused me more, causing me to finally say, "I can't."

Jenna's grin widened, and she slowly ran the back of her index finger up my stomach and my chest to finally stroke my cheek. Her nails, which she kept trimmed short, were painted light pink, matching her lipstick. She tilted her head and smiled teasingly. "Tell me you want me, Mr. Phelkar," she said in barely a whisper. "Tell me you want me right now."

"I want—"

But Jenna pushed me roughly back against the wall and pressed her body up against mine before I could even say it. Her lips parted, and her breathing increased in pace. She forced her mouth onto mine, although I was hardly resisting. I couldn't believe this. As our tongues entwined, tasting some sweet liqueur, her hand slipped down to my waist, and she began to unfasten my belt. Fireworks were going off in my head, and I no longer had doubts I was in love with this woman, whatever may come. I pulled up her shirt and slid my hand around her back, and I pinched the clasp of her bra. Jenna gasped as it sprang open, and she rested her forehead on mine. "Why, Mr. Phelkar, you're quite talented," she said, chuckling as she pulled out my belt and unfastened the clip to my trousers.

I said nothing and moved in to kiss her again as my hand reached up to cup one of her firm, pert breasts. I made to rip off her shirt, but she stopped me. "No, no, no, this is a twelve-hundred-dollar blouse, and I'm not likely to see another store again for a while." She unfastened the locket, dropped it on my desk, and swiftly unbuttoned the blouse.

As my lower garments fell, I stepped out of them and pulled off my shirt. She spun me around, pushed me back down upon the bed, and let herself fall on top of me with a gasp. I looked into her bright blue eyes as she crawled up to straddle me and looked down at me with a grin. She pushed her mouth down onto mine again, kissing me long and hard. Her skin was soft under my touch, perfectly smooth. My arousal pressed hard into her abdomen as my hand ran down her side until I found her buttock. As I moved to her calf, I found it to be firm and muscular, in stark contrast to Stacey's softness. Stacey, why was I thinking of Stacey?

The brain-numbing sensation that all men have came over me. She raised herself on her knees and directed me into her slowly, deliberately, lowering herself upon me with a soft moan. I let out a gasp. Her long brown hair hung down, tickling the sides of my face. She moved herself to a rhythm only the two of us could hear. With each movement, the beat got faster as I stared up at that virtual work of art, Jenna Plural.

Then it all went so wrong, for me at least. She began to climax, and I neither expected it so soon nor was I prepared. I tried desperately to stay in the moment, but as she bit her lip and closed her eyes, whimpering, I struggled to maintain my arousal. Thoughts of the difference between her and Stacey came back again. The little spitfire did that thing with her hips, followed by the other thing with her teeth, pulling me over the edge. I was at full mast again and erupted with Jenna. She tensed, her eyes still closed as she dug her nails into my chest. As she relaxed, she opened her eyes, grinned down at me, and fell against me, kissing me again. She lay there for a while before rolling over next to me.

"That was so good," she said softly, curling up against me and resting her head on my shoulder. I just hugged her to me, my head filled with confusion. I had dreamed of this moment. I was in love with this woman. So, why the hell was I thinking of Stacey Grant?

Chapter Nineteen
Rendezvous

Waking late the next day and finding the empty space next to me, I concluded that it must have been a dream. There was no way Jenna Plural would have slept with me, but as I heard the shower go on in my bathroom, I sat up. I saw the high-heeled shoes sitting on the chair where she had thrown them. I climbed out of bed and put on a robe. I saw our various garments scattered throughout the room and began to pick them up. I smelled the aroma of coffee and saw a pot brewing away on my desk.

It had all been real, and in my bathroom, right now, was the woman who captured all of my senses, including my heart and mind. As the night's memories returned, I smiled, wanting this to last forever, and pushed my thoughts of Stacey from my thoughts.

I noticed the locket sitting on the table and picked it up. I flicked it open and saw two pictures, one on each side, both of young men. I wondered who they were and why they were so important to her. I didn't recognize one of them, but there was something familiar about the other. I couldn't place where I had seen him before, but the sandy-haired man was definitely someone I knew. I heard the shower go off, and I realized what I was doing could be perceived as invasive. I closed it and returned it to the table.

When Jenna stepped out with just a towel, I did not turn away this time and just smiled at her. She gave me the sweetest smile. "Well, good morning, Mr. Phelkar," she said softly.

I chuckled and replied. "And good morning to you, Major Plural." However, unlike me, she did not seem to notice the idiosyncrasy of retaining our formal titles.

"I ordered breakfast to be sent here. Made a joke about treating you." She tilted her head to one side, drying off her hair with another towel as she talked. "I don't think it would be appropriate if I were seen here."

This instantly bothered me. "You're not ashamed by it, are you?" I asked, concerned.

She chuckled as, still drying her hair, she poured us out both coffees. "Don't be silly, Mr. Phelkar. Although you may not be officially military, you have placed yourself under my command. It wouldn't be good for people to think your authority, as my adjutant, is based on our relationship." She handed me the coffee. Dropping the towel she had been using on her hair over the back of my office chair, she picked up her own coffee and stepped over to sit on the edge of the bed.

I smiled. "So, this is indeed a relationship?"

My heart sank as she looked startled and said with surprise, "A relationship?"

"Never mind," I responded and looked down at my coffee, avoiding her gaze and feeling like the prize idiot she always called me.

"Wait. No. I'm sorry," she said earnestly. "You just surprised me, that's all."

"But still, it was just sex to you, right?" I took a sip of my coffee to avoid looking up at her.

This took the smile from her face, and, with an intense frown and irritation in her voice, asked me, "Do you think I just fuck anybody in my command?"

Even after all that we had shared, I still found that gaze intimidating. "No, of course not. I was just establishing where we stand."

She sighed. "I like you, and you really mean a lot to me. I wanted to share this time with you."

At that, I did look up. "Just not enough for more than a roll under the sheets."

Her face fell, and she looked sad. "You misunderstand me. It's not about me not wanting a relationship. It never remotely crossed my mind that you would want a relationship with me."

"Why the hell not?" I snapped.

There was a long pause where she stared at me with an expression of confusion. Eventually, she said, "Because I'm a Gen-Mod, Mr. Phelkar. You know the old saying?" I shook my head. "'Too good not to fuck but don't take it home to Mom.'"

"Oh my God, is that what you think I'm thinking?" I said, quite offended. She shrugged but said nothing. "I'm sorry, but I'm confused. If you think I felt like that, why did you even come to me last night?"

She shrugged again. "Even a GenMod needs to feel close to someone now and then. As I said, I really like you, and I feel close to you."

I felt stunned as I worked this through my head. It was the first time I'd seen frailty in her. "If I had known that, I would not have done what we did last night."

"I understand." She looked upset now and a little embarrassed. "Perhaps I should just get out of here." She got up and started to grab up her clothes, but I stepped over to her and took her by both hands.

"No, I don't think you do. You see, it is not your physical appearance I'm attracted to." She raised an eyebrow questioning the integrity of that statement. "Well, yes, okay, I'm physically attracted to you, obviously, but it is not what interests me about you."

She laughed lightly, breaking the tension. "Well, please do tell me, Mr. Phelkar, what is so interesting about me?"

As I sat next to her, I paused and looked into her eyes with sincerity. "Your passion, your dedication, your strength," I started. "I have never met a woman with such confidence and who instills such confidence in me. I would run into hell at your command." Then it came out before I could stop myself. "I would die for you."

Her reaction to that surprised me. The confidence in her demeanor returned, and she leaned in, and we kissed long and slowly. She pulled back ever so slightly with her hand resting on my shoulder and whispered in a teasing voice. "So, you wanna be my boyfriend?" It was a question, not a request.

I chuckled. It sounded silly, put like that. "At least till after prom night," I replied.

She laughed. "My actual prom night was a disaster, so let's skip that, okay?" She sat back and became serious. "You must understand, everyone in my life grows old and eventually dies. I carry on getting older, but I keep the face of an Oklahoma Thunder cheerleader. Everyone leaves me in the end, whether by choice or by death. You already look as if you're old enough to be my father. What will people think of you? Will they see it like a normal relationship?" She shook her head slowly. "No, I will be viewed as some sort of trophy partner and you as some dirty old man."

"I don't care what other people think!" I stated determinedly.

"You say that now, but what about in twenty years?" She snorted disbelievingly.

"I don't know. I'll sit on the porch under a blanket while you play volleyball with the grandkids." I laughed.

"It's not funny," she said irritably. Then in a quiet, subdued voice stated, "And we cannot have kids anyway." She added irritably, "My body would reject your D.N.A. as substandard."

"Charming," I muttered, but she either did not hear me or chose to ignore it. "Look, I understand your life is very different to mine," I said. "But what we are discussing is not even an issue yet. We just got together last night. Should we worry about this stuff now?"

She sighed, staring into space for a few moments before looking up at me. Then she smiled. "I'm overthinking all this, aren't I?"

I shrugged and smiled. "Possibly."

She studied me carefully, deep in thought. "You know, I swore I'd never get into another relationship." She paused as if she wondered whether to say what she would say next. "Somehow, it feels right with you."

There was a knock at the door, and Jenna jumped up and slipped into the bathroom, closing the door behind her. I opened the door and took the tray from the steward. After he left and I laid the tray on the table, she returned. She was now dressed in her typical khaki briefs and a matching tank top that made up part of her uniform. I frowned. "How is it you have a change of clothes here in my room?"

"Oh, I only need about two hours of sleep a night, and with my quarters only being next door, I picked up a few things I would need this morning. I have been up for hours. I will tell you this." She grabbed a slice of toast off of the tray. "I'm glad you're in my life. I trust you, Mr. Phelkar, which I very rarely do. The only other people I trust completely on this ship are Sakamoto, Harlow, and Stacey."

"Stacey?" I said, surprised.

Jenna laughed, almost spitting out her toast. "Would it surprise you if I told you Stacey Grant is probably my best friend?"

I nodded. "Yes, it would. The pair of you do not seem to have much in common."

"We don't. However, we have been through a lot together over the last few years, and while she annoys the hell out of me on frequent occasions, she is still very dear to me. I would go as far as saying she Is like my kid sister."

It did surprise me. However, I said nothing, wondering what Jenna would think if she knew I had been intimate with her 'little sister.' Jenna retrieved a hairbrush from the bathroom and returned to brush out her damp hair.

"You're the one person I expect to be completely frank with me even if I don't like it. Even if it makes me angry or upset. You're my counterbalance, and I trust you to keep me level. I'm not good at diplomacy, and I'm going to need to be if I'm going to bring a fleet together."

"Well, we certainly have a long road ahead," I said before sipping my coffee.

"Yes." She stopped brushing and pondered. "Maybe this is the wrong time to get involved with someone."

"Maybe it's what you need—to know what you're fighting for," I said, not wanting to lose what I had only just achieved.

She looked at me and grinned. "Don't worry, Mr. Phelkar, I'm not backing out here." She laughed. "When I met you, I thought you were a creep. After all, within seconds of meeting me, you were checking out my legs."

I blushed. "Oh my, was I that obvious?"

Jenna chuckled. "No, but I'm more observant than most people. My peripheral vision is just as acute as my direct vision. I see everything all the time." She ran a finger along my cheek and gazed into my eyes. "However, your ability to put our differences aside when the chips were down said a lot about your character. I value that loyalty. Anyway, I have to go to a meeting with Tracker" She headed back into the bathroom. When she came back out, she had trousers and a pullover on. "Stay and finish your breakfast, and then perhaps you can meet up with us later." She stepped past me and gave me a quick kiss on the cheek. She turned back to me just before the door opened. "Thank you for being here for me, Mr. Phelkar," she said softly. "And I'm not just talking about last night."

Without another word, she stepped out. I looked down at the breakfast, realizing I wasn't hungry. I heard Jenna talking to someone outside. "Strategy meeting? Oh yeah, right. Sorry, Hardy, maybe some other time."

I was grinning from ear to ear for several hours that day. I ate the breakfast, but only because she

had got it for me.

Later that day, Stacey reported she had picked up the first American ships on the long-range scanners, and there was a buzz of excitement among everyone. It was like our story was coming to an end. It wasn't; it was just the beginning of a trip through hell, but we enjoyed the moment.

They came from all directions and in all sizes. Jenna was in an ebullient mood until Stacey called

her up to the bridge.

"Boss, I'm picking up transmissions from the U.S.S. Constitution to most of the fleet," Tracker told her as we entered.

Jenna took the headset from her and put it on. She turned to face me. "That Iowan pig fucker is trying to convene a meeting over the comms without us."

"Baines?" I asked her.

"Who else?"

"That's not exactly protocol. The Peons could be listening in," I responded.

Stacey interjected. "Yes, well, since we've taken out the Peons' primary communications hub, he

is claiming they are not currently able to pick up our radio signals for several days."

I looked to Tracker. "Is that possible?"

Tracker shrugged. "Yeah, it's possible, but it's also possible they have comm buoys scattered between here and wherever."

Jenna looked like she would burst a blood vessel. "Try telling him that."

I thought about this, then replied, "If you will let me?"

Jenna turned her blue eyes up at me. "What?"

"Let me talk to him." I smiled. "I'm the diplomat, after all."

"But—"

"You say you trust me," I interrupted, shrugging. "Prove it."

"Okay, Mr. Phelkar." She tried to hide the unease in her voice as she removed the headset. "Go

for it."

I turned to Tracker. "Put it on speakers and give me an open line to the admiral's ship."

Her brow furrowed. "Mr. Phelkar, an open line will enable all the other ships to hear you."

"I know," I said with a grin. "Give me that line."

Stacey grinned back at me. "You're a wily pommy bastard, Phelks. What are you up to?"

I just winked at her as Tracker turned back to her console. "You have the line."

Although they couldn't see me, I stood upright and spoke calmly and concisely. "This is Michael Phelkar of the U.S.S. Lady Liberty to the U.S.S. Constitution. Do you read me?"

A young female voice came back. "This is the U.S.S. Constitution. Please state your designation code. I don't see you listed as a United States vessel."

"Cut the bullshit. You already know we don't have a designation code for the Lady Liberty. She is a spoil of war, all above board and following the Galle Convention. Command was transferred here from the U.S.S. Lewis Puller."

There was a long pause before the voice returned with an awestruck tone. "You're one of Jenna Plural's crew?" Apparently, Jenna's reputation had already spread, and I smiled at the major, but she was just listening intently.

"That is correct. I have the privilege to serve under Major Plural, and this is her flagship." It was a hell of a gamble, and I will freely admit that now, but I thought establishing our intent right off the bat would save any confusion later.

Then, there was another pause. "Um, I have Admiral Baines on the line for you."

The admiral's voice held the tone of the authority of an older veteran. "Mr. Phelkar, I demand to speak with Lieutenant Plural."

"*Major* Plural is currently unavailable. She is in a strategy meeting and cannot be disturbed. However, she demands to know why you're arranging inter-ship communications in a time of war where the enemy can overhear them."

Baines almost spluttered out his words in his response. "You insolent ass. As you well know, the war is over, and the military has been dissolved until further notice. And that genetically modified freak you follow is certainly no major. I have stripped her of *all* rank until a formal court-martial can be held."

"I'm sorry, admiral, but what you're saying does not make sense. If there is no military, in your opinion, you cannot strip her of her rank. You don't have the authority to do so by your own admission." "What are you talking about, boy?"

"Unlike you, *Mister* Baines, the genetically modified freak still recognizes the authority of the United States military." Stacey snorted with laughter and covered her nose and mouth as I repeated Baine's insult. "You have made it clear to the entire fleet that you intend to surrender to the enemy. As a result, you have abdicated authority in these matters." I was flying by the seat of my pants now, but it came to me like a gut reaction.

"Is this fleet-wide?" Baines said suddenly, and he wasn't talking to me.

"Umm, yes, sir," the woman who answered the call replied.

"Turn it off, you stupid—" And their end of the line went dead.

But I continued to talk. "Major Jenna Plural requests all ships indicate their intent not to turn themselves over to European authority." I waited nervously for a response. Jenna sat stoically, arms folded and legs crossed. I couldn't help wondering if I had played my hand too soon or incorrectly. I almost gave up when we picked up a transponder signal from the U.S.S Los Angeles. I triumphantly raised a fist and punched the air as another signal came. I soon lost count.

Baines's voice burst once more over the communications. "Discontinue these transmissions at once. That is an order."

I indicated to Stacey to end our transmission. Then I turned back to Jenna, who was grinning like

the Cheshire Cat.

"Stacey, how many ships out there did you say?" she asked.

"One hundred and forty-two"

"And how many are now broadcasting their transponders?"

"One hundred and thirty-one."

"We can assume the remaining ten will follow Baines or have already conceded defeat," I said. "However, I believe your position in the playing field has just increased. You may still not get your rank recognized, but you will get heard."

Jenna stood up. "Mr. Phelkar, you truly are a phenomenon. Thank you. Stacey, bring us into the

fleet."

As we moved into visual range, we could finally see a wide variety of American, British, and other allied ships of various shapes and sizes, from small transports to the larger battleships; however, as the U.S.S. Constitution came into range. It dwarfed us all. The flagship of the United States was the gleaming pride of the fleet, and upon its hull sat hundreds of smaller attack craft that could swarm an enemy vessel at a moment's notice. I swallowed hard as I realized if this came to a conflict, the entire fleet couldn't stand up to the Constitution.

Once more, I had Stacey cut the transmission so I could not be heard.

"Was one of the ships which signaled its transponder code the U.S.S. Los Angeles?"

Stacey glanced down at her screen. "Yup!"

I looked at Jenna. "Would your old friends be willing to host us?"

Jenna looked at me quizzically. "What have you got in mind?"

"Arrange a strategy meeting. Not to discuss your leadership, although that will undoubtedly come into play. Set it up as an inter-ship discussion on the way forward, as if leadership is already decided." She nodded. "Stacey, give me a secure line to the Los Angeles if you please."

"Encrypted and secured, you have a line," Stacey replied.

"This is Jenna Plural to Captain Addison. Do you read me?"

"Reading you loud and clear, Jenna. You certainly know how to throw the shit at the fan, don't you?" Addison said, coming in strong.

"I'm doing my best, Claire."

"That dick, Baines, is probably going apoplectic right now." Addison chuckled.

"Major," I interrupted. "I'm very sure that Baines will be hacking into this transmission as we talk.

We need to move along."

"Understood, Mr. Phelkar," Jenna said, nodding.

"Well, hello, who's the guy with a cute English accent?" Addison said with a hint of amusement.

"That's our Mr. Phelkar. It's a long story, and I will bring you up to date with it as soon as possible," Jenna said, speaking faster now. "How do you feel about hosting a fleet-wide conference?"

"Not a problem. I trust Stacey still knows how to dock a ship?" Addison said, sounding serious. "Yeah, yeah." Stacey rolled her eye. "Fuck you, Claire."

Chapter Twenty
Powerplay

I t took about two hours to dock with the U.S.S. Los Angeles, and during that time, I went over my plan with both Jenna and the one person we would need, Helen Tracker. Once we were tethered, the three of us crossed over to join the much larger battleship.

Addison met us at the airlock. She was a tall, muscular woman and somewhat masculine in her features, yet not unattractive. She was in her late forties, possibly her early fifties, but what stood out most was that she was about six-foot-two or so, making her a couple of inches taller than me.

She and Jenna embraced. They tried engaging in small talk, but I kept coughing and tapping my wrist. They got the message. The U.S.S. Los Angeles was a beautiful state-of-the-art battle cruiser that dwarfed both the Liberty and the Puller in power and size.

"I took the liberty of informing the ships that indicated their support that we will be doing a virtual conference at oh eight hundred hours," Addison advised us as we went down to the virtual conference room. They chatted about old times and various missions they had shared while I talked with Tracker.

"To hold this meeting without inviting Baines would be considered unreasonable. "I advised Helen Tracker. "However, we really don't want him to speak or even hear if possible."

Tracker nodded. "Disrupting his communications is not a problem. However, the hard part is making sure it's not traced back to us. It would be easier if we had someone aboard the Constitution, but since we don't, I have arranged for the Lewis Puller to move into a position where it can imitate a tachyon burst. If Batty could do that directly between the Los Angeles and the Constitution, it would disrupt communications. He would then put out an alert regarding engine problems. It is a minor issue, so it won't be like anyone will respond to them as if it was an emergency."

"Won't the Chesty's association with Jenna arouse suspicion?" I asked.

"Possibly. However, it can't be proved unless they want to diagnose the Lewis Puller fully." Tracker grinned.

"And if we're successful, we can make sure that doesn't happen, and if we are unsuccessful, it

doesn't really matter," I concluded.

"Exactly," she said, nodding.

We sat at a conference table, and a young tech handed Jenna a helmet similar to the one I used on the Chesty to watch Jenna's spacewalk. She put it on. To her, it would appear that she was sitting at a virtual conference table. Upon their respective ships, the captains would be doing the same, and it would be as if everyone was in the same room. No one would be able to see that I was at her side, potentially coaching her.

Jenna was taking deep breaths, and as I slipped into the seat beside her, I asked if she was okay. "I'm not a public speaker, Mr. Phelkar. I'm so out of my comfort zone here."

"You're a natural leader, Jenna. Just be yourself, and don't let anyone piss you off," I said, watching as Addison was set up for the conference on the other side of the table.

Tracker sat down at the communications interface, ready to play her part in controlling who could speak and who couldn't. I had a prearranged signal for her to cut anyone's feed if we needed to, and I prayed that we wouldn't.

Finally, ready or not, when oh eight hundred came, Tracker switched on the transmission. I watched on the screen as many captains began to appear down an impossibly long table. At the far end sat Captain Addison. Many voices started talking urgently, some confused or even angry. Jenna waited patiently until finally, silence fell, and all eyes turned towards her. That is when she spoke.

"Ladies and gentlemen, I'm most delighted that you can meet with me today and that you have chosen not to acquiesce to the European Union. "

"That hasn't been decided yet, Lieutenant Plural," came back Baine's voice. His image appeared in the same place as Captain Addison and then flickered in and out. He had wanted to sit in a position of authority and was trying to override the Los Angeles' image of its captain. I could not help but grin. No one could get the better of our Helen Tracker, and the sad untimely loss of her would eventually hit us hard in more ways than one. But for now, she simply made Baines look stupid and petty. "And let's start as we mean to go on. As ranking officer here, it is appropriate that I conduct this meeting. You, Lieutenant, do not hold ship command rank and have no place here."

"Admiral Baines, you have already conceded that there is no longer any U.S. military command structure," Jenna responded just as I had prepped her. "You're part of the hierarchy that got us in this position. We did not lose this war. The leadership led us to it, and it's time for a change in that leadership. You intend for us to surrender. You have made that clear to everyone present here today. You're already in the pocket of the enemy."

"I'm not interested in listening to you, Lieutenant Plural," Baines retorted. "I'm only here to address the senior officers of the fleet. Not some upstart girl with her delusions of grandeur."

"Admiral Baines, this is a conference about fighting back, not how we roll over and play dead."

"Now listen here, Plural—" He had said enough. I nodded to Tracker, and she sent the signal to Batty. We did not hear what Baines said next because his signal started to break up. Jenna made an excellent pretense of trying to call him back but eventually appeared to give up.

"What the hell is going on?" demanded one of the captains.

"Can we please be patient and allow the major to speak," Addison said curtly. "A little bit of professionalism here would be appreciated."

Jenna waited patiently for silence before speaking again. "We are in a desperate situation. Betrayed by the government that was supposed to lead us to victory. I intend to unite all the free forces that the Europeans haven't yet taken. To form a resistance and fight back."

"My God, you're barely more than a child," one of the captains rudely interrupted. "I don't even understand how you are in this position, yet you are here saying you intend to command an entire fleet. I see now. I'm just wasting my time."

"If I may, Major Plural," Addison requested to speak, and when Jenna nodded, she stood up. "Captain Lewis. It may have escaped your notice, but Major Plural is genetically modified. The only reason she held the rank of lieutenant is because of that fact."

"You think I'm going to sit here and listen to a damn Gen-Mod?" Another captain argued. "Does no one remember the Grozny uprising?"

"Shut up and hear her out," said one of the other captains.

Addison continued. "I served under Major Plural as a rookie thirty years ago. She trained me, and she mentored me. Then she watched me being promoted over her."

"There is a reason we don't allow GenMods to hold senior officer positions," someone argued.

"And those reasons no longer hold true. If they ever did." This was another captain who came in unexpectedly. "The face of this war has changed. The old rules no longer apply. We need the best of the best. And Jenna Plural is even better than the best, and you can all damn well check your prejudice at the door."

A young captain indicated his desire to speak. Jenna nodded to him. "I, too, have served under Jenna Plural, as probably many people around this table at some time in their careers. Her leadership has saved my life and the lives of literally millions on many occasions."

"That is all well and good. Yes, yes, you have fluffy feelings about the lieutenant, but Baines is the obvious commander. He holds the current rank." Inputted the bigoted speaker.

Jenna responded. "That is something to which I would agree if it were not for the fact that Baines intends to join with the surrender. He has made that very clear to everyone here."

"And that is an option that is not yet off the table."

"It is off of any table I'm seated at. That is non-negotiable," Jenna snapped back. I nudged her, warning her to stay calm.

"Who the hell do you think you are that you get to set the agenda, Lieutenant?"

"I'm an American patriot who won't concede defeat until I'm dead with my gun still in my hand." "You sound like a fanatic, Jenna Plural."

"And you sound like a defeatist coward, Captain," Jenna growled. I placed my hand on her thigh and squeezed gently to warn her again.

"We are digressing," put in Addison. "If we are to fight back, we cannot do that as long as Baines stands in opposition to us and sowing discord."

"You expect us to take on the U.S.S. Constitution? Attack our own people?" someone blustered.

"Anyone unwilling to stand up and fight our oppressors is no longer one of our people," Jenna stated. "If Baines does not stand down quietly, he needs removing by force."

"Even if we agree, I still don't see how you're the best person moving forward. There are men and women around this table with thirty or forty years' command experience." An objector stated.

Addison laughed unapologetically at that and said something that shocked me to the degree I couldn't hide it, and I gasped. "Sir, Jenna Plural has served in the United States Marine Corps for more than a hundred and seventy years. Most of those were as a four-star general within the Department of Defense. She has more experience around this table than probably all of you combined. So, don't anyone dare suggest she does not have the experience."

"What about Phobos?" another captain said with contempt in her voice. "I'm hearing all sorts of horrific reports of a massacre of unarmed civilians by Major Plural."

At least she referred to her as "major," I thought.

"I've heard that too," said the original objector. I could not help but wonder how anyone could have heard about events on Phobos since it was only our crew who knew.

"Enough," Jenna shouted and slammed a fist down upon the table. "I don't know what you've heard about Phobos, but I know you haven't heard it from anyone who was there. Do we take our information from the Europeans now? I'm not going to explain my actions on Phobos beyond saying I did whatever was necessary. This is no longer a war of convention and treaty. This is no longer a war of rules of conduct. This is a war of resistance against seemingly insurmountable odds. Old rules, old laws, and old ways of thinking are out of the airlock. Hard decisions need to be made. They may not be pretty. They may not be popular. But they are necessary if we want to be free of the yoke of European oppression."

"You make a good case, Major Plural," said a captain who had been silent until now. "However, I think we should all get a vote on it."

Jenna looked like she was about to protest this, but I leaned in to advise her it was a good move.

She gave a slight nod and stood up. "Very well, ladies and gentlemen. Decision time. Those who wish to support me should indicate by flashing their transponder signals." Jenna removed her visor and turned on me aggressively. "Is the United States military now a democracy, Mr. Phelkar?"

I shrugged. "The vote will achieve two purposes," I told her. "First, if you win that vote, it will be clear-cut and unarguable. Secondly, we will know exactly who is in opposition to you."

"Assuming that I even win the vote," Jenna said gruffly.

"If you don't have support to win the vote, you will have trouble maintaining authority anyway. However, I think it's unlikely that you will lose."

However, the result surprised even me. I was expecting it to be a narrow margin one way or the other, but it was a landslide. I had severely underestimated the regard in which Jenna was held within the Marine Corps. Only sixteen ships voted against Jenna.

I told Addison to close the meeting as soon as the result was announced in case the validity of the vote was challenged. "It is the decision of the free Pacific Alliance forces that Jenna Plural assumes command of what remains of the United States fleet," Addison said. "I recommend we conclude this meeting and ask ship captains to stand by to await our new commanding officer's orders."

I signaled to Tracker to cut the broadcast before anyone could respond.

We sat quietly, reflecting for a few moments. We all knew it wasn't as simple as this. Baines wasn't gonna accept this vote. Jenna was far from having control while the Constitution was in his hands.

Jenna removed the communication devices from herself and sat back. First of all, she thanked Helen Tracker for her diligence. Then she addressed Addison and me. "We should hold a more private meeting now."

"Can I assume you will be transferring your command to the U.S.S. Los Angeles?" Addison enquired.

"You can. You can also assume that, as of now, you're my second in command." This did not surprise Addison or the rest of us, and she simply thanked Jenna for her trust.

"Of course, we are only dealing with the Americans here," Addison said as we headed to the captain's briefing room. "Many other nations out there will start arguing about putting themselves under the command of an American," Addison advised.

"I think that is where Mr. Phelkar will come in," Jenna said as we entered. "Do you think you can start sounding people out about their allegiances?"

"Of course, Major," I replied.

"Claire, could you call up Stacey, Sakamoto, and Hardy and have them come over? We need to discuss strategy."

As we waited for them to arrive, a steward served us drinks, and when all were together, Jenna surprised me with her opening words, for I thought it to be a resounding success. "The meeting went partially well. By a majority vote, I'm now the fleet commander. However, the problem arises because the remaining dissenters haven't sworn allegiance to me. This means I cannot trust them not to side with Baines."

"I can't see there is much you can do about that, Major," said Addison. "If you try to replace them, you may push them to do just that."

Stacey scoffed. "If we remove them permanently and off the radar, that's not something they can do."

A silence fell, and I looked up at Stacey in horror at the suggestion, but Jenna, who was smiling at her pilot, said, "That was my thinking."

Addison's eyes widened. "That is a dangerous step, Major, and one that could hit you in the face if not done correctly."

Jenna looked at her carefully. "I'm not hearing you object to the concept, though."

Addison toyed with a strand of her hair, something I would notice she often did when she felt uncomfortable. "I must admit you have completely hit me broadside with this suggestion, and I want to hear more before saying anything else."

Jenna nodded. She looked around the room. "Does anyone else wish to share an opinion?"

After a brief pause, Tracker spoke up. "If you want me to be totally honest, Major, I want no part of it. However, having said that, I will accept whatever it is you do. I believe in you and the path that we have started to follow. I'm even aware that we may have to kill fellow Americans in the coming days, but for me, that can only be in battle."

"I can accept that." Jenna nodded. "You're non-combat personnel, and I will try to ensure your ethics are not compromised." Jenna then looked at her closest follower. "Sakamoto?"

"I'm not happy about this direction," Sakamoto said pointedly. "Not happy at all. However, I think you're right. I don't think we can allow the opportunity of dissent."

Jenna turned back to Addison. "Well, Captain?"

The captain sighed. "I never thought that day would come when I would have to make this decision. I will support you, but I will warn you of this. You may find yourself in total revolt at the death of the captains of these ships."

"If I may share an opinion?" I said, raising my hand and looking around the room.

"Always, Mr. Phelkar," Jenna said, nodding to me.

"There is an alternative to killing them. It won't take much to place documents or other evidence to show these captains were cooperating in a conspiracy to assist the Europeans."

Jenna frowned. "It would have to be very convincing."

"I can do it, but...." I looked over at Tracker. "I will need some help."

Tracker sighed and looked down at the table, and then she sat back and bit the nail on her thumb.

After a pause, she looked up. "You can count on me, Mr. Phelkar."

"I don't think you should be involved in this any further," Captain Addison said pointedly to Jenna. "Throughout this endeavor, you need to have... let's say... clean hands."

Jenna pondered this, then looked back at Addison. "Find out if Charlotte Kensett is anywhere in this fleet. If she is, it will be in some form of security somewhere. Have her brought to me."

Everyone except me seemed to recognize this name, and not all reacted positively. Stacey clearly muttered something egregious, and Tracker looked startled. Addison nodded and radioed through the instruction to one of her team.

"Moving on," Jenna continued. "We have to discuss how we will take the Constitution. The issue is we have to cause minimal damage and as minimal loss of life as we can help."

"I think that will be most unlikely," said Addison. "She is the most advanced warship in the American fleet."

"Tracker, is there any way we could disable the ship's defenses remotely," Jenna asked.

Tracker did not even have to spend time thinking about it. She replied instantly. "Not a hope in hell. She maintains a tech team that constantly monitors for viruses and intrusions into their computer systems. The computer system itself is the most advanced we have. R&D has been working on upgrading all ships with one of them. It is the latest trans quantum computer and runs a billion times faster than anything we have. The only way I could shut anything down is if I was actually aboard the ship in the computer room."

"Then we must work on a way to get you aboard," Jenna said as if it was as easy as that.

"That is a tall order, Major," said Addison.

"Add that to the list for Charlotte Kensett if you find her," Jenna stated as she sat back and yawned. "I think we should call it a night. I, for one, am tired, and I think we should all get a good meal and some sleep."

Addison raised her hand to her head, receiving a call on her earpiece. She looked at Jenna. "We have found Charlotte Kensett. She is on board the Quincy Adams."

"Great, have her transferred to the Los Angeles and report directly to me," said Jenna, pleased.

"Can you set her up in a secure room?" she asked. "With any equipment she needs?"

"Of course," Addison replied. "I will secure a conference room for her."

"She will resolve the issue with no loose ends and can liaise with Mr. Phelkar here."

I couldn't help but wonder what she meant by that, but I soon found out during my first meeting with Charlotte Kensett.

"Excellent," I said. "I look forward to meeting this Kensett."

"Okay!" said Jenna wearily. "If there is nothing else, I'm out of here. Mr. Phelkar, you're with me."

Chapter
Twenty-One

Charlotte
Kensett

V ery early the following day, I met Charlotte Kensett in a prearranged conference room. I was most surprised to see that she was not military. She was a tall, slender woman with straight shoulder-length hair and what appeared to be an expensive designer business dress. It was blue and came down to just above her knee, contrasting with the black stockings. Her shoes matched the dress and had a two- to three-inch heel. She looked more set for a board room than a battleship.

The conference room had been turned into a command center with hastily erected computer terminals and screens around the walls. Kensett was seated behind the desk as I entered. She stood up, but I just waved her back down with a smile. "Good morning, Miss Kensett," I said, heading straight towards the drinks dispenser and ordering myself a coffee. "I'm sorry you have to be up so early." It was only four a.m.

"That is not a problem, Mr. Phelkar." She smiled but shook her head as I indicated the machine

and offered her a drink. "It's not like we can do this during regular business hours."

I glanced back, surprised by her accent, "You are British?"

She smiled, studying me for a moment before answering, "Expat. I became an American citizen some time ago."

"Why?" I asked, curious.

She smiled at me, "I don't think we are here to discuss my background. Are we Mr. Phelkar?"

I gave her a shrug that indicated a fair point, and I stepped in front of her desk, proffering my hand. "Please call me Michael."

She smiled graciously and took my hand. "Charlotte," she replied.

I took my seat opposite her. "We haven't had a chance to speak before this. Do you truly understand what it is we're doing today?"

She looked affronted by this. "Of course I do, Michael. We are removing obstacles to the smooth transition of Major Plural's command of the fleet."

"I guess you could put it that way," I said, actually amused at this unamusing situation. "And you have been fully briefed, but this operation is classified most secret?"

Her face narrowed into a frown of someone who now took offense. "Michael, I do know my job responsibilities, with all due respect."

"My apologies, Charlotte. You must understand that I'm just looking out for the security and safety of Major Plural."

Charlotte frowned again, and rising, she stepped around from behind the desk. She may have been dressed as a civilian, but her bearing was military, although her heels clip-clopping on the floor stood out. She leaned back against the desk right in front of me. She folded her arms and stared down at me with cold, intimidating eyes. "May I speak freely, Michael?"

"Of course," I replied pleasantly. "I'm not military and don't follow the military protocols."

"Thank you, Michael. Then with all due respect, the responsibility for the major's safety and security is now my job and not yours. She put me in this position personally and set the levels of my authority in carrying out special operations to maintain that safety and security."

"Indeed." There was something unpleasant about her extreme politeness while also putting me in my place. "Did she say what level of authority that is?"

There was a long pause before she responded. "My authority, Michael, is unlimited and unrestricted." She looked at her watch. "We have about ten minutes before this operation will commence. If you wish to confirm this with Major Plural, we can wait."

"That won't be necessary," I responded, a little intimidated.

She smiled at this. "Michael, I'm aware you are adjutant to the major, and in that position, you carry much power, albeit without military authority. I have to answer to Major Jenna Plural, albeit, at times, through you. But not to you. I answer to Major Plural and Major Plural alone. That is what she wants. Am I clear, Michael?"

Well, that certainly put me in my place. Trying to retain some dignity, I replied, "I'm just here to assist you, Charlotte, not usurp your authority."

"I'm so glad we understand each other, Michael. Your assistance is most valued and appreciated." The smile, this time, was quite a warm one, which only enhanced her creepiness. "Shall we get on with it?"

"Yes, of course. Perhaps you'll do me the courtesy of guiding me through your plans."

Again, she smiled, and it irritated me a little. "Of course." She sat back down in her chair, rolled it back to a terminal, and crossed her long legs. As I am sure you are aware, as you have followed this chronicle, the shapely form of a woman's legs was a weakness of mine and a frequent distraction. Especially when ending in an expensive pair of designer patent leather stilettos.

She picked up a remote control from the counter. Pressing a single button, all the monitors lit up. Dozens of them. Various corridors throughout the fleet. In each of those corridors stood four Marines armored with snap pistols. She turned to face them. "You're seeing my men outside the cabins of those captains who are intent on treason or mutiny against the major.

They will enter those rooms at precisely four-thirty and make the arrests."

"Can you speak to the personal loyalty of each of those Marines?" I asked.

Charlotte turned her chair back to me. "I cannot give you a confident answer to that. This is an odd situation. I can confirm they are loyal to the cause of fighting back. However, given time, I'm sure I can establish a security force loyal entirely to Major Plural, personally."

"Understood. Carry on," I replied, confused, for it did not sit right with me, and I was sure that was not Jenna's intent.

Kensett turned her chair back to the monitors, and after hitting another button on the remote, she said, "This is Kensett to unit leaders. We are four minutes out from a go. Report readiness." One by one, the unit leaders reported back their readiness to go. "Confirmed unit leaders," Charlotte replied. "Three minutes to go. Await my command to make entry. Remember, we want you to take them alive if possible. Do so unless they give you no alternative. If anyone interferes, you may respond with extreme prejudice. I repeat, if anyone interferes, respond with extreme prejudice."

I must admit I was impressed by her efficiency if not her style. She clicked another button, and another monitor came on with the clock counting down. When it got down to thirty seconds, Charlotte alerted them. I watched as each trooper did a final check on their arms and lined up on either side of the door of the rooms they were about to enter.

"Ten seconds, ladies and gentlemen." When she got down to five, she started a count-off. "Five, four, three, two,...." Then fast and urgently shouted, "Operation Badger is a go, make entry, go, go, go."

My eyes darted over each monitor, trying to follow what was going on. There was no sound, but I could almost hear the shouts of the unit leaders as they entered the rooms, and the cameras switched to the unit leaders' helmet cams.

Each small group made their way into the quarters of the captain they had come to arrest, some of whom jumped out of bed at the sound of the doors opening while others had their sheets pulled off them in a most undignified manner. All of them looked surprised but yielded to what was happening. Each was grabbed and pushed face down on their beds while another trooper cuffed them.

Charlotte pressed another button, and there was suddenly sound. Troopers were shouting aggressively at their new prisoners.

Charlotte hit yet another button. "If I may have your attention," she said calmly, and all the guards fell silent. A couple of the captains were still shouting protests. Charlotte waited patiently, her legs crossed, with her arms now folded, swinging back and forth in her chair ever so slightly. She did not speak again until all was quiet. "You're under arrest for crimes against the United States of America and our allies. Under new rules established by the fleet commander Major Jenna Plural, acting under emergency procedures, your rights in this matter have been suspended. You will be taken from here to be detained for an unspecified time until a court-martial can be held and this matter adjudicated. Take them away."

The captains were hauled off their beds and dragged back out into the hallway almost in unison. The last I saw of them was being frog-marched down the corridor.

Charlotte pressed yet another button, and the screens went off. She turned to face me again and smiled. "Operation Badger is a success, Michael. All perpetrators are in custody, and there were no fatalities."

"When will their courts-martial be held?" I asked. "I don't think it would be wise for them to be able to speak in a public forum. At least not until Jenna's position is firmly established and unquestioned."

There was a long pause as Charlotte studied me, but eventually, she smiled again and spoke quietly. "Oh, I have no intention of convening any courts-martial, Michael." I was completely confused by this, but my confusion was instantly dispelled before I could speak. "Please just trust me." Her voice was genuine, perhaps for the first time in our encounter. "The matter will be dealt with by myself and my team." I was about to protest when she simply said, "Plausible deniability. I'm not only protecting the major. I'm protecting you."

"I see," I said uneasily, "But how are we to explain this to the rest of the crew?"

"When they decline their rights to a trial and provide me with a full confession, that should be the end of the matter."

"But how can you—" I started to say, but she interrupted.

"That is not your problem, Michael. Please just let me do my job."

Another long silence hung between us as I reflected on her words. Finally, I said, "I see." Then I sighed and sat back in my chair, getting ready to stand up. "I will make sure the major knows how efficiently you dealt with this matter," I said curtly.

Charlotte raised an eyebrow. "I don't understand how you can do that since you were never here."

Again, I paused as I wrapped my head around this. I gave her a nod. "A pleasure working with you, Charlotte."

Charlotte nodded back. "Likewise, Michael."

And with that, I turned and left, unsure about what I felt about the situation. Did Jenna approve of this? I was not sure I wanted to know the answer. Of course, since that time, I have come to realize that all of this was absolutely necessary. After all, Jenna Plural is our only hope.

It was not the last I saw of the covert operations officer that day. She had been working with Jenna and Addison on the plan to disable the Constitution from within. I was not part of the planning, but I did attend the final briefing. Charlotte had changed clothes, and she now sported a black designer two-piece with matching heels that once more clip-clopped along the floor. "My operatives are preparing a distraction and will blackout cameras and alerts briefly," she was saying as I entered and took a seat between Tracker and Hardy. It was the only one available. Jenna gave me a brief smile, then returned her attention to Charlotte. "It will give you just three minutes to get Gunnery Sergeant Tracker into the Constitution's service airlock."

Addison looked to Hardy. "That enough time for you, Sergeant?"

"It will be tight but doable," the big oaf responded.

"One of my people will be there to let you on board, and once you are, well, that's my part over," Charlotte concluded.

Addison spoke next. "With her two guards, Tracker needs to make her way across the ship and down two decks to the quantum computer room. You will have ditched your EMUs and will be in the uniform of Constitution officers. Hopefully, you won't be challenged. However, you will be stopped at the computer room. It's unlikely you will get in without violence."

It was Tracker's turn to take over the briefing. "Once inside, it will take about ten minutes to decrypt the computer and shut down all power. With power down, the airlocks will unlock to enable evacuation."

Jenna looked at Addison. "Nothing personal to your pilot, but I would like to have Stacey at the helm of the U.S.S. Los Angeles for this mission. I'm giving her command of the Lady Liberty in the long term, but nothing personal to your pilot, but I trust Stacey more to pull this off."

Having worked with Stacey Grant for four years, Addison simply smiled and nodded. Stacey already knew that Jenna was going to announce this and spoke up. "On my lead, I will take in the Los Angeles close enough to release troops for a noncontact assault. That will be the signal to the other ships." By noncontact, she referred to troops in jetpacks who would fly across to the Constitution and burn their way through the hull without docking the ship.

Silence fell, and all eyes turned to Jenna, who sat back, legs crossed and deep in thought. "So many things can go wrong," she said at last. "If we screw this up, we are done for. Baines will throw everything he has at me." She glanced at Hardy. "Who are you taking with you?"

"I'm still going through personnel to decide," he replied.

"Take Dodgson," Jenna said, almost interrupting him.

"Dodgson, Ma'am?" He looked confused. "Dodgson is a fine Marine, but she lacks experience. I'd prefer—"

This time Jenna definitely interrupted. "Wasn't a suggestion, Hardy. I trust Dodgson's loyalty over anyone else's experience."

"But..." he started.

Addison shot him a glare. "The major gave you an order, Hardy, not an invitation to afternoon tea and a chat."

Hardy sighed. "Yes, Ma'am."

I could not help but show my amusement, and I, too, got a glare from Addison.

We watched from the bridge as the trio floated out of the Los Angeles, with Hardy and Dodgson each holding one of Tracker's arms as they set the thrusters towards the U.S.S. Constitution. It would take three hours to get there, and it was probably the bravest thing she had ever done. Tracker was no combat vet and certainly no spacewalker. However, after the painfully long wait, our hopes began to fail when no one came to open the airlock. Jenna called down to Charlotte, who came up to the bridge.

"What the fuck is going on, Charlie?" she growled at Charlotte as she entered the silent bridge with a clip-clop, clip-clop.

"Patience, Ma'am, I promise you my man won't let us down," she responded calmly.

We waited, Jenna growing ever more tense and curt with Charlotte.

"Two minutes to the point of no return," the pilot reported, meaning they would not have enough air to return to the Los Angeles. We had no way of talking to them, or them to us, without it being picked up by Baines. I was surprised Hardy was not aborting.

"Charlie!" Jenna growled again.

Charlotte raised a hand. "Patience," she repeated softly.

"And that's it. They have no chance of getting them back before they run out of air." The pilot sighed.

"Charlie, if you have just cost me—"

"Airlock opening," the pilot cried out. "They are going in."

Jenna jumped up to look at her monitor. When she turned back, Charlotte had gone.

Now we played the waiting game again. The covert team was heading for the central control room, and all our hopes were pinned on them. Failure now meant game over. Stacey came onto the bridge and stepped over to the pilot.

"Nothing personal, Mr. Samuels," Jenna said to him as he gave up the seat to her.

"No problem, Major, everyone knows Lieutenant Grant's reputation," he said smiling, "but do you mind if I stay and watch?" Jenna nodded with a smile.

"Take a seat beside me, mate," Stacey said, patting the co-pilot seat right before he joined her. Stacey then studied the scanners and waited with the rest of us. About thirty minutes later, she whooped and punched the air. We had no clue what she had seen as she powered up the engines and started to pull the Los Angeles around towards the Constitution.

"Are you sure, Stacey?" Jenna jumped up and went over to her.

"Yes, boss. She is listing like a drunken wombat." Stacey grinned, and suddenly the lights on the Constitution blinked out.

Jenna grinned and slapped Stacey on the back. "Well, get us in there."

"What do you think I'm doing? Waltzin' Matilda?" She laughed.

"Plural to Addison," Jenna called to the first officer who was down with the assault troops. "Ready on Stacey's mark."

"Affirmative, Major, ready on Stacey's mark."

The young pilot was now pouring on speed towards the behemoth that grew larger with every passing second. It looked at first as if we were going to smash right into it. Then at the last,

Stacey dipped the Los Angeles, and we shot underneath as she fired the retros to slow us. "Drop troops go," she shouted.

"Go, go, go." Addison could be heard on the intercom, and we saw tiny white pinpoints of troopers jetting across the abyss to the ship. We could also see the U.S.S. Houston and the New York come in at adjacent angles to perform the same action as we were. They began releasing their troops as I looked up at Jenna, who I had never seen happier than she was that day. "I can't just sit here and watch, Mr. Phelkar. I really can't."

"Well, you don't have much choice," I said, knowing I spoke to deaf ears.

Jenna looked up at me with a grin. "Idiot, you know I'm going over there."

I slowly shook my head disparagingly but said, "And you know I'm coming with you, then."

Chapter
Twenty-Two

22 Civil War

Thirty minutes later, we were aboard a shuttle with four Marines, including Thompson and Neuman, and a Marine I had not met before, Anna Grayson. I was sure I had never seen her on the Puller and assumed she was from the Los Angeles, but my assumption was wrong.

We exited out of the docking bay and headed towards the Constitution. Jenna was in full battle dress with an array of armaments. I, on the other hand, just carried my trusty snap pistol. The shuttle slipped through the dark and made its way over to the Constitution as Neuman passed around light-intensifying goggles to each of us, and we put them on. It seemed to take an eternity for us to reach the ship and attach ourselves to one of the airlocks. Jenna went ahead first, despite my protests. Thompson and Neuman followed behind her, and Grayson indicated for me to go ahead of her so she could bring up the rear. It was eerie stepping into the darkness of the ship yet being able to see everything as if it was daylight. Jenna moved ahead cautiously, rifle raised at the ready. "Let's head for the bridge," she said.

Occasional bursts of gunfire could be heard in the distance both ahead and behind us. The hope that the crew would stand down as they had on the Chesty had been in vain. There were many still loyal to the admiral.

We encountered a group of techs running towards us, and they stopped in fear, raising their hands as they engaged us. "Get in a room. Wait till this is all over," Jenna ordered. "You can come out when the lights come back on."

They raced away with a look of relief, and we continued carefully forward. Anna Grayson suddenly grabbed me by the arm and called abruptly to Jenna. "Stop, Major!"

Jenna stopped and glanced over her shoulder. Grayson indicated to the small limpet mine placed against the wall. It was the type that had a motion sensor. The moment we stepped past, it would have exploded. Neuman stepped up beside it and pulled a small gadget from his belt. He placed it next to the mine, and there was a high-pitched noise. The Marine nodded to Jenna that it was now safe to continue. We slowed down even more on the lookout for such other devices and traps. We encountered three more, all of which Neuman carefully deactivated. Just as he nodded that the last one was cleared, gunfire suddenly erupted from further ahead. He flew back into the wall amid a hail of bullets and slumped to the ground. My blood ran cold as I saw how close they had come to taking out Jenna. Swiftly, the Marines and Jenna returned fire. Grayson pushed past me and stood at Jenna's side. Two Constitution crewmen went down. Grayson bent down to briefly check for Neuman's pulse but stood up and stepped over his body without a comment. Thompson relieved his corpse of the small device for checking the limpet mines. I was startled, for I knew this guy fairly well. He was the Puller's great fry cook when not on duty, and it seemed wrong to just leave him here. But we carried on. We heard voices up ahead, and Jenna indicated for us to stop. She signaled Grayson forward, and together they turned the corner, ready to gun down any who resisted.

"It's okay, come on," Jenna called back to Thompson and me, and as I caught up, I saw it was Marines from the Los Angeles.

Jenna smiled at the unit leader. "Good to see you again, Nathan. I did not know you were aboard the Los Angeles," she said, fist-bumping the young man.

"Good to be fighting alongside you again, Lieutenant." The man then rapidly corrected himself.

"Sorry, I mean Major. Wow, you didn't waste time causing some heavy shit while we were in storage."

"You know me, Nathan, stars and stripes forever." She chuckled.

Nathan Dodd smiled back. "Well, we have got your back, Major, and in return, all we expect from you is our country back."

Jenna grinned. "I shall endeavor to oblige you, Corporal."

We continued to the bridge, unsure if the lack of gunfire was a good sign or a bad one. As we reached it, we could smell burning metal, which caused some concern that we had lost the bridge. However, we saw a group of Army rangers from the U.S.S. Houston burning through the door's seal with a laser cutter. The group leader turned and leveled his weapon at us, only lowering it slightly when he saw the U.S.S. Lewis Puller insignia. We had yet to update the crew uniforms.

"Identify?" he ordered.

"Major Jenna Plural," she said sharply.

The trooper instantly lowered his weapon and saluted, and the guy on the laser cutter wobbled slightly as he turned around, distracted by the arrival of the new fleet commander.

"We will be through the bulkhead here in a few minutes, Ma'am. I suggest you stand back as no doubt they will open fire upon us."

Jenna raised her gun and spoke calmly. "That won't be necessary, Lieutenant."

I gently rested a hand upon her back and shook my head at her. She looked back at me with frustration. "Very well." She lowered her weapon and stepped back to the side of the door.

There was a resounding crash of metal as the ranger kicked the improvised panel open, but there was not the expected gunfire, and the rangers looked quite surprised as the bridge crew filed out with their hands raised. Thompson and another Marine from Houston led them further down the corridor and made them stand against the wall with their hands against it.

Jenna and the leader from the Houston stepped inside, and I, as always, followed closely.

Baines was sitting alone in the captain's chair, and he turned it around to face us as we came in. "You really are quite the strategist, Jenna Plural."

"I do my best, Admiral," she said softly. "I'm sorry that it must come to this, but the cause is more important than any of us."

"I hope you remember that when the time comes. Don't let the power go to your head. Today you have proven yourself an exemplary leader of men and women. I salute you." He stood up and gave her the sharpest salute. Jenna handed me her rifle and returned it.

"It's not too late for you, Admiral Baines. You can help remove all doubt and unify this fleet by standing down from your present position and acknowledging me as the commander in chief of the free forces.

Baines looked surprised. "To be honest, Major Plural, I expected you to put me out of an airlock."

"That is still an option, admiral. However, you're more useful alive than as some martyr who will continue to fracture this new alliance."

"Very well, Major Plural, I concede to your command. I will send a message to those remaining loyal to me to transfer that loyalty to you. I have one condition."

"Which is?"

"I retain command of the U.S.S. Constitution, although it will be a part of your fleet."

Jenna nodded. "Agreed." That surprised me. I could not imagine her not taking her place on the most significant ship in our fleet. But I was soon to understand. "I will return to the Los Angeles while techs work on getting this ship up and active again. I look forward to working with you, admiral."

"It will be interesting, Major Plural." He smiled.

And with that, Jenna stepped out of the bridge as she strode down the corridor. She nodded to Anna Grayson to fall in with her. When it was just me, Jenna, and Grayson, the major turned to her and spoke with grim determination. "As soon as that cunt sends that message, shoot him and throw him out the airlock, but be discreet about it." Grayson nodded and fell back to the bridge.

A cold chill ran down my spine at this instruction, but all I said was, "How did you know that Marine would accept such an order?"

Jenna looked back at me. "Who? Oh, Anna. She's one of Charlotte Kensett's people," she said casually as if that answered everything. Unfortunately for me, it did. "Got a good solution for his death?"

It surprised me that I did not so much bat an eyelid when I replied. "Wait twenty-four hours. Then we will announce his suicide. 'Couldn't take the strain of losing the war. Yadda, yadda, yadda.'"

"That'll work," she responded, but as we headed back to the shuttle, I felt unease at how easily I had delivered that solution to a situation people may well have questioned the ethics of.

When we reboarded the Los Angeles, a cheer went up, and throughout the ship, the chant "Plural, Plural." As we entered the bridge, we were met by Captain Addison.

"Good to see you again, Captain," Jenna said.

Addison grinned. "Same goes for you, Major."

"Any news on the status of Helen Tracker?"

"She is safe back aboard this ship," she reported.

"There is an incoming transmission from Admiral Baines on ship-wide communications," said a young communications officer.

"Play it," Jenna ordered.

"This is Admiral Baines to all ships. It has been my honor to command the United States Outer System Fleet for these past seven years. However, times have changed, and me with it. I realize now that new leadership is required. Many of you heard my objections to turning over command to Jenna Plural, but she has proven herself to be a greater strategist than I. I withdraw my previous objections and formally stand down as admiral of this fleet. I asked those of you who also doubted the leadership of *Admiral* Jenna Plural to put aside that distrust now and join with me in supporting her. God Bless America, Baines out."

I looked at Jenna, and she looked back at me with the broadest grin on her face. She had achieved what many would have said was impossible. Jenna Plural was in command of what was left of the United States military.

The celebration did not last long. About ten minutes. I had never seen Helen Tracker angry. She stormed onto the bridge shouting and cursing. "That dumb motherfucker you sent with me blew up the fucking computer room."

Jenna looked startled by this outburst. "What are you talking about?"

"Hardy. I was having trouble getting through the firewalls, and he stepped in and blew the damn thing up,"

"He was just making sure the mission succeeded," Jenna said, defending the big lummox.

Tracker now sounded exasperated. She threw her hands into the air. "Major, that was a tri-quantum computer system. Only six of them are known to currently exist in the entire solar system. The ship was built entirely around them. Without it, the U.S.S. Constitution is a floating piece of scrap metal." Jenna sighed, remaining remarkably calm in the circumstances. "And I take it you can't repair it?"

"Possibly, but I can't guarantee it. There will be parts that need to be replaced and are difficult to find for a start. Even then, it's weeks of work."

I won't repeat all the words of profanity that came out of Jenna's mouth. I will stress that they were not aimed at Tracker but at the situation in general. I have to be honest and admit that I hoped she would do to Hardy what she did to Stephanie Morris. No such luck.

"This looks like a job for you, Mr. Phelkar." Jenna turned to me. "Take as many people as you need and go through the entire inventory of the damned fleet to find everything Tracker needs." I nodded in response as she turned back to Tracker. "Get to work on making Mr. Phelkar a list of everything you want. Strip every ship apart if you need to, goddamn it. I will personally shoot anyone who gets in his way. I'm not going to lose the Constitution."

Going from commanding a small ground unit to a fleet that was in disarray before we even arrived kept Jenna constantly busy with meetings late into most nights. I rarely saw her over the next couple of weeks.

I frequently found myself in one of the U.S.S. Los Angeles mess halls in the evenings. I had been drinking more than ever and even when on duty but was oblivious to what was becoming a problem.

I spent the time alone with my thoughts and a beer and a whiskey chaser or three on the side. However, one night I had a surprise companion.

"Hey there, Mr. Phelkar." Dodgson drew me from my thoughts, and I looked up. It was a busy night, and she had to speak loudly to be heard. "Mind if I join you?" She said, her stammer a little more obvious.

I smiled up at the young corporal and indicated the seat opposite me. "I will be delighted by your company."

"Thank you, Sir." She smiled sweetly and slipped into the chair as I waited for one of the stewards.

"So, how are you doing?" I asked her, trying to put her at her ease. I had always thought that the stammer was due to nervousness. However, I would eventually find out that it was due to an inoperable brain injury Caused by childhood abuse by her father. Even in these days, there were some things medicine couldn't fix.

"I'm okay," she said, but she had a look on her face as if she wanted to ask me something but was unsure of herself.

"Is there something you want to talk to me about, corporal?"

"Well, Sir, there is a rumor that Admiral Plural it's going to give me a commission. Make me an officer."

I knew that Jenna was making changes to the command structure and replacing people with those she knew she could trust without reservation. We were living in strange times, and the usual promotion procedures were no longer to be applied. "I have not heard anything specifically about you, but I will say this. If Jenna Plural thinks you have what it takes, then you have what it takes."

"Yes, Sir," she replied but did not appear quite placated.

"You know, I'm not an officer. You don't have to call me 'Sir.' You don't even have to call me Mr. Phelkar. My name is Michael."

Before she could reply, someone else responded. "What sort of a name is Phelkar?" Stacey Grant jumped over the back of the couch and fell into the seat beside me. I couldn't help but notice a sudden disappointment on Dodgson's face. Stacey was pressed against my side and slipped her arm into mine. "I mean, it's not like it's even a real name."

"My parents were born on Mars. It was a tradition back when Martian independence was a thing. People started making up names that had no national boundaries. My name would have been Phillips had they been born on Earth. That was before the war, and both sides decided that discussing independence for Mars was treason."

Stacey looked up at me with disinterest in what I was saying. She then looked at Dodgson. "Phelks is an okay bloke, but he can be such a long-winded wanker sometimes."

Dodgson smiled, but it was clearly feigned. "Yes, Ma'am."

Stacey waved the back of her hand at the young corporal. "We are off duty. Cut the Ma'am shit and call me Stacey. Actually, cut the Ma'am shit altogether. I don't go in for that."

Dodgson shifted uncomfortably in her seat but nodded. "Yes, ma... Stacey." She was clearly not at ease with the suggestion.

I felt the tension in Stacey's body dissipate. Something I had not noticed was there until it was gone. "Seriously, Dodgson," she said in a tone that I had not heard before from the young Australian. It was as if that crazy outback girl persona was some-what of a façade. "Tonight, we leave the war behind us." She smiled, not that cheeky smile she perpetually wore, but a more sincere one.

Dodgson relaxed slightly and smiled back. "Then please call me Emma."

Stacey grinned, and that inane look was back. "How about I call you Em and make it more Aussie-like?"

Dodgson laughed. "As you wish."

"I have worked with you a while now, but I don't know much about you," I told Dodgson. "Why did you join the Marines?"

"Bloody hell, Phelks," Stacey interrupted, "you have two of the hottest women in the damn fleet sitting here, and you wanna talk shop!" She winked at Dodgson, who chuckled lightly.

At that moment, the steward finally arrived, and I ordered a light beer for myself, but Stacey once again interrupted. "Screw that, Phelks. Hey mate, do you know how to make Melbourne firebombs?" The steward indicated that the barman did. "Make that three and throw in another three as a chaser." He nodded and departed as Stacey sat back and snuggled further against me. "So how come a cute girl like you is all alone?"

Before she could think, Dodgson replied. "Well, I wasn't alone." She instantly regretted the statement and colored up slightly, glancing at me and then away. I, too, colored somewhat, for I had completely forgotten that the young corporal appeared to have an interest in me.

Stacey couldn't help but grin. "I'm sorry. Did I interrupt something?" Dodgson shook her head and looked away, biting her thumbnail. "You know, I always thought you preferred girls."

Dodgson looked back, wide-eyed, at Stacey. "What have I ever done to give you that idea?" Stacey shrugged. "You remind me of a friend of mine. My best mate, actually. She liked the ladies."

"You must be worried about her with everything going on," I said.

Stacey sighed and stared off into space. "Not really, mate. She's dead."

I recalled the picture on her bedside cabinet of her with a young woman. "I'm sorry to hear that."

However, Stacey simply shrugged it off. "It's what happens during a war. It comes to all of us eventually."

Dodgson reached up to take a Melbourne firebomb from the tray as the steward returned. Both Stacey and I followed suit. Uncomfortable with the way the conversation was going, I downed both of mine in one and took the next, saying, "Same again, and keep them coming." I could barely get the words out as the drink burned in my throat.

"Nice one, let's call this a party." Stacey grinned.

"Actually," Dodgson said uncomfortably, "I should probably go."

"I'm sorry, mate," Stacey said, her tone soft again. "I have made you uncomfortable. I didn't mean to. Please stay."

"Stacey's mouth is more active than her brain," I said to Dodgson.

"Ain't that the truth." Stacey smiled. Dodgson smiled and forced herself to relax a little as I called the steward to hurry up with the refills. "Actually, you're quite a cute girl," Stacey said appreciatively.

Dodgson gave a genuine chuckle. "I'm really not into women."

Stacey shrugged. "Nor am I. At least, I wasn't until I met Jenna Plural. Now she is hot."

Dodgson laughed. "Now that I cannot deny."

"You cannot help but wonder what she's like in bed with all that genetic perfection." Stacey downed her third firebomb as soon as it arrived.

"I don't think that's an appropriate way to talk about our commanding officer," I said impatiently, waiting for my fourth firebomb to arrive.

"More inappropriate than rooting her, Phelks?"

I couldn't hide the startled look on my face. "What are you talking about?"

Stacey grinned. "Rumor has it that you're fucking the major... sorry. I mean admiral."

As the steward returned, I took two more firebombs from the tray. "I don't know what you're talking about." I looked towards Dodgson, who was staring at me wide-eyed.

Stacey noticed it too. "Looks like we are both outmatched when it comes to gaining the affections of Mr. Phelkar," she said with a chuckle.

Rather than get embarrassed this time, Dodgson grinned. "Well, it certainly increases the challenge." The firebombs were taking effect, and the customarily reserved Dodgson started to come out of her shell. Her stammer had all but disappeared.

"Well, he knows what he is missing with me." Stacey grinned, glancing up at me.

After downing another firebomb, Dodgson raised an eyebrow and looked back at Stacey. "Is there anyone that Mr. Phelkar isn't sleeping with?"

"Well, it's not like he's an amazing stud or anything, but there was an amazing lack of men on the Chesty."

I took Stacey's arm and pulled it from mine, pushing it away. "Well, thank you," I said curtly, somewhat offended by the statement.

She elbowed me playfully in the ribs. "Oh, come on, Phelks, I'm just joshing you, ya moron." She slipped her arm into mine again, and I did not resist. My head was seriously buzzing now, and all of our speech was becoming slurred slightly. "So, you and the boss. That's just a rumor?"

"Of course it is," I said. At the time, I was only thinking of how Jenna wanted to keep our relationship on the down low. It wasn't because I intended what would happen later. I had made inappropriate decisions, but none of them were planned.

Stacey looked up at me. She had a brief quizzical look, and then that silly grin returned. She looked over at Dodgson. "So, what do you think of a young Emma here? She's quite a cutie."

"She's younger than my daughter."

Instantly the inebriated Dodgson came back. "I like older men."

Stacey, however, glared up at me. "How old do you think I am?"

"Never thought about it, to be honest. How old are you?"

"I'm twenty-seven." She then looked at Dodgson. "How old are you?"

"I'm nineteen."

I grinned and shrugged. "And my daughter is twenty-two, so I stand by my statement."

"You're such a fucking arsehole." Stacey pouted.

I reached over and kissed her on the side of the head where her hair was shaved. She pulled her head away, but I could tell she was only feigning contempt. We ordered another round of drinks. I was somewhat aroused at the intimations of the conversation. I looked at Dodgson, wondering what it would be like to have her. She noticed me looking and had that look on her face as if she knew what I was thinking, and a smile crossed her lips. I finished the next firebomb and ordered yet another.

I had enough sense left to realize I was walking down a dangerous road with my young assistant. So, I finished my final firebomb. "As nice as this has been, I think I'm going to retire. I have to be up early in the morning."

"You see, Em, that's the problem with older guys. They may know what they're doing in the bedroom, but they have no stamina."

Dodgson laughed. "It's the knowing what they are doing that makes them most interesting."

Yes, it was time for me to get out of there. Untangling myself from Stacey, I rose unsteadily to my feet. "And on that note, I will bid you ladies goodnight."

"Yeah, yeah, fuck you, mate." Stacey grinned at me. Dodgson smiled at me but had a disappointed look in her eyes as I turned and left.

Chapter Twenty-Three

Rules of the Navy Way

I wasn't back in my room for more than twenty minutes when there was a knock on my door. I had taken an Alcorin pill, and it had already had its designed effect, sobering me and leaving nothing more than a faint buzzing in my head.

Stacey stood in the doorway and looked up at me. There was a long silent pause before she said, "You could have had both of us tonight."

"Maybe." I shrugged. "But I would have regretted it in the morning and had a complicated relationship with someone working as my aide."

"Life is always complicated, Phelks. Like it makes no sense why I'm interested in you again." She lifted up on her toes to kiss me, and, once more, without thinking of any consequences, I went with it. At that moment, Jenna was the furthest thing from my mind. Memories of our previous time together came flooding back. All I knew right then was that I wanted Stacey Grant. All that mattered was that I had her right here and right now.

I made to pull her into the room, but she resisted. "No, not here, mate. I want to show you something."

She took me by the hand and led me back out into the corridor, and I quickly realized we were not heading in the direction of the crew cabins. "Where are we going?"

Pulling me along, she looked back at me. "Come on. I'll show you."

She led us down a corridor towards the engineering section but suddenly stopped. Letting go of my hand, she looked around conspiratorially. Then, pulling out a small utility knife, he turned toward an air vent and, using the point, started to unscrew it.

"What are you doing?" I asked, a little concerned.

Looking back over her shoulder, she frowned at me, "Bloody hell, Phelks. Just keep a lookout, would ya?"

Despite my strong reservation, I did as I was told, and soon, she pulled off the grating. "Get inside."

Reluctantly I complied, and the young pilot crawled in after me. "What the hell are we doing?" I asked nervously.

"Just keep going, turn right so as you get towards the end." She said, pulling the grating back in behind her.

I continued following her directions as she whispered them to me from behind. The sound of the ship's engines grew louder, and the ventilation shaft began to vibrate.

"Okay, you can stop now," Stacey instructed.

I turned on my side. There wasn't even space to sit up, and I looked back at Stacey, who crawled up to me, then lay on her side, facing me and resting her head in her palm. "Do you feel it, Phelks?"

"Feel what?

Stacey chuckled. "The vibration of the ship."

"Of course I do. What of it?"

"Have you never fucked in a vibrating ventilation shaft before, Phelks?" She said with a cheeky grin.

"You want to do it here?" I did not even try to hide my surprise.

"What can I say?" She shrugged a shoulder. "It's the Navy Way."

I chuckled at this. "Is everything the Navy Way?"

Stacey grinned mischievously and said seductively. "Oh, my dear, Phelks, the rules of the Navy Way are very simple." She kissed me long yet gently, our tongues exploring each other. She pulled back and raised a finger. "Rule number one, the Navy Way is any way a Navy girl wants it." She slid her hand down and started unfastening my belt. "And, two, what this Navy girl wants, she gets."

She reached up and pulled my head to hers, and kissed me hard. I ran my hand across her hip and down to her leather-clad thigh. I became aware once more of the marked difference between the two. Jenna, well-toned, muscular. Stacey, softer, curvier.

She let go of my head and pulled back. Once more, that cheeky-looking grin returned. I jumped as a hand suddenly grabbed my crotch, and she chuckled lightly. "Relax, mate," she said as she started to unfasten my pants. I leaned in and kissed her again, softer this time. I then inhaled sharply as her cold fingers closed around me. She grinned wickedly and slipped down out of my view. I moaned softly as her mouth enveloped me. I reached down to run my hands through her hair and was momentarily startled again by the amount of gel and other products she used to keep it in position. She knocked my hand away, clearly not wanting me ruining her style. When she came back up to me, we struggled in that cramped ventilation shaft to remove her leather skirt, becoming almost comical. Eventually, still half-dressed, we made love, and it was, as before, the most amazing experience I had ever had. We had tried to keep our noise at the minimum throughout the encounter, but finally, as we came together, she let out a cry, and it echoed down the ventilation shaft. I swiftly covered her mouth with my hand grinning with pride. As her body finished convulsing against me, she let out a soft sigh, and I removed my hand, and she grinned up at me, "Bloody hell, Phelks, you have suddenly improved."

I chuckled, and I pulled out, falling on my back next to her. We lay there for a minute or two, just catching our breath. She turned to face me and reached out to stroke my cheek. I was startled to see a single tear running down her face. "What's the matter?" I asked, almost distraught with concern. The last thing a guy wants to see is a girl he just made love to cry.

She shook her head, and wiping away the tear, she said, "It's nothing, don't worry about it."

"Please tell me. If I have done something wrong, I would like to know."

She shook her head again and smiled at me softly. "You haven't done anything wrong, mate, you make me happy, and that's the problem." Confused, I just looked at her questioningly, and she sighed and, lying on her back, stared up at the roof of the ventilation shaft. "Did you want to be with me tonight, or would you have preferred to have been with Jenna or Dodgson?"

Had she asked me this during our last encounter, I would have lied, but I could be sincere this time. However, I was surprised by the question from this usually overconfident young pilot.

"There was nobody on my mind, but you, and that's the truth."

She looked at me and smiled weakly. "You're full of shit, Phelks. But thank you." She leaned over and kissed me softly.

"So, what has got you in this negative frame of mind?"

She shrugged. "Just been thinking about home a lot lately. And the last day I saw Oz."

"Want to tell me about it?"

She stared down the ventilation shaft. "When my country fell to the Peons, I was there. I was piloting an aircraft during the final battle."

"The Battle of Cape York?" I clarified.

She nodded and continued. "Most of my squadron were blown out of the sky, and just three of us were left. The order came through to cut and run. I didn't want to. I initially refused. But my best mate, my gunner, convinced me to. We had nowhere to fly to in Australia unless you wanted to put down in the Outback. New Zealand had already fallen, so we headed to the only safe location. We made it to Japan, where we finally learned that we had surrendered. I swore that day I would never be happy again until our flag flew over Canberra once more." She turned and looked at me once more. Tears trickled down the side of her face. "Can you understand that, Phelks?"

"Yes, I can," I said softly. "So, how did you end up in the U.S. Navy?"

"I'm not really. I'm in what they call the Australian Free Forces, attached to the U.S. Marines. Jenna wanted me as her pilot, and the Puller is a Navy ship. So on paper, I'm Navy. Hell, Jenna would have me listed as a sanitation worker if it kept me as her pilot."

"Fair enough. Tell me more."

"Well, I crashed my aircraft in Japan. And that's when I lost my eye. While I was in the hospital, Jenna visited me. She wanted to recruit me for a mission that required my piloting style. I agreed with some conditions." She chuckled at that last point.

"Which were?" I said, curious about the sort of conditions this unconventional woman would have demanded.

Stacey grinned. "That I don't have to call anyone Sir or Ma'am. Everyone calls me Stacey. And the case of Portobello Brandy."

I laughed. "I take it that is the same brandy we drank back on the Chesty."

"The very same. I have three bottles left. One I'm saving to drink on the banks of Wagga beach when I get back." Her face turned sullen once more. She reached up and stroked the name exquisitely tattooed on her neck. "I can't tell you anything about that mission. It's still classified, but I lost my best mate, which was the final straw."

"Is that the girl in the picture I saw in your quarters?" I asked gently.

Stacey managed to smile. "Yep, that is Harper Davis. She was just a kid when she died—nineteen years old. So desperate to become a pilot. She idolized me. I don't know why. I'm not exactly what role models are made of." She paused and gave a gentle sigh, "All I live for now is to kill Peons, and for the day I get to go back Downunder."

"I can understand that," I said, but she frowned when I added, "though I am sometimes concerned about how we go about it."

"Meh," Stacey shrugged and looked back up at the shaft. "I used to think like that. Jenna's methods may be considered brutal, but she gets the job done. I trust her. Probably the only person I trust. She told me once, 'There should only be one rule to war, and that's not to start one, but if you do, then all bets are off.'" I could not agree with that statement, at least not back then. There was a moment of silence before she looked at me again. "So, Phelks, what I'm really saying is that it has been four years since I allowed myself to have feelings for anyone. Been close a few times but being around you makes me happy. I get the feeling you feel the same. Have we got something here, or am I just making a fool of myself?"

It was only then that the weight of guilt descended upon my shoulders. She had no idea that I was involved with Jenna, and I had not only just cheated on her, but I had also done so with someone she considered a very close friend. However, before I could reply, a voice boomed out, "Whoever is in there, come on out. You have ten seconds to comply before we flood the vent with neuron gas."

I sat up sharply, banging my head on the roof of the ventilation shaft with considerable force. I cried out, and Stacey burst out laughing as she scrambled to pull on her underwear and skirt.

"Wait! Stop! We are coming out," I shouted down the ventilation shaft. Hastily dressing, we headed to where the voice came from. It was at a different grate, and we had to lower ourselves to the ground. I helped Stacey out even though she did not need it and followed her. A young official-looking lieutenant stood with his arms clasped behind his back, looking daggers at us. Behind him stood four armed guards with their snap pistols pointed at us.

"What were you doing in the ventilation shaft?" he demanded aggressively.

"Bloody hell, mate, we were just exploring," said Stacey with mock innocence.

He glared at Stacey with contempt, "Civilian crew are not allowed in this area." He looked her up and down. As per usual, she was not in uniform. "Goddamn Aussie refugees," he sneered, shaking his head slowly. "Vagrants of the solar system. I will never understand why we ever let you on to our ships."

I tried to stop her. When I heard those words coming out of his mouth, I knew there would be a problem. Stacey stepped forward casually, then suddenly head-butted him squarely into the face. His nose blossomed into a crimson flower of blood, and it splattered everywhere, and he staggered back with a cry.

She moved in to inflict more damage, but my hand was on her shoulder, and the rifle muzzles pulled up to her face made her back off. She stepped back quickly, raising her hands.

"Easy now," I said, stepping between Stacey and the guards. The officer, holding onto his bloodied nose, stepped towards her. I blocked his way with my hands raised towards him. "Let's calm it down. You know you asked for that, Lieutenant."

He stood staring at me for a long moment, weighing up his options until he finally said to Stacey, "Who do you report to?"

Stacey stared death at the young officer until, eventually, she said, "Jenna Plural."

The man's face went from anger to surprise, and he hesitated before asking nervously, "Name, rank, and number?"

"Captain Stacey Grant, commanding officer of the U.S.S. Lady Liberty. And I don't just give out my number to any guy. Especially to dumb American mother fuckers."

The men with the guns looked at each other and rapidly lowered them. The Lieutenant paled, and looking at me, he nervously said in a gentler tone, "And you, Sir?"

I smiled, hiding my irritation at his treatment of my friend. "Michael Phelkar, I have no rank, for I'm a civilian. I'm an adjutant to Admiral Plural."

He swallowed hard, "my apologies, Captain." He said to Stacey.

"Fuck you," Stacey replied in her delicate way.

The officer stiffened, clearly frustrated at how he was being spoken to yet neutered by her newly

revealed rank. "I still have to report this incident to Captain Addison," he said, sounding stuffy.

"Lead the way, you fuckwit." Stacey indicated for him to go ahead.

Twenty minutes later, we were standing in front of the desk for Captain Addison. To my surprise, Stacey stood at attention. Addison sat reading the officer's report as if we were not even there. She then let out a sigh and, dropping the tablet onto the desk, she looked up at each of us in turn. "Okay. Let's hear it."

Stacey and I looked at each other, but neither spoke at first. "I'm entirely to blame, Ma'am," Stacey said eventually.

"No, you're not. I knew what I was doing," I said to her.

Addison banged a fist on her desk. "You will address me, Mr. Phelkar, and not Captain Grant. Do you understand me?"

"Yes, Ma'am."

"We were exploring the ship," Stacey said.

"You were fooling around in the ventilation shaft," Addison corrected.

"How could you possibly know that, Captain?" I asked.

Addison raised an eyebrow. "Because, my dear Mr. Phelkar, you are apparently so good that Captain Grant's ecstasy was picked up on audio sensors." Instead of being embarrassed, Stacey snorted and brought her hand up to her mouth to stop from laughing. "It's not funny, Captain Grant."

"No, Claire." The young Australian struggled to keep a straight face.

"Stacey, I worked with you for four years. I would go as far as saying I consider you a friend. But you have now been given command of a ship, and your old ways won't work anymore. The major has always given you a lot of latitude due to some bizarre agreement you had when you joined her, but you do need to start becoming an example to those you command. We need you out there."

"Yes, Ma'am," Stacey said, but with a tone of disinterest.

Addison sighed and shook her head, knowing that her words were falling on deaf ears. "Very well. Stacey, you ought to confine yourself to the U.S.S. Lady Liberty and not leave it unless directly ordered to do so by myself or Major Plural. Am

I understood?" Stacey nodded. "You're dismissed." We turned to leave, but Addison wasn't finished. "Not you. Mr. Phelkar." Stacey shot me an apologetic look before heading out the door. I turned back to Addison, who sat glaring at me. "What the hell do you think you're doing?"

"What do you mean, Captain?"

"Are you, or are you not, in a relationship with Jenna?"

I stared at her incredulously. "With all due respect, Captain, I think that is none of your damn business."

"With all due respect, Mr. Phelkar, the well-being of this fleet and its commanding officer are very much my damn business. We need her to focus. We need her head in the game, and we don't need her to be distracted by your shenanigans with other women."

"Again, with all due respect, I'm not in your chain of command. If I do or do not have a relationship with Admiral Plural, I can assure you that I will always have the best interests of her and her mission at the forefront of my heart."

Addison sighed. "You need to be there for her if that is what she wants. Everything is riding on her."

I tried to quell the rising anger. I admit that my relationship with Jenna Plural had given me a self-absorbed feeling of importance. "Captain Addison, it is not appropriate of me to discuss my relationship with the admiral. I assure you everything is fine."

"I hope so, Mr. Phelkar," she said, and before I could say anything more, she added, "Dismissed."

As I returned to my quarters, the reality of what I had done was just beginning to sink in. I had cheated on Jenna Plural and had deceived Stacey Grant into thinking I was available. As I climbed into bed, I wondered how Jenna would react when she found out. But what bothered me more were the feelings I was developing for that coarse little Australian.

Chapter Twenty-Four

The Battle of Deep Space

There were many changes in personnel over the coming weeks. It was quite unconventional, but these were desperate times. Tracker was given a field commission and promoted to captain to take over as Head of Technical Services. Stacey officially got the command of the Lady Liberty with the new rank of captain, and Sakamoto took command of the Chesty with a similar promotion. The only real change that affected me was that I lost Dodgson, who, along with Hardy, was now permanently assigned to the U.S.S. Constitution. Dodgson was indeed getting a commission, but it would not come into effect until they had someone to replace her current duties.

Abigail Thompson, who had joined us on Phobos, also received a commission and became my official military aide as I took up the role of Chief of Civil Affairs. I'm not about to knock the efficiency of Lieutenant Thompson, but she was not an experienced logistics officer. Less than a month before, she was a sergeant whose primary skill was as a sniper. Now, however, she was assisting me in responding to the whining complaints of dozens of ship captains, from garbage haulers to luxury liners. One such ship, the Twilight Wanderer, was a state-of-the-art vessel. A cruise liner that had been taking some of the richest people in the U.S.A. and other allied countries on a luxury trip to see the rings of Saturn.

And along with wealth also comes superior expectation. I received many calls in my office for demands, mostly from executives believing they had the right to speak to Jenna directly. I was compelled to instruct the captain of the Twilight Wanderer to restrict all outgoing calls. But there were others. Ones with true emergencies, such as a lack of fuel or food. Thompson and I began a redistribution program to ensure everyone's needs were met. This was frequently met with reluctance from the ships having to give up some of their stores. On one occasion, I had to threaten to board the ship with Marines to take what we needed. So, as you can understand, tensions were running high; however, despite the hiccups, Thompson and I managed to organize the civilian fleet into some semblance of order.

It also befell me to negotiate with and appease the non-American forces that were initially unwilling to fall under the command of an American. While I extolled the virtues and abilities of Jenna Plural, I was stymied at every attempt to get an agreement.

It was Jenna herself, in a surprising act of anti-diplomacy, that resolved the issue. She canceled my transfer of all resources from U.S. ships to non-U.S. and sent a message to the foreign commanders stating they were welcome to leave and fend for themselves if they were unwilling to accept their position in the new fleet. She then gave them twenty-four hours to depart. Within twelve hours, every nation, except the Japanese, had signed on to Jenna's authority. The Japanese would join us later, but that is more Stacey's story to tell.

Four days later, something happened that was about to potentially undo all our hard work. Ships on the outer edge of the fleet started to report picking up incoming vessels which would not transmit transponder codes. We had hoped this was more American ships, as seventy-five percent of the original fleet was unaccounted for. However, by the following day, that hope died when it was realized they were Peons and heading towards us. Jenna was about to begin her new command in a baptism of fire.

I was summoned to a briefing, the first in a few weeks that Jenna headed. I arrived slightly late as Addison was given an account of the current situation. "At the current rate, they will arrive in about five days, but if the faster cruisers detach from their main fleet, they could make it here in three."

"If we head in the opposite direction, can they catch us?" An officer, who I had not seen before, asked.

"Not If we traveled at the speed of the slowest ship, and we would also have to abandon the U.S.S. Constitution," Addison advised.

"Damn it to hell," Jenna cursed. "I'm not giving up the Constitution. Our priority is to get that ship back online. She's the real hope in this situation."

"Tracker already has every advanced technician in the fleet aboard the Constitution as we speak," I stated.

Jenna sighed with frustration. "Call her now."

Seconds later, the tech came online. "Tracker here, go ahead, Admiral."

"We have an incoming Peon fleet five, possibly three, days out. I need the Constitution back up and running," Jenna said determinedly.

"I don't wish to be the bearer of bad news, Admiral. There is no hope in hell that I'm going to achieve that deadline. I need two weeks, minimum."

"If you turn your attention just to the battle systems, can you at least get her to move and launch her craft?" Addison asked.

Tracker pondered. "Well, it's doable, but it might be flaky. Every system runs on the old computer, and it's going to require my team and me to bypass the failsafe constantly during the battle. I don't recommend it."

"I'm sorry, Helen, but we don't have a choice. See that we can move that hunk of junk when we need to and that we can dispatch infantry."

"We will do what we can." The line went dead.

Jenna rose from her seat, and she began to pace back and forth, thinking hard. She then looked up at Addison. "Take all the heavy combat ships, the fastest ones you can think of. Set a direct course for the nearest Peon base no matter how far away it is and head full speed toward that."

"I don't think we're in a position to attack a Peon base at present." Addison looked shocked. "The crews haven't nearly had enough adjustment times with all the rearrangements we've done."

"You're not going to attack. You're just going to make the Peons think you are. What do you think the Peons will do if they detect our heaviest warships heading towards one of their bases?"

"They would change direction to intercept," I backed her up, grinning as I realized her plan.

"Exactly, Mr. Phelkar. They will think we have abandoned the slower ships on some crazy hair-brained scheme by a dumbass lieutenant to take out their base. It would be like we were trying to perform the last hurrah. It will extend our time to ready the other ships, and once the Peon fleet is between us, we will come up them from the rear."

Addison smiled. "That might just work."

I interjected at this point, "One of the objectives of the Peon will be to take you out, Admiral. I suggest you transfer the slowest and most unlikely ship in the fleet. One that they are likely to ignore."

Addison didn't like this idea. "But what if they do take notice? She will be defenseless. We can't risk losing the Admiral."

"I don't think they will," I insisted.

Addison shook her head. "That's a big risk if you ask me."

Jenna ended the debate in my favor. "I trust Mr. Phelkar's judgment. What ship has the least crew and is furthest behind in preparation?"

"U.S.S. Kamchatka, it's a Chechnyan garbage freighter. It dumps waste from various bases into deep space," Addison advised after checking the roster.

Jenna laughed, "Well, that's an interesting place to start my new command. Have them come dock with us."

"Actually, Major," I interjected. "It's probably a good idea if we even keep this from the crew. I don't think they will think the Kamchatka is here to pick up garbage, and we don't want to draw attention to it. Let's just take one of the shuttles over to the ship during routine ship transfers."

"Very well," Jenna agreed.

"It would also be good if we blast the airways with multiple traffic signals as you leave," Addison recommended. "That way, if anyone is listening in, they won't pick up your transit comms as you fly out there."

Jenna nodded, "Smart thinking, do it."

A moment of silence hung between us as we all contemplated what would happen in the next few days. Addison broke it by saying, "This is where you make your mark, Jenna. The results of this conflict will set the mark for everything to come. It won't be just about winning. It will be about *how* we win."

"We will make a show of it, trust me on that," Jenna said determinedly.

We watched the Los Angeles and the alpha ships of the fleet depart the flotilla from the small shuttle piloted by Anna Grayson as we headed for the small garbage hauler. We had not informed the Kamchatka that we were coming, and as we approached, we got a bizarre call. "Um, hi there, can you hear us? This is the Kamchatka. What do you want?"

The words were in Russian, and only I could understand them. "This is shuttle one four nine seven. Please be prepared to receive us," I informed them.

"Oh, okay, um, we really weren't expecting company."

I translated for Jenna, and she stifled a grin and shrugged back at me.

"Yes, well, this is a priority situation. I assure you we do have the authority to be here. However,

I'm not going to discuss anything else over an unsecured channel. Please prepare for us to dock with you.

"Well, okay then," replied the Kamchatka. "We will be prepared to have you aboard. Would you be staying for dinner? Petrov gets really pissed if we don't let him know ahead of time or any changes we want."

"Petrov?" I inquired.

"The ship's cook."

I smiled. "Well, Kamchatka, you let Petrov know we will be there for some time and prepare for three guests."

"Will do. We are looking forward to meeting you. We haven't seen anyone in months. It would be nice to have some company. Kamchatka out." As the communications line went dead, I could not help but burst into laughter at the strange informality of whoever had called us.

It took about an hour to dock with the Kamchatka and ensure our airlocks were sealed tight. I had them double-checked, not quite having confidence in the ship's crew. It's hard to describe the look upon the faces of the two crewmen that let us in the entryway. Seeing the two Marines and myself step into their ship was not something that happened to them regularly. They did not exactly instill confidence in us when we saw they were dressed in civilian clothes that had probably seen better days. I realized now why they had the nickname "garbage monkeys." "Welcome aboard the Kamchatka. I'm Captain Peter Delaney, and this is my copilot, Ksenia Bortnick," he said in broken English.

Delaney was a slightly overweight man in black cargo pants and a greasy white t-shirt, while Ksenia was a tall, long-legged woman. What stood out the most about her was her distinct lack of clothing, wearing a pioneer crop top and cut-off denim shorts. She looked more confident than her captain, but there was an uneasy look in her eyes as she studied the three of us. I stepped forward. "Captain, allow me to introduce the fleet commander. Admiral Jenna Plural."

I thought the captain was about to shit his pants as his jaw opened wide, and he stammered out, "Seriously?"

Jenna smiled at him. "Relax, captain, your name will go down in the history books in the next few days. Who knows? They may even start naming high schools after you in years to come. Let's go to the bridge, and I'll let you know what is going on." He led the way as Jenna asked, "How many in your crew do you have aboard?"

"There are just three of us."

"Forgive me, major, but I must question why you come here?" Ksenia asked. "When the surrender order came from the Chechnyan government, we did not know what to do. I did not want to end up in a European labor camp. When we intercepted your message for military vessels to rendezvous at this point, we considered this a safe harbor. However, the battle is now imminent, and the leader of the free forces is on our ship. So, forgive me again. I just want to know we are safe."

"I understand your concern, ma'am," Jenna said in soft tones, but her voice grew hard, "none of us are safe. Not while the predatory European Union enslaves our homelands. We are at war, and we must all play our part. I won't insult your intelligence by saying you are not at risk. I will do whatever I can to ensure you are safe, but I cannot promise it."

Ksenia smiled. "Well, I must say your honesty is more reassuring than any attempt to reassure me."

"What is the nature of your operation on this ship?" I asked.

The captain responded. "We just spent the last six months dumping radioactive waste from the mines of Saturn's moons."

At these words, I shot a look to Anna Grayson, and she understood my concern. "I will check for radioactivity." She turned to the captain. "Would you direct me to the cargo bay, please?"

"Sure, Ksenia, would you take the young lady down to the cargo hold?" she nodded, and the pair headed off in the opposite direction. As we reached the bridge, we found it to be small and cramped with an old-fashioned launch chair. "You may find this unusual," Jenna said, "but we have to use your ship as the command base for the upcoming battle."

The captain raised his eyebrows, "Major, you must respect we are a very old haulage ship. We were on our way to Earth, where the company would decommission us. We won't last two minutes in an attack."

"The whole idea is to ensure we don't get attacked," I told him. "I assure you, but your life and the lives of your crew will be our top priority." It was a lie but a necessary one.

The captain brushed down a seat with his hand and offered it to Jenna. She glanced at me, trying not to smile, and sat down, "Did I hear you say you have a real chef?" She asked the captain.

"Yes, we do, Petrov Truman. You know, he's not a bad little cook."

Jenna smiled. "You know, I haven't had a non-processed meal in some time. Right now, that sounds like heaven itself. Any chance you can see to it?"

"Yes, of course." The captain headed out.

Anna returned to report. "Admiral Plural, I'm pleased to report minimal radiation levels."

"Thank you, Lieutenant. Okay, Mr. Phelkar, Miss Grayson, let us see what fair this Petrov has for us."

I chuckled. "Don't get your hopes up, Major."

Petrov turned out to be a stereotypical overweight fast-order cook. He served up eggs, bacon, and grits, all swimming in grease. It was quite heavenly if I'm honest. The crew turned out to be your typical garbage monkeys, salt of the Earth, hard-working, independent contractors, your regular labor class. They were tense around Jenna at first, but she slipped into her "just one of the crew" persona, and they started to relax. She chatted with them about going back to Oklahoma and waxed lyrical about the sea to shining sea and amber waves of grain. They were missing home. "We were heading back to Earth after being out here for two years," Delaney told us. "We were mighty pissed--excuse my language--when the report came in that we had surrendered, and we were mighty pleased when we heard of your transmission. We had no idea what we were going to do. We had no orders to go back to Earth or turn the ship over to anyone."

"I hope you don't have any problems that we rig the ship for military use now?" Jenna asked.

The captain shook his head. "Not at all. We can't do much, but we will do anything we can."

Jenna smiled at him. "That's the attitude we need to win this war, captain. You and your crew are true heroes. I wish everyone had your sort of dedication in the United States."

The captain beamed with pride, "Never really thought about myself being a hero before, but if it means I can get back to Grozny, I'm ready to fight."

"Well, that was certainly a delicious meal. Thank you. However, we are rather tired. I'm assuming you don't have spare rooms for us." She sighed heavily.

"You have my quarters, sorry, but it's not much," Delaney said. "I'll bunk down with Petrov, and your crewman can have the first officer's room."

"Oh, we don't mind sharing. We are Marines, Captain." Jenna smiled.

"As you wish, Major." Although he looked uncomfortable at the idea of the three of us sharing.

The quarters were small but adequate. I assumed I would give up the bed to them, but Jenna and Anna found this amusing. "We are not princesses. You are the soft civilian, Mr. Phelkar. When you have slept under the yellow sky of Titan in an E.M.U. suit, you can sleep anywhere," Jenna stated. "You take the bed."

Grayson said very little, and as they curled up to sleep on the floor under a shared blanket, they were soon snoring softly. I dozed fitfully but did not really sleep, and I rose very early.

Chapter Twenty-Five

Unchallenged Power

Jenna and Grayson were still asleep, so I decided to leave them in peace, and I headed out to the bridge. Ksenia was there. She was seated in the pilot's chair with those long legs up on the console. She was barefoot, her trainers scattered across the floor as if she had just kicked them off. She was leaning back, her eyes closed and arms folded. A pot of steaming coffee sat haphazardly up on the navigation console. I picked up a mug, and it didn't concern me that it had been previously used as I poured myself a coffee. I turned, she had not moved, but her eyes were now open and watching me. Her grim Slavic features brightened as she smiled at me, "Good morning, Michael," she said to me in Russian.

"I'm sorry. I didn't mean to disturb you," I replied in her language. "Unfortunately, a caffeine addiction made that coffee just too inviting."

"Don't worry about it. We are not on one of your United States military ships now." She chuckled. "And I appreciate the company. I don't get many visitors in my line of work."

I slipped into the copilot seat and turned it to face her. I took a sip of my coffee, delighting in the realization that it was, in fact, authentic and not synthesized. I had not had any real coffee since that first breakfast with Jenna. She noticed my surprise and smiled wider. "It is good, isn't it?"

"Indeed." I said."

Ksenia shrugged, "this is not glamorous work, but I like the occasional luxury."

I suddenly felt guilty about having one. "I'm sorry, perhaps I should not have...."

Ksenia chuckled. "You are fine, Michael. You need to relax. As I said, this is not a military ship. I'm only too willing to share my coffee."

"Well, thank you." I relaxed and sat back in the chair. 'How long have you been out here?"

"Do you mean out here in the solar system or since we were last back home?"

"Either."

"Well, it's been about three months since we last made landfall. But just over two years since we were on earth."

"That is a long time to be away from home."

Ksenia looked noncommittal. "It's a living of sorts." She yawned slightly and stretched her arms out behind her back. Her large breasts strained against the top. I tried not to stare, but I could not help it.

"Sorry to interrupt this cozy little meeting," said Jenna as she stepped into the cockpit. As I looked up, I noticed her shoot a nasty glare at Ksenia, who either didn't notice it or chose to ignore it.

Ksenia gave up her seat to her without being asked, and Jenna took it without comment, but I noticed her glance slightly as the young first officer of the Kamchatka came and stood beside me.

"Perhaps you can see about getting us some food if you would?" she asked Ksenia, who smirked and left the cockpit.

An ominous silence hung between us. "What's the matter?" I asked.

Jenna suddenly sighed and relaxed, "Nothing but a little stupid jealousy, don't worry, Mr. Phelkar. She was flirting with you."

I grinned, "You were jealous of me talking to the little garbage monkey?"

Jenna flushed slightly, and grinning, she told me to shut up. I chuckled as I poured her a coffee and handed it to her. "Idiot," she muttered.

She sat back and sipped the coffee, looking out into space, watching fleet mass in front of her.

Her fleet.

"All this waiting is..." and as if in answer to her words, the call came over. "This is the U.S.S. Benjamin Franklin. We can confirm Peon fleet is now directly between us and the Addison flotilla. It's now or never, Admiral."

"Thank you, Franklin." She rose to her feet, handing me the coffee. She folded her arms. "Plural to Beta Fleet. This is it, boys and girls. Engage your engines, full thrust towards the Peons. Captain Addison, about-turn, prepare to engage the enemy.

"Aye, Major," came Addison's voice. "Alpha Fleet one-eighty on my mark." A pause for all ships to plot the maneuver then. "Mark!" The legendary Battle of Deep Space had been joined.

The Kamchatka's captain came into the cockpit, and Jenna jumped out of her seat as Ksenia came running back in. They took their seats at the pilot and copilot positions. "Take us in with the fleet carefully, Mr. Delaney," Jenna ordered softly, looking out grimly at the ships moving into formation. "We're just one of the crowd."

"But keep her near the rear, captain," I said. "Don't let anyone get suspicious of our activity."

"I'm just going to mosey along like it's a walk in Gorky Park," said the captain as he pulled the ship in line with the others heading towards the Peon fleet. As soon as the Peons realized we were coming up from the rear, they began to turn around but stopped when they realized that Addison's alpha fleet was heading back towards them. Our forces took advantage of their confusing situation. We swept in between them from all sides, and our ships were first into the battle, launching troop pods at battleships. Jenna whooped as reports came in that nearly all the pods had hit their marks, and our forces were burning into the hulls to board.

Smaller ships engaged other smaller vessels, and the sky was filled with thousands of tiny glowing dots of flying troopers from both sides jetting across the abyss. The first ship victim was one of ours. A cutter lit up the night as its ion drive detonated. Those minutes turned into hours as I tried to follow the stream of reports coming in.

Suddenly, I heard Stacey's voice above the hubbub of intercom traffic. "Admiral, the Chesty is under heavy attack," she said urgently. "Much more than other ships."

"They must think you're aboard," I said.

"At the least, they're working on that possibility," Jenna replied tersely. "Get me the Lewis Puller on the line."

"Yes, ma'am," responded Ksenia.

As the connection was made, you could hear the sounds of explosions and gunfire, but calm, professional Sakamoto came online. "Are you holding your own, Tomi?" Jenna asked.

"That's a negative. We are compromised with Dutch commandos on board. Engines destroyed. We have lost key personnel. I'm losing troopers faster than we can download them. Implementing self-destruct."

"That is a negative, Sakamoto. I repeat, that is a negative." Jenna jumped up, "You are to abandon ship. Do you read me?"

"That is not protocol, major. My duty is to ensure that this ship does not fall into enemy hands."

"Fuck protocol, Sakamoto. You are of more value to me than that piece of shit ship. They can grow goddamn tulips on it for all I care. I want you alive."

There was a long pause before Sakamoto came back again, "The ship's captain is the last to leave."

"Damn it to hell, Tomi. I'm not going to continue repeating myself. Get off that ship, and that's a fucking order."

"What about the rest of the crew?"

"Evacuate as many as you can in the life pods and eject the M.E.T. Anyone who doesn't make it then tough luck, but I need you, Batty, and Harlow off that ship. No more talking, do it."

"Harlow is already dead, Admiral."

Jenna's body briefly tensed, and she closed her eyes. It was the only reaction that she showed, and, steeling herself, simply stated in a soft tone, "Get yourself off that ship."

"Yes, ma'am." the line went dead.

"Keep an eye on them and update me on the situation," she ordered and returned her attention to the battle.

The formations began to break up as the ships of both fleets entered into what was known as the dance of death. Ships of both sides twisted and turned to either make a purchase on their enemy or avoid them.

Just then, the Chesty lit up the sky in a massive explosion, and I said a silent prayer for the young Batty and the others. Sakamoto would later be picked up in a life pod unharmed.

Then another ship went up, then another. Jenna cursed. "They're not trying to board our ships there, simply planting mines on them and blowing them up," Jenna snarled. She hit the communications line. "Plural to all ships, break protocol, now bring your ships in close to the enemy. They are not trying to board. They are trying to blow you out of the sky. Make sure you stay close so that they have to destroy their own ships to get to you." She watched as her ships drew closer to the Peon vessels, which immediately began to try to back away to carry out their plan. The fleet seemed to be in chaos, but then two more of our ships disintegrated in front of our eyes. I was concerned, but Jenna just seemed just more determined.

There was good news that we had taken control of three Peon heavy cruisers from their crews. "Get those ships out of the fight. As soon as you have control of an enemy vessel, take them out of here." Several inquiries came in about prisoners. "I made it clear. We don't have the resources to take damned prisoners. Don't accept any surrender, and don't leave survivors."

The battle raged on, and we lost several more ships. But all in all, we had lost eight ships but captured twenty-three. Ships started flashing their transponders, and Jenna grinned and cried out, "The damn shit-eating mother fuckers are running away." She laughed, and as I watched even, I saw the ships disengaging.

However, Jenna's joy turned to fear after the radio message came over the com lines. "The last two Peon cruisers are heading directly for the U.S.S. Constitution. Collision speed."

"Turn us around. Turn us around now," Jenna snapped, and the captain spun our clunky ship around. "Full speed ahead," she no longer cared about discovery. She would not lose her new flagship that still hung like a dead hulk in space. "Get me the Constitution." Seconds later, "Tracker, you have Peon cruisers coming in on you. Can you get anything online?" there came no reply "Addison, disengage now and protect the Constitution."

"Admiral, all ships are in the process of picking up troopers. We've got thousands of shuttles out there in space. If we stop now, we will lose a lot of our men and women."

"Damn it to hell! I won't lose that ship." She turned to the captain. "How good a pilot are you?"

"I can do at a pinch." He shrugged.

"Get us in there. Get us into the docking bay. Don't spare the thrusters. Carry on, Addison, disregard my last order."

Suddenly a large Peon heavy cruiser overshot us. "Holy crap!" Delaney stared wide-eyed. "They are going to ram her."

Jenna just stared in desperation. There was nothing she could do. Then, just before it hit, another ship seemed to come out from nowhere and slammed into its side. "I.D. that ship." Jenna barked, as confused as the rest of us.

"Ma'am, it's the U.S.S. Lady Liberty," Ksenia reported.

"Stacey!" I stepped forward, my heart leaping up into my throat as I watched the front of her ship break up as it disappeared into the side of the heavy cruiser.

"For Harper and Wagga, you fuckers." Her voice came over the commlink, grinding and twisting metal almost drowning her out. As both the enemy ship and the Liberty started to break up, she barked orders at her crew, "Okay, you pack of rabid dingos. Time to disembark this joy ride. Abandon ship, I repeat, abandon ship. Move it, you shits, that's a fucking order."

"Stacey Grant, I love you." Jenna laughed. "Don't die, or I'll bring you up on charges."

"Ahh, you only get all kissy-kissy when I save your genetically designed arse from hot water. Love to chat, but I gotta get these arse holes moving to the escape pods." The line went dead.

"Addison, make picking up Stacey's escape pod a priority."

"But Major..."

"Just do it!" Jenna snapped irritably. "And send out as many troopers as you can to board the Constitution."

"On it, Major."

The Kamchatka bucked and weaved as Delaney tried to keep away from the jetsam of the exploding ships. The little ship strained under the pressure of the speed that the captain was pouring on now, yet still, it moved like a desperate slug with salt on his back. The cruiser came past but ignored us as an insignificant gnat. This one had no intention of ramming and moved into boarding position.

"Captain, what personal arms do you have?" Jenna asked urgently.

"We just have our sidearms, Admiral."

"Are you prepared to board the Constitution with us and fight?"

"I can't speak for Petrov, ma'am, but I can assure you, Ksenia, and I will be in there with you."

"Thank you." She turned to Anna. "Go find out if Petrov is willing to fight and see about fetching their sidearms."

The captain swung the ship towards the Constitution's main cargo hold. "Bay doors are closed, Major. We are not getting in there." Tiny dots of people came out of the last Peon cruiser and headed towards the Constitution.

"Call the Constitution. Tracker, come in, please. Plural to Tracker."

Finally, the familiar voice of Helen Tracker came back. "Reading you, Major, sorry for not responding earlier. We had trouble with the communications."

"Tracker, you have inbound bogies. Is there anything you can do to stop them?"

"We are working on it, Admiral. I can't say anymore because we've detected the Peons are intercepting our calls." Suddenly the U.S.S. Los Angeles passed overhead and began releasing its troops at the Constitution.

"Can you open the cargo bay doors?" Jenna barked at Tracker.

"Yes, ma'am, opening the doors now."

"We will see you soon. Get your troops ready to prepare to repel boarders."

The doors opened, and the captain thrust his way into the cargo bay, then slammed on the reverse thrusters and spun the ship around to slow it even faster. It hit the deck with a silent shudder. We headed down to the airlock. It seemed to take an eternity for the cargo bay to repressurize.

Then Jenna Plural boarded the U.S.S. Constitution.

Our people were already putting up a good fight when we stepped aboard, but despite my objections, Jenna went ahead. "I took the ship away from Americans. I'm damned if I will let the Peons take it away from me." She said to my protests. We entered the dark corridor with a sense of Deja Vu view, but suddenly the ship lit up with lights. "Wow!" The captain said as he looked around at the brilliant cream-colored walls lined with chrome, "You sure have a fighting ship here, Admiral."

"Why thank you," replied Jenna. "If we make it through this, I'll find a place for all of you on its crew if you want."

Before he could reply, a sudden burst of electricity danced along the chrome.

"What was that?" asked a surprised Ksenia.

Jenna grinned from ear to ear. "Oh, that beautiful girl has ionized the hull," she said, referring to Tracker. "There will be no more Peons landing or leaving."

"Tracker to Admiral Plural, I have done what I can. We only have a few Marines on this ship, but we have to move fast. I'm picking up distress signals from escape pods. They're homing in on this ship, but they'll get fried if I have the full field on."

"Patch me through ship-wide." Jenna barked.

"Ship-wide communications open."

"This is Admiral Jenna Plural. All the enemy troops landed on the starboard side. Concentrate your defenses there."

And with that, we headed down into the corridors, opening fire on any Peon uniform we saw. Realizing that they had lost any opportunity to return for their ship unless they took this one, they fought in an almost frenzied manner. I wanted to stand in front of Jenna to defend her from incoming fire, in a rare act of bravery on my part, but she was determined to push forward. "Mr. Phelkar, much as I may care about you if you try to get in front of me again, I will shoot you myself." To this day, I cannot be sure if she meant it or if it was just an idle threat said in frustration, either way, it had its intended effect, and I stayed back.

Tracker again came online, "Admiral, are all your troops wearing tracer pins?"

"No, I have the crew of the Kamchatka with me. Why do you ask?"

"I think I've got internal defense systems back online, but you have to hurry. We have Peons pounding on the door down here."

"How long can you hold out?"

We heard an explosion, and Tracker cried, "They are through!"

"Set it off, Tracker. Set it off now!" Jenna screamed.

A large double-barreled machine gun dropped from the ceiling ahead of us. Jenna pulled Grayson and me in front of the Kamchatka crew, hoping it would block them from what was about to come. I grabbed Ksenia, who was nearest to me, pulled her to the ground, and lay on top of her, but it was no good. I was lucky a stray bullet did not hit me, as bullets danced around me, hitting her. The firing stopped, and I looked into Ksenia's wide, shocked eyes.

"Watch out for that Jenna Plural. That genetic freak has no soul. We remember Grozny."

I did not get a chance to respond to that, for the lights went out in her eyes, and she let out a last long breath. Jenna pulled me off of her. "I had no choice," she said softly. "We would have lost the ship and possibly the battle." I was shaken, and all I could do was nod. Jenna turned away, and with a last look at the three bodies, I followed her.

We headed up to the bridge to find Tracker had already made it there. She smiled at Jenna and snapped her fingers at the pilot seated in the control center. His fingers darted over the controls of the engines of the U.S.S. Constitution purred into life.

Jenna grinned, "Helen Tracker, I could kiss you."

"I still wouldn't object to that, Major." Tracker grinned.

Jenna just raised an eyebrow at her. "How long before she's fully functional?"

"A few weeks, maybe two, I promise."

"Take a few hours off. You look beat. Meet us back on the bridge at zero-eight hundred."

Tracker smiled and nodded at Jenna, "Thank you, ma'am."

Jenna looked over at one of the bridge officers. "Status Report."

"Lowering the ion field and bringing aboard survivors."

"As soon as that's done, set a course for deep space. We need to get out of here before they regroup. Mr. Phelkar, please get me full run-down ships and personnel we have lost."

"Yes, ma'am," I nodded and sat down at a console, and began collecting reports as they came in.

Dodgson came in looking worse for wear with a torn uniform and a bruised and cut face. "Are you okay?" Jenna asked.

She nodded but looked worn out, "Was good to get some payback after what happened to the Chesty, ma'am," she said with a tired smile.

Jenna turned to her with a wide grin on her face. "Amen, sister!" she said, "now go wash up and get that face seen too. And change into a uniform more fitting to your new rank, Lieutenant Dodgson."

Dodgson's face lit up with a wide grin, "Yes, Ma'am." As she turned to leave, Jenna asked, "Where is Sergeant Hardy?"

Dodgson looked back with sadness in her eyes, "I'm sorry major. He didn't make it. I..."

Jenna sighed, "That's war for you, Emma. Don't let it get to you, and don't forget it either."

As Dodgson turned to leave again, she saw the huge grin on my face and frowned. I turned away from her quickly and noticed Jenna looking at the captain's chair. "Aren't you going to sit down in it?" I asked. "It *is* yours now, after all."

She shook her head and said, "No, not yet. I'm not ready yet." Without further explanation, she stepped outside.

Chapter
Twenty-Six

Genesis

When the news that the M.E.T. from the Chesty was re-covered, it was the icing on our victory cake. I ordered it delivered to the Constitution and wanted to be there when they downloaded my old crewmates. Tracker gave me one of her assistants to help with the downloads. It was larger than I had expected, and most of it had been hidden away either behind the wall or under the floor. Ironically, it was about the size of a coffin, and it sat in the middle of the storage bay like some ancient relic.

The bay was so empty that my voice echoed off the walls. "Start bringing them back, please, Corporal." I nodded to the tech.

Clip-clop, clip-clop. The sound echoed around the room, and I turned to see Charlotte Kensett casually walking across the bay. "Belay that order if you please, Mr. Phelkar."

I looked at her questioningly, but her stoic face gave nothing away as she looked down at the datapad in her hand. Behind her, a young man in a tech uniform followed closely. As she reached us, she dismissed the tech next to me, who looked at me and then headed out. Kensett handed the pad to the tech with her and said, "These are the people to download. Only these."

"Care to explain?" I asked as the tech complied with the command and downloaded the first Marine.

"It is the list of those who stated their loyalty to the major when she took command of the Lewis Puller." The first Marine appeared. Kensett smiled at them. "Welcome back, private. You are on board the U.S.S. Constitution, and it has been six weeks since you were uploaded. Fall out."

He saluted her and headed out to the bay. The tech continued to download the troopers, and I lost count of how many as each followed out of the room in a well-rehearsed manner. My greatest surprise happened when young Neville Batty appeared. The gormless grin on his funny little face smiled up at us before heading off.

"That's everyone on your list, ma'am." The tech advised her.

"What about the rest?" I asked.

I will remember what Kensett said next to the day I die, even without an eidetic memory chip. She leaned over the tech and looked at the data, "I see no one else on this list."

"There are still fourteen people in this M.E.T."

Kensett appeared to look genuinely bewildered, "I think you are mistaken, Mr. Phelkar."

"What games are you playing, Kensett," I said, too shocked to even get angry.

"I can assure you, Mr. Phelkar. I'm not playing games. Every loyal American has been downloaded."

"And what about the others? They can't permanently stay in the M.E.T. The patterns will start to degrade."

"Oh, that is such a pity, Mr. Phelkar," she stated with a half-smile. "Don't worry. I can assure you that it won't happen."

I felt some relief for a moment, but when she next spoke, my blood ran cold. She carefully and deliberately turned back to the tech. "Format the M.E.T and reset it to factory settings."

"Yes, ma'am," the tech replied and turned back to the panel on the side of the M.E.T.

"Kensett, you can't be serious?" I said, lunging forward in horror, but she stepped in front of me.

"I'm frequently told, Mr. Phelkar, that I don't have a sense of humor. However, I do have a sense of loyalty to the Admiral. Corporal, what are you waiting for?"

An alarm went off when he tried to erase the patterns within, but she quickly overrode it, and within seconds a green light came on, indicating the device was reset and ready for use.

Charlotte Kensett said nothing more and turned away and, with a clip-clop of her heels, headed out of the docking bay. After a brief pause, I raced after her. Catching up with her, I said, "Why the hell did you do that? There were men and women still in there?"

"They were only traitors in there, Mr. Phelkar. Each one is a potential threat to the authority of the Admiral. It is my job to eliminate such threats."

"They were just grunts. Jenna promised them a safe harbor. How do you propose explaining this?"

Kensett smirked, "Oh, the signals were too degraded, the poor things." Just as she heard me sigh, she stopped walking and turned to me. "Are we going to have another problem, Mr. Phelkar? This is the second time you've questioned my responsibilities. Admiral Plural has made my position clear. I am to protect not only the physical bodies of certain crew members which she has named, one of which is you but also to ensure there are no challenges to the authority of those individuals." she sighed and then reached out and placed a hand upon my arm. "I ask you to trust me, Mr. Phelkar. I haven't only the Admiral's best interests at heart but also yours." She looked at me like a schoolteacher protecting a student. I struggled with the concept this attractive, young, innocent-looking woman could perform these duties with such ruthless efficiency. "I do what I do so that you don't have to. Please let me do my job." she did not wait for an answer and simply turned away and headed down the corridor with a clip-clop, clip-clop.

Celebrations were so wild you would think we had won the war. They could hardly be blamed. They had gone from absolute defeat to once more having hope. Ships blasted out their transponder signals morning, noon, and night. Almost immediately after the last trooper had got on board, Jenna had us hightail it away from that region. Four cruisers attached to the Constitution to tow it while Tracker continued to complete her restoration.

The following morning, I was going to the bridge when I saw Stacey heading down the busy corridor toward me. I had not spoken to her since our night in the ventilation shaft. Our eyes met briefly, but she swiftly turned around and headed in the opposite direction. Confused by this, I called out to her, but she just sped up. When I reached her, she turned away from me. I grabbed her arm, but she immediately snatched it away and spun to face me but did not meet my eyes. "Please, Phelks. Don't make this any harder." Her usual smile was gone, and there was a pain in her usually cheery expression.

"What are you talking about?" I asked, genuinely bewildered.

Stacey looked around at the crewman coming and going down the busy corridor. She lowered her voice, "I know about you and Jenna." She glared at me.

"What about us?" I responded.

Stacey lowered her head but kept her eye looking up at me. "I thought it was just gossip, and you even told me it was. If I had known, I would never have..." her voice trailed off.

"Stacey, what's the problem?" I asked.

She sighed, fidgeting uncomfortably, "Do you realize what that makes me, Phelks? Do you?" I shook my head. "At best, it makes me your mistress. At worst, it makes me your whore."

"It's not like that, Stacey. Truly, it's not," I said earnestly.

"Really? Then explain to me exactly what I am and what Jenna is to you."

"You're one of my very dear friends, and I care about you greatly." But I had hesitated too long before saying it.

"Is that all?" She tilted her head to one side, and even her false eye shone through her hair as she gave me her foulest look.

Silence hung hard between us because I knew that wasn't all. Her grey eye stared up at me, and I knew she wouldn't let me off the hook on this one. Weakly and barely audibly, I said, "No." I sighed, "That's not all, but it is the way it has to be."

"Damn you to hell, Phelks." she said in an angry whisper, "you let me fall in love with you when you knew nothing could come of it."

"I'm sorry, I had no idea. Honestly, I just thought you were letting out the stress." I pleaded.

"The first time, yes, that was just something between comrades. But there's something about you, Phelks. You never treated me like some conquest. You're a total wanker in many ways, but you did something most men don't." She frowned, anger turning to hurt.

"And what is that?"

"You treated me with respect. It's been a long time since any guy's done that."

"That's because I do respect you, Stacey. I respect you a lot. I'm sorry for any hurt I've caused you."

She shook her head vigorously. "Oh no, mother fucker, you achieved something few men ever have. You got one over on me and played me for a fool." She suddenly deflated. "I knew it was too good to think you may feel the same way about me. I guess I was just making a complete arse of myself."

'No, you weren't." I stepped towards her, but she stepped back.

"No, don't," she shook her head. "You're the Admiral's man. And I love her too much to mess with that."

"Does it help if I told you I had feelings for you?" I said softly.

She frowned and, sneering up at me, said, "Don't be a cunt."

I looked at her, startled, "what?"

"Don't fucking mess with me."

"I assure you, Stacey, I'm not. I'm confused, yes. But I know my feelings for you are more than friendship, even if I try to deny it myself." I said uneasily, knowing I was probably making this worse.

Stacey laughed dryly. "Well, you sure know how to confuse a girl."

"I'm sorry. I just didn't want you to think you're meaningless to me."

"And you also told Jenna this?"

I blushed. "Not exactly."

Stacey laughed mirthlessly and shook her head. "So, you're saying that instead of being a cunt to me, you're being a cunt to Jenna?"

I shrugged and reluctantly admitted, "I guess so."

"Do you have any idea of how much I respect that woman?" I shook my head. "Do you have even the remotest fucking idea how men have treated her over the years? I thought you were better than that."

"I'm ...." I started, but Stacey pushed the palm of her hand in front of my face.

"I don't want to hear it. That girl has had my back more times than I can count. I would have been cashiered long ago if it weren't for her. She gives me hope that I will sit on Wagga Beach again. Have a barbie on Christmas Day and return to that land that I love. No, Mr. Phelkar, I'm never going to hurt her." She sighed and looked away from me. "At least, not intentionally."

"Nor do I expect you to." A silence fell once more between us. We looked at each other as if we had run out of things to say. "So, where do we go from here?" I asked.

"We don't. We stay apart as much as possible and make sure we're never in a room alone together. We put this down to some bad decision-making on both our parts."

"But..."

"No buts. Go fuck yourself." She shook her head and calmly offered me a hand to shake, and I took it, held it, and relished her cool soft touch. "It has been a pleasure, Mr. Phelkar."

"Likewise, Captain Grant. Clear skies to you."

"Clear skies to you, too." She smiled politely and, taking her hand back, she turned and walked away.

I watched as she disappeared among the crewman coming and going. It simplified my life, but the pain I felt from this encounter was almost too much to bear.

Stacey, not perfect, but perfectly imperfect.

However, I did not have time to think about it as I received a surprising call from Charlotte Kensett. "I need to meet with you, Michael," she casually said.

"Is it urgent?" I said, sounding more irritated than I intended to.

"Urgent, no, important, yes," she said, an edge to her voice piqued my curiosity.

"Want to meet in my office?" I asked.

"No, I would rather keep this meeting on the down-low, if you don't mind. " Now that had my full attention. "Meet me in the mess on deck four."

"I'm on my way."

The deck four mess was small and rarely used, as the poor design had placed it next to the recycling system, and the faint odor of rubbish permeated the room. Kensett was already there and looking quite out of place in her expensive red dress and matching heels. She was seated at a table, looking at her tablet with a coffee in front of her and one she had got for me. She did not look up as I took a seat opposite her. "We have a problem, Michael." She said softly, still not looking up.

"We are in a fleet in rebellion against our parent nations. I think we have quite a few problems." I chuckled.

Kensett glanced at me, "I need you to take this very seriously, Michael, very seriously indeed." She lay her tablet down, sat back, and picked up her coffee. "We have a traitor within the ranks of Jenna's inner circle."

"What makes you think that?" I asked as my brow now furrowed in concern.

Kensett sighed and looked at me as if she was reconsidering telling me. "Whoever it is, is very clever, and I almost missed it. I probably wouldn't have even investigated it if it were not for my suspicious nature. You see, the coordinates for the fleet rendezvous were sent with a purely American encryption code. One that I know has not been broken. The only ships that should have received it would have been American military vessels. However, allied and civilian vessels started arriving almost immediately. Some even before Jenna got here. That seemed odd to me. Undoubtedly, the word would have gotten out eventually, but not that fast and not to that many." As she said this, I remembered the Chechnyan crew telling me how they received Jenna's message. "It was as though the code had been cracked or the information passed on, but I was suspicious." She paused and sipped her coffee, looking at my face to gauge my reaction, but I gave none that I was aware of. I said nothing and let her continue. "So I had my people go back and track the communications logs. The coordinates transmitted from Phobos were indeed only picked up by American military vessels. However, while en route to the rendezvous, other ships picked it up. All of them. And it was unencrypted."

"Maybe someone was just trying to inform a family friend or relative," I said dismissively, thinking this was no more than paranoia. "People act desperately at desperate times. Inappropriate and probably illegal but hardly tantamount to treason."

Kensett nodded, "That is something I considered. But I delved further and found that this unencrypted message was sent on a Peon carrier wave. It was sent directly to the Europeans, Michael. Directly telling them exactly where we intended to rendezvous. Someone deliberately betrayed us." She fixed her eyes upon me.

A silence fell between us as I pondered this, and a single one-word question formed in my head that I was not sure I wanted to hear the answer. "Who?"

Kensett shook her head. "I don't know. At least not yet. Whoever did it is very clever and hid their tracks well."

"Come now, Charlotte, I have not known you long, but I know you well enough to know you have suspicions."

Kensett smiled, taking what I said as a compliment, "I do indeed. The list is not a long one. Whoever did it has unfettered security access and the confidence of Jenna Plural. They also need to have the technical know-how."

"Don't keep me in suspense, Charlotte," I said, trying to sound lighter than I actually felt.

She hesitated, "this list includes friends of yours."

"I'm a grown-up Charlotte. I can take it. My first and foremost concern is the security of Jenna."

Kensett smiled. "So, I believe, Michael." Then the smile dropped, and without needing to look at anything for reference, she recited the list, "Helen Tracker, Claire Addison, Stacey Grant, Rockford Harlow,

Neville Batty, and several others that are lower on the list, and, of course, you."

At that, I sat up, "Me?" I said incredulously.

Kensett chuckled. "Don't worry, Michael. If I really believed it was you, I would not be talking to you about this." She paused and then corrected herself. "Well, actually, I would, but it would be an interrogation chamber and not over a cup of coffee."

"That's reassuring, I think," I said, relaxing a little. "Well, Harlow is already dead, so you can hardly question him, and I can vouch personally for the loyalty of both Grant and Tracker."

Kensett's eyes widened, and it was her turn to look incredulous. "Really?" she said. "You have known them a mere few months. I served with both of them for nearly three years before being transferred off the Lewis Puller, and even I am not ready to swear to their absolute loyalty."

"I take your point, but I have become very close to Stacey, and I highly doubt that she would engage in such activity," I stated confidently.

"Let's not beat around the bush, Michael. You fucked her a couple of times, but that does not mean you know her. Stacey doesn't exactly make forever friends out of her lovers."

"Is there nothing you do not know about?" I asked with irritation.

She shrugged, "I don't know who the traitor is, Michael, but I know that I will find out. I have a perfect record, and I'm not about to lose that."

I pondered this over the long silence that followed. "So why come to me with this? Aren't you supposed to answer directly to Jenna?"

"Yes, and I'm breaking her orders in not doing so. However, she needs her head in the game right now. Suddenly distrusting who she presently trusts the most will cause her to be distracted. I cannot go to Addison, our official number two, for she is a suspect. So to cover my arse, I'm coming to her unofficial number three. I want your authority to proceed in this matter."

"You are quite a piece of work, Charlotte." I grinned disparagingly at her. "If you screw up, I get the blame, and if you succeed, you get the credit."

This did not faze her one bit. "When you get to know me better, Michael, you will learn that I don't get credit for anything. My actions are always under the radar and should never come to the attention of anyone. I bring this to you because I play a dangerous game with a very clever opponent. An opponent who could very well turn the tables on me. I need someone I can be open with, and I have selected you. I need someone that someone will have my back if the chips go down."

There was a long silence again. I certainly did not trust Charlotte Kensett. Indeed, I considered her an abominable excuse for a human being, but I feared for Jenna, and finally, I said, "Take whatever action you deem necessary, Charlotte, and I promise you I will have your back if any concerns arise with Jenna."

Kensett smiled, put down her unfinished coffee cup, picked up her tablet, and said, "Thank you, Michael. I will talk to you again when I have some news." And with that, she rose, and with the familiar clip-clop of her heels, she headed out of the room. I sat there momentarily pondering everything before getting up and heading back to my quarters.

My new accommodation aboard the U.S.S. Constitution was unbelievable. Unfortunately, I did not get the first officer's quarters as I had aboard the Lady Liberty. That privilege went to Jenna, who let Addison keep her former Captain's quarters. However, it was larger and more comfortable than even my apartment in London. It was a suite of rooms with a lounge, bedroom, bathroom, kitchen, and office. There was even a side room attached which should have been for an aide. However, as integrated as the U.S.M.C. was, it was certainly not wise to move Abigail Thompson there. I considered moving Bridgette there only to discover she had moved in with Thompson without my knowledge.

Jenna had forgotten entirely about the idea of keeping our relationship secret. Each night, she came to my quarters as if we lived together. It even got to the stage where I had arranged for the steward to bring our meals there.

We had not been intimate for a while, and she seemed more distant. Considering what she had on her mind putting together the remnants of our fleet, it wasn't surprising. However, my insecurities made me broach the subject. One night, I came home to find that, for once, she was there before me. She was seated at a desk going through some reports. She barely looked up and did not even acknowledge me as I came in. "Have you eaten today?" As of late, she had become known to skip meals.

"I had breakfast with Addison."

"That was more than twelve hours ago. "

She did not reply as she continued to read the data in front of her. I hit the intercom and instructed her steward to arrange for a light meal to be delivered to our room. "I have to let some ships go," Jenna said at last.

"What do you mean?" I said, pulling up a chair adjacent to the desk.

"We have ended the battle with more ships than we started with. The gains we made from the Europeans require crews, and we are already spread thin. I will have to start putting in people who may not even be ready for the job just to fill the positions. Even then, it's going to be tight. We might have to cut loose some ineffectual ships and transfer their crews to other positions. I was trying to avoid making such major changes."

It was the first time I'd ever seen her looking so weary. Dark lines had managed to break through that genetic coding. "Take a break. You look exhausted."

Jenna looked back at her tablet and shook her head. "I don't have the time, Mr. Phelkar."

I reached over and hit the power button on the tablet. As it went off, she looked up at me angrily. "What do you think you are doing?"

"Right now, I'm not your adjutant, and you're not my commanding officer. I'm your partner."

"That can be changed very quickly," she said aggressively.

I was taken aback, but I retained my composure. "Is that what you want, Admiral Plural?"

Jenna sighed and calmed down. She rested her hand gently on my leg, "No, Mr. Phelkar. Sorry, I'm just getting rather frustrated,"

"So, what is it you do want? With regards to us, I mean."

She looked at me, biting her lower lip as she pondered an answer to this question. "You have become important to me, Mr. Phelkar. And I don't just mean for your diplomatic skills. Of which I can honestly say we would not be here without." She stood up and turned her back to me and, with a heavy sigh, stated, "I don't think I can get past the difference between us due to my genetic nature."

"Why do you have to?" she was surprised by my curtness and glanced over her shoulder, but I didn't give her a chance to respond. "You get frustrated with people's attitudes about GenMods, but you have the biggest hang-up." I stepped up to her and placed my hands on her shoulders. "Instead of you worrying about the effect on me, it should be me worrying about the effect on you. You're the one who has to watch me grow old as you stay young."

A smile slowly crossed Jenna's face as she turned to look back at me, "to be honest, I have never quite thought of it like that."

I took her hands and looked into her eyes, "whatever you feel about me, I honestly don't know. I love you, Jenna Plural."

She leaned in and kissed me softly. Then she backed away. "I'm afraid of that commitment, Mr. Phelkar. It is probably the only thing I'm afraid of." No was not the time to mention the whole spacewalk thing. She sat back down and stared at me, deep in thought. "Twice in my life, I've committed to someone. Twice it did not last."

"What happened?" I asked.

"In one occurrence, as I believe I have told you before, my husband died. In the other, as he grew older, it became more complicated. He died in the battle we just went through."

I must admit that startled me, "Did I know him?"

At this, a wistful smile came to her face, and she said, "Yes, Mr. Phelkar, you did. It was Rockford Harlow, the chief engineer on board the Chesty." The very thought that the overweight elderly engineer had once been the partner of Jenna Plural was beyond my imagination. Then I remembered the picture in that locket and the man I recognized on our first night together. I could see it now. Rockford Harlow. She saw the surprise on my face, "Now you see what I mean."

"I see what you mean, and I'm sorry about your loss. However, that is the price to be paid if a relationship is based on appearances. It should not have mattered what he looked like or how he aged." "I think you misunderstand, Mr. Phelkar. It wasn't me that broke it off. It was him. He felt guilty about being my partner and ended it after twenty-three years."

"Jenna, all I know is I love you. If we have to keep it on the down-low, so be it, but I won't accept some lame excuse that it's because you're a GenMod. You're a woman and have the right to whatever any other woman has."

Jenna stared at me for the longest of moments. Then she stood up, threw her arms around my neck, and kissed me. Looking into my eyes, she said softly, yet quite clearly, "I love you, too, Michael."

Epilogue

I stepped onto the bridge, walking confidently in my new suit and tie. I stood at the center behind the empty captain's chair, looking around at the newly refurbished Control Center of the U.S.S. Constitution. Tracker looked over to me from her console. She smiled and nodded, and I responded likewise. I looked down into the pilot's well. Stacey looked up at me, and we briefly made eye contact before both looking away. At her side, Batty was chatting away, as he usually did. I saw familiar faces from the chesty and smiled as I realized Jenna was surrounding herself with those she could trust. My smile faded as I remembered one of these people was a traitor. I pushed the thought from my mind.

The first battle was over, and Jenna had asserted authority over the remnants of the allied fleet. We had sent the Peons running across the solar system with their tails between their legs. It was a time of victory and one much-needed during these days of many losses. I turned to look back at the door as the media crew came in. I nodded to them, and they began to set up their camera equipment at the front of the room. "Captain

Tracker, are you ready to break into that German communications hub?"

"Just say the word, Mr. Phelkar." She smiled.

"How long do you think we have before they shut us down?"

"About six minutes would be my guess. Give or take a minute."

Captain Addison came into the room, and I turned and looked at her questioningly. She nodded in response. "She's ready."

I felt nervous as I stepped up to the podium in front of the camera, about to beam my image and message to all corners of the solar system. The camera operator gave me a nod, and I looked over at Tracker. "Whenever you're ready, Captain Tracker." I gave the command.

"Breaking into German broadcast communications in three two..." She gave me a thumbs-up, and I looked into the camera.

"This is Michael Phelkar speaking to you from the bridge of the U.S.S. Constitution. I present to you the new leader of the allied resistance forces, Jennacia Plularian."

The camera turned as the doors opened, and Jenna entered, looking resplendent in a new black nonspecific dress uniform. She strode purposely forward, knowing she was already on the camera. The crew all rose and stood at attention. As she stopped, taking my place at the podium in front of the camera, she raised her hand to indicate they should sit and then looked ahead. She paused and looked around at her crew before looking back at the camera and speaking.

"I pray that I come to you today as a beacon of hope. I have assumed command of the loyal remnants of the allied forces. You should have already heard about the great victory over the Europeans in the Battle of Deep Space. We emerged from it stronger and more committed to the cause of freedom than ever before, for I say to you now, as clear as I can be." Her voice rose aggressively, and she slammed a leather-gloved fist on the podium. Anger and passion were vehement in her eyes. "We completely and utterly reject the surrender of the leaders of the Pacific Alliance. We won't roll over like a dog under the tyranny of the European Union. We won't hide. We won't run. We won't capitulate. We did not ask for this war." Spittle flew from her mouth. "I did not ask to sacrifice the lives of our young. I don't love war." She paused, then shouted, "I love freedom, and I will fight, bleed, and die to see that restored." Her voice lowered, "It is not going to be easy. You are bloodied and bruised, but we have shown the Europeans that we *will* be masters of our destiny. I say to you all," She raised a clenched fist and shouted once more. "Rise up. Rise up and be counted as a hero. Rise up and turn on your oppressors. We will be out here, growing in number every day. Taking the fight to wherever a European cowers and hides. We are battered, but we are unbroken. We will strike at the very heart of European domination. We will destroy every ship. We will destroy every base. We will destroy every European we encounter until no more Europeans are left." She paused and took a breath before continuing. "We will take no prisoners. We will pursue the enemy with our hearts filled with vengeance for the loved ones we have left behind on Earth. I dedicate myself, and I ask you to do the same to the total eradication of the European Union. I don't bring you victory today, but I do bring you the promise of victory tomorrow. It may take months. It may even take years. I promise you, with everything that I am. We *will* prevail. And to you Peon scum out there. I am coming for you. The day will arrive when the European Union is no more than a footnote in the history books. This is total war, and we are coming home."

From Down Under to Out There

They took her country.

They killed everyone she knew.

They are going to wish she hadn't survived.

It is a desperate time as the forces of the Pacific alliance are losing the war.

Stacey Grant has seen her country burn.

Escaping the invasion of Australia, the veteran Air Force pilot finds herself recruited by the Americans to help steal the prototype of the most advanced fighter craft in the solar system from the enemy.

When she suffers even more loss on that mission, she fights back the despair with a renewed determination to play her part in turning the tide of war and one day return to Australia at the head of the greatest liberating force since D-Day.

Nothing will stop... That Girl From Wagga